Voyeur

Voyeur

Lacey Alexander

HEAT

Heat
Published by New American Library, a division of
Penguin Group (USA) Inc., 375 Hudson Street,
New York, New York 10014, USA
Penguin Group (Canada), 90 Eglinton Avenue East, Suite 700, Toronto,
Ontario M4P 2Y3, Canada (a division of Pearson Penguin Canada Inc.)
Penguin Books Ltd., 80 Strand, London WC2R 0RL, England
Penguin Ireland, 25 St. Stephen's Green, Dublin 2,
Ireland (a division of Penguin Books Ltd.)
Penguin Group (Australia), 250 Camberwell Road, Camberwell, Victoria 3124,
Australia (a division of Pearson Australia Group Pty. Ltd.)
Penguin Books India Pvt. Ltd., 11 Community Centre, Panchsheel Park,
New Delhi - 110 017, India
Penguin Group (NZ), 67 Apollo Drive, Rosedale, North Shore,
Auckland 1311, New Zealand (a division of Pearson New Zealand Ltd.)
Penguin Books (South Africa) (Pty.) Ltd., 24 Sturdee Avenue,
Rosebank, Johannesburg 2196, South Africa

Penguin Books Ltd., Registered Offices:
80 Strand, London WC2R 0RL, England

First published by Heat, an imprint of New American Library,
a division of Penguin Group (USA) Inc.

First Printing, May 2007
1   3   5   7   9   10   8   6   4   2

Copyright © Lacey Alexander, 2007

Heat is a trademark of Penguin Group (USA) Inc.

LIBRARY OF CONGRESS CATALOGING-IN-PUBLICATION DATA
Alexander, Lacey.
Voyeur / Lacey Alexander.
p. cm.
ISBN: 978-0-451-22119-3
1. Voyeurism--Fiction. I. Title.
PS3601.L3539V69 2007
813'.6--dc22   2006034771

Set in Centaur MT
Designed by Ginger Legato

Printed in the United States of America

PUBLISHER'S NOTE
This is a work of fiction. Names, characters, places, and incidents either are the product of the author's imagination or are used fictitiously, and any resemblance to actual persons, living or dead, business establishments, events, or locales is entirely coincidental.
 The publisher does not have any control over and does not assume any responsibility for author or third-party Web sites or their content.

The scanning, uploading, and distribution of this book via the Internet or via any other means without the permission of the publisher is illegal and punishable by law. Please purchase only authorized electronic editions, and do not participate in or encourage electronic piracy of copyrighted materials. Your support of the author's rights is appreciated.

Chapter One

Laura Watkins stared at the blank computer screen, her mind spinning with desperation. *Write something! Anything!* The black cursor kept blinking at her. Nothing came.

She never had writer's block—*never*.

Well, until her recent breakup with David. Even now, as she lifted her gaze to the gently falling snow out the window in front of her, she couldn't quite figure out why ending the relationship had affected her so severely. She'd never seen David as a stimulant to her creativity—after all, he was all business, the quintessential suit and tie guy, the corporate icon, partner in one of Seattle's most prestigious law firms at thirty-two. Had she loved him that much? Had she loved him at all?

You're pathetic. Twenty-nine years old, and you still don't know exactly what love is. And your promising career is going to die an early death because you're not smart enough to sort out your emotions.

Maybe Monica was right. Over pizza and beer at Laura's apartment two weeks ago, she'd said, "It's sex. You've gotten used to it. Without it, you're just sort of . . . clogging up or something. No *sexual* release equals no *creative* release. I'm sure of it."

"That's ridiculous," she'd replied. "I wrote books before David—I can write books *after* him. And as you know, I'm not even sure why we stayed together so long."

"Because you need sex to create—it's that simple."

Monica was a graduate student going for her Ph.D. in psychology at the University of Washington and thought she knew everything about the human mind, but in this particular instance, Laura didn't buy it. Her best friend was usually a terrific problem-solver, but Laura just couldn't believe her *creative* flow had anything to do with her *sexual* flow.

Her real fear was that maybe she'd underestimated her feelings for David—maybe she did love him, deeply, and just wasn't recognizing it until now, when it was too late. Another valid fear? Her next Riley Wainscott Mystery was due to her editor in less than a month, at the beginning of March, and so far, she didn't have a plot. Or a crime. Or a criminal. Or even a good group of suspects. All she had was her intrepid heroine, Riley Wainscott, living with her eccentric Aunt Mimsey in a quaint New England town.

"A getaway," she'd told Monica enthusiastically, when the idea had hit her after her second beer. "Maybe that's what I need. Just a change of scenery. A . . . retreat. Isn't that what writers do when they need to get absorbed in their work? They go on a retreat someplace quiet and secluded. Maybe if I do something like that, so that it's just me and Riley, the story will reveal itself."

Monica had looked skeptical. "That sounds way too simple, if you ask me."

Laura had only flashed a scowl, having truly felt she was on to something.

"And even if you really wanted to pursue that, I see a major problem."

"Which is?"

"You're broke. And I'm just guessing, but I don't think secluded hideaways come cheap."

Laura had let out a huge sigh. Leave it to Monica to throw another crimp in her plan—even if she was right. She had, unfortunately, spent her partial advance for the current book long ago, on things like food and shelter, and was now living off her savings account. Until she turned in the completed novel, she had to count pennies.

She'd looked up to find Monica's lips pursed, her eyes narrowed. "This is against my better judgment, but luckily for you, I happen to have a cousin with a vacation home in Colorado. He's always inviting me and the rest of my family to use it."

Laura lowered her chin. "So you're saying?" This sounded good—*perfect*, even—but she didn't want to jump to conclusions.

"I'm saying I'm sure he'd be happy to let you retreat there. If you really think it would help."

"I do, Monnie, I really, really do!"

Monica had delivered one of her typical superior looks. "I still say you need a good lay way worse than you need to lock yourself up in a big, lonely house, but if this is what you really want, girlfriend, consider it done."

Looking back on that night, Laura remembered the instant sense of relief, sureness, that this was the answer. Yet true to Monica's predictions, here she sat, staring out on a beautiful mantle of Colorado powder through the picture window of a fabulous mountain home she had all to herself, and Riley's story was no closer to completion than it had been in her tiny office back in Seattle.

What the hell was she going to do?

She couldn't sleep, damn it. At first, she'd thought it was worry over the book, but then she'd realized she was hot, sweating. She got up to adjust the thermostat and lay back down. Then she realized her nose, mouth, throat, were as dry as the Sahara. Altitude. She rose once more and padded to the bathroom in her long blue cotton pj's with white and black snowflakes all over them. She drank a little water and lay back down. Pulled the covers up, then pushed them off.

She finally shot upright in bed in utter frustration and walked with determination toward the kitchen. She'd brought a few bottles of wine for relaxing by the fire in the evening, and now seemed like a good time to uncork one—surely a little wine would help her sleep.

She didn't bother turning on a light as she brought a glass and open bottle into the two-story living room. Instead, she just flipped on the handy gas fireplace, watched as the orange flames cast a glow across the room, then sat down on the sofa, ready for some serious relaxation.

But what if Monica was right? What if her block truly had something to do with sex? After all, she didn't really *miss* David. She didn't miss his company, or his face, or his voice. But as she swallowed the last sip of wine in her stemmed glass and poured another, she couldn't deny that she did miss being touched, being entered.

She'd never thought she was a highly sexual person, unlike Monica, who *lived* for sex. In fact, Monica's sexploits were a big reason Laura was able to dismiss Monica's theory so easily—her best friend was a nympho and, like Freud, thought *everything* related to sex. But as a sip of wine moved warmly down through her chest, she couldn't deny that the crux of her thighs ached at the thought of intimacy, that her breasts felt tender, sensitive.

Pushing to her feet, she moved across the room toward the same huge wall of windows she'd worked next to earlier in the day. There were no blinds or shades, and the deep carpet of snow beyond shone silvery in the moonlight, doing its part to light the room.

Slowly, deliberately, she lifted one hand to her breast. Her nipple jutted through her pajama top, hard against her palm. She squeezed gently, vaguely wishing the touch were that of a man—a bigger hand, a slightly rougher caress. She raked her thumb across the pearlized peak and felt a *whoosh* of desire sweep through her crotch.

Maybe if sex *was* the problem here, she thought as she made her way back to the couch and drained her glass a second time, she should attempt to do something about it. Hell, for all she knew, a good orgasm *would* loose her creativity. If nothing else, it might help her sleep.

Lowering her glass to the coffee table, she raised her hands to her breasts, covering them, slowly massaging. Her pussy flooded, just from that. She hardly ever did this—got herself off—but clearly she needed to come. She hardly ever thought of her vagina as her pussy, either, yet something about the moment almost called for it—that certain bluntness the word provided. A rose by any other name is still a rose . . . and in the quiet stillness of the dimly lit room where she was becoming intoxicated with wine and desire, there was no reason not to think of it that way. Just like if a man had been there—*he* would think of it that way, so she would, too. Sometimes even *she* needed to quit being her conservative self and just act without thinking.

Unbuttoning the two top buttons of her pajamas, she reached inside, moving her left hand to her right breast. Once again, she found herself wishing it were a masculine touch, but desperate times indeed called for desperate measures.

She twirled her erect nipple between thumb and forefinger, relishing the fresh rush of blood to her cunt. Mmm, yes. Pleasure. Want. And another dirty word. It, too, fit the moment—the raw arousal echoing through her. She *did* need this. So bad.

Still, as she slipped her other hand between her legs, she harbored that same helpless wish—for a strong, virile, sexy man.

But stop it. Quit wishing. Quit thinking. Just do this. Rub yourself.

It took only a gentle massage to keep her pussy humming with eagerness. Maybe it was the solitude that made the self-caress easier than ever before, the knowledge that no one else was around—it was just her and the fire and the snow. Of course, the wine had certainly helped, too. It hadn't made her any sleepier, but it had relaxed her—way more than a mere two glasses usually did.

That's when it hit her. Alcohol increased the effects of high altitude. No wonder she felt so . . . loopy. Pleasantly drunk. Free. To do . . . whatever.

Reaching up, she untied the drawstring at her waist and eased out of the snowflake pajama bottoms, letting them drop to the floor. She leaned back on the sofa, legs parted, two fingers stroking through her pink cotton bikini panties. Mmm, the pleasure began to spread, echoing down through her thighs, up into her already sensitized breasts.

That's when she noticed the tiny little light across the room. A minute green dot on a gadget next to the colossal computer screen—the homeowner's computer, but Monica had told her to feel free to use it.

She froze in place, her hand going still as she realized she'd totally forgotten Monica's giggling warning. "By the way, you might want to avoid walking through the living room naked." It had come during the phone call when Monica had been giving her directions from the Eagle-Vail airport, instructions on how to get inside the house, all that.

"Well, I hadn't planned on it," she'd said, "but why?"

"My cousin has a webcam on his computer there."

"He's going to spy on me?"

Monica had laughed. "No, nothing like that. He just uses it to check in on the house occasionally when he's not there. He once told me that when he knows someone's coming to stay, he sometimes peeks in just to make sure they arrived okay. So no worries—just figured I should mention it."

Now Laura couldn't help wondering if there was any chance she was being watched. Surely not. It was late—after 2 A.M. Monica's cousin, a rich guy who had something to do with corporate takeovers, was surely asleep by now. As she should be. But she was not. So what if he was awake, too?

Unlikely.

Yet . . . she couldn't ignore the slight feeling that someone *was* watching her, that same feeling you get when someone in a crowded room hones in on you. Only this was no crowded room. It was complete seclusion. Wasn't it?

She swallowed nervously and let her fingers glide lightly over her mound once more. They left little trails of fire. She bit her lip, her skin tingling with the new questions surrounding her. What if Monica's cousin *was* witnessing this? Shouldn't she stop? Shouldn't she snatch up her pj bottoms and flee the room this instant? And still, to her surprise, the idea that maybe he was taking in her private touches added to her arousal, made her cunt pulse with an even harder need.

She tried to remember what she knew about him. Shockingly little. There was the corporate takeover thing. "He's like those guys in the movie *Wall Street*, but nicer," Monica had said. What else had her friend told her? He wasn't married. He was some kind of pilot in his spare time—as evidenced by the vintage flying paraphernalia decorating part of the mountain home. He was in his thirties and handsome, Monica had supplied. "Your basic rich, confirmed bachelor type." With horror, Laura realized she didn't even know the man's name.

And yet she was rubbing her pussy for him.

If he was even watching. Again, she reminded herself that chances were slim—surely he wasn't.

But in that leaning-toward-surreal moment, she almost *wanted* him to be. Her breasts seemed to bloom with new desire at the confirmation. She wanted this man she didn't know to watch her play with herself.

In fact, the concept excited her so much that she decided to just pretend he was. Likely that light on the computer burned all day and all night, all the time, not really indicating if anyone was using the webcam thingy, but for now, she was going to follow the simple, delicious urge to indulge in a fantasy and believe that a dashing, worldly pilot-slash-corporate raider was watching with bated breath as she touched herself for him.

Moving her fingers in slow, deep circles over her clitoris, she closed her eyes and tried to feel his pretend gaze on her as warm pleasure spread through her. With her other hand, she unbuttoned the pajama top, all the way down, and pushed it open, revealing her breasts, both nipples taut when she ran her fingertips over first one, then the other. She imagined her voyeur's delight and was almost tempted to look into the camera, but then decided—no, let him think she had no idea anyone could possibly be there. Let him think this was just her, sensual and sexy, pleasing herself by the light of the fire.

She opened her eyes, glanced down at her nipples, dark and rosy in the room's warm glow. She used both hands to pinch them lightly, letting out a sigh at the sharp sensation between her thighs.

Easing one hand back down, she slid her fingers inside the pink elastic band and down into her wet folds. "Mmm," she purred, thinking, *Watch me. Watch me touch myself for you.*

Her fingertips sank deeper into her drenched flesh, massaging, feeling, stroking. She'd probably never explored her pussy this thoroughly before, and the thought hit her that it was about time she had!

Part of her was tempted to take off her panties and spread her legs wide so her imaginary voyeur could see how pink and wet she was with his own eyes—but no. She didn't want to give him *everything.* She wanted to titillate, tease. She wanted to make him ache for a glimpse of her swollen cunt.

She never stopped rubbing her fingertips over her clit as she used her other hand to ease down one side of her undies just a bit, then the other. She drew them only to the tops of her thighs, playing with him, torturing him as she continued to massage herself, letting out a light moan as her pleasure grew. "Mmm," she purred and felt a soft smile curve her lips. She was so close to coming, and the idea of being watched continued to escalate her heat, ratcheting it higher and higher.

Are you watching? Is your cock hard for me? She worked her clit in tight little circles, thrusting gently, gently, against her hand. *Are you waiting for me to come?*

"Oh, mmm . . ." she moaned when the orgasm hit, waves of hot, swallowing pleasure buffeting her whole body as she kept rubbing, rubbing, sighing heatedly with each crushing pulse of the climax. Oh God, it was good.

Had she ever come like this before? Had her pussy ever throbbed with such intensity? No, never—but she rode it out, still pumping, still stroking, until the last little pulsation ebbed.

As sanity returned, she bit her lip and resisted a glance in the webcam's direction. If that even *was* the webcam. She didn't hang out with any high-tech types—she'd never actually *seen* a webcam before.

Either way, though, the fantasy was over. It had brought her truly shocking pleasure, but it was done now.

And she was even more sure than before that no one had watched her masturbate, thank goodness. Stimulating as a fantasy, yes—but it was nothing Laura would ever want to live out. It just wasn't her style. And with a stranger, no less? Nope. Monica would probably *love* living it out, but not her.

Now she only had to hope that perhaps her orgasm had given her the needed release so she could concentrate on her book tomorrow and get Riley's story moving.

Plucking up her pj bottoms, she stepped into them and tied the drawstring waist, then buttoned her pajama top. Flipping the switches that killed the fire and turned the room dark but for the reflection of the moon on the snow shining through the floor-to-ceiling windows, she finally allowed herself to take another peek toward the supposed webcam.

Was there anyone there? She tilted her head, allowing herself to sincerely wonder once more, now that she was hidden in shadow.

No. Impossible. Or at least highly unlikely.

Good night, my imaginary voyeur.

Chapter Two

When Laura awoke the next morning, she still didn't find herself bubbling with a plot for Riley and Aunt Mimsey. *Damn it.*

But that was okay, she assured herself. After a cup of coffee and a bagel eaten while peering out on the snow-encrusted mountains in the distance, she put on a pair of jogging pants and a comfy long-sleeved T-shirt and situated herself before the computer, still convinced last night's release would surely be followed by a burst of creativity. On some level, she'd decided to believe Monica's theory—since maybe believing would make it so, helping her put some words on the computer screen today.

As she pulled up the file in which she was utterly determined to start writing a novel within the next few minutes, she glanced absently out the window, the view too beautiful to be ignored for long. But then her gaze stuck on the presumed webcam. A sense of relief washed over her when she saw that, yes, the little green light remained lit, meaning it was *always* lit and that no one had really been watching her last night.

"All right now, Riley, what mystery can you solve this time around?" she said to the computer. She'd completed seven Riley Wainscott Mysteries thus far, the last two making the *USA Today* best-seller list, and she'd come to rely on her "relationship" with Riley, the innate understanding she had of her character, to guide her when writing. She knew Riley wouldn't fail her now.

Slowly, the first seed of an idea began to grow in her mind. And whereas her plots were usually well thought-out before she ever committed a word to the page, she knew that this time she needed to simply take this kernel and run with it. She began to type.

Aunt Mimsey came bursting through the front door of her cottage quicker than Riley would have believed the old woman could move. "Riley, come quick!"

"What's wrong, Aunt Mimsey? Did Mrs. Dorchester's cat dig up your flower bed again?"

"No, it's a man."

Riley raised her eyebrows in doubt. "A man dug up your flower bed?"

Aunt Mimsey shook her head, clearly in distress. "No, silly girl. There's a man outside. I saw him lurking around the Dorchesters' guesthouse."

Just then, the computer let out a beep and a window appeared on the screen atop Aunt Mimsey's tirade. An Instant Message box.

FLYBOY1: Good morning.

Laura couldn't have been more stunned. Flyboy. Must be Monica's pilot/corporate raider cousin.

Well, maybe he was being polite enough to check on her arrival like this rather than with the webcam. Even so, given her exploits last night, it was unsettling.

The reply box that automatically opened was labeled FLYBOY2. She figured she had no choice but to answer. After all, the guy was letting her use his vacation home for free.

FLYBOY2: Hello.

FLYBOY1: I trust you arrived okay. How do you like the house?

*FLYBOY2: The house is fabulous. A per-
fect retreat. Thank you for letting me
use it.*

*FLYBOY1: Glad to have you there. Mon-
ica told me you were having some trouble
writing in your usual environment. Are
your creative juices flowing yet?*

FLYBOY2: Starting to, I think.

*FLYBOY1: Good. Are any other juices
flowing?*

Laura's stomach pinched tightly. She hesitated, trying to figure out how to respond. *FLYBOY2: Um, not sure what you mean.*

*FLYBOY1: Come on, Laura, you can be hon-
est. Your secret's safe with me <g>.*

Her pussy clenched, along with the rest of her body. She simply sat there, frozen, unable to think clearly . . . or reply.

*FLYBOY1: I saw you last night, Laura. I
saw you make yourself come.*

Her breasts ached as her chest tightened. Her heart threatened to pound right through her rib cage. Again, she couldn't answer. She couldn't fathom that he'd really seen her, that she'd really been performing, touching herself, for a real, live voyeur!

Yet another message appeared.

*FLYBOY1: Forgive me. I didn't do it on
purpose. Was just up late working and it
occurred to me I hadn't checked on your
arrival, so I flipped on the cam, and
there you were. I shouldn't have watched,
but what can I say? I'm a red-blooded
American male. And you're an incredibly
hot little houseguest, honey.*

Laura stared at his message in awe. Sensible responses to what had just happened raced through her mind. She should shut down the computer right now. More than that, she should pack up and leave, head right back to Seattle. Every logical instinct told her to run, to take whatever measures necessary—no matter how extreme—to get herself out of this situation that was so very *un*-her.

Yet her pussy pulsed under her jogging pants.

And Monica's description played back through her head. Handsome. Thirty-something.

How handsome? she should have asked Monica.

She bit her lip, felt her heartbeat speed up, and dropped her gaze to her fingers because she was nervous and wanted to make sure she hit the right letters. She could barely believe the reply she'd typed, even as she hit Send. FLYBOY2: Did I make you hard?

FLYBOY1: As a rock.

Mmm, the words on the screen turned her breasts heavy, achy. Could she actually do this? Have cybersex? Without even any wine to fuel her?

She wasn't sure what had gotten into her, but to her surprise, maybe she could. FLYBOY2: Did you suffer all night?

FLYBOY1: No, honey, afraid not. I took matters into my own hands, just like you <g>.

The image that entered her mind turned her crotch even warmer than it already was. FLYBOY2: Right at the computer? Or later, in bed?

FLYBOY1: Right at the computer. I came just a few seconds after you. Watching the pleasure wash over your face while you worked your hot little pussy pushed me over the edge.

Despite herself, despite what a dangerous game this might be, she yearned for more of that image—details. She suddenly longed to know exactly what she'd made happen to this man, this stranger. FLYBOY2: Did you come on the screen? The keyboard?

FLYBOY1: *No—caught it in a tissue. Computers are expensive. ;)*

If his computer at home was as extravagant as the one she worked on right now, he was right. She typed the first thought in her head without weighing it. FLYBOY2: *I would like to have seen.*

FLYBOY1: *Sorry, honey, the webcam only works one way.*

FLYBOY2: *That's not exactly fair.*

FLYBOY1: *Is your pussy wet right now? From talking about this?*

Oh God, was it ever. And her heart beat so hard it hurt. But maybe she should lie. Maybe it would be wise to say something jocular, or sarcastic, something to lighten the mood from the deep and dirty direction it had taken.

Only . . . she slowly realized that she *wanted* to tell him, wanted him to know. FLYBOY2: *Yes. My panties are already soaked.*

FLYBOY1: *Mmm, nice, baby.*

Then a rather horrifying thought occurred to her. FLYBOY2: *Can you see me right now?*

FLYBOY1: *Yes, Laura. I'm looking right at you.*

The knowledge made her want to shrink away. They weren't on equal footing—he seemed to have all the control.

FLYBOY1: *In fact, while we've been talking, your nipples have gotten hard. I know you're wearing a bra—I can see the outline through your shirt, but those pretty nipples are jutting through anyway.*

And growing harder by the second—she could almost feel it happening.

FLYBOY1: *You're blushing.*

She'd never felt so trapped between embarrassment and arousal. FLYBOY2: *I feel like I'm on a stage.*

FLYBOY1: I'm the only person in the
audience.

She bit her lip. FLYBOY2: Is that supposed to make
me feel better?

FLYBOY1: Yes. I like watching you.

Even that fed her desire, making her pussy flutter. Still more nervousness flitted through her as she asked the next thing that came to
mind, arousal beating out embarrassment, at least for this brief moment. FLYBOY2: Are you hard right now?

FLYBOY1: Very.

She didn't know why, but she chose that second to finally glance
down at her breasts, shrouded in a comfortable cotton bra today.
Maybe she'd thought now that they'd turned the attention to *his* body,
he wouldn't notice if she looked at *hers*? As he'd promised, the taut peaks
poked visibly through.

FLYBOY1: They're beautiful, Laura.

She played dumb, sorry to have been caught studying herself. FLY-
BOY2: What are you talking about?

FLYBOY1: Your breasts, of course. Fucking
beautiful. Watching you play with them
last night made me want to slide my cock
between them.

Oh God. Now her heart beat between her legs. And her breasts felt
huge, bigger than their C-cup size. This situation was already insane,
and it seemed to be spinning more and more out of control. What was
happening to her? Why couldn't she resist the forbidden allure of their
conversation? Before she could weigh the consequences, she found herself perpetuating it. FLYBOY2: How big is it?

FLYBOY1: My cock?

FLYBOY2: Yes.

FLYBOY1: Big enough :)

What guy *wouldn't* say that? FLYBOY2: Big enough for
what?

FLYBOY1: Big enough to satisfy you. I promise.

But she needed more. *FLYBOY2: Too vague. Could you be more specific?*

FLYBOY1: Well, at the moment, it feels about the size of the Washington Monument.

She couldn't help laughing lightly. *FLYBOY2: I'm looking for a number in inches, please.*

FLYBOY1: Sorry, honey, can't say I ever measured.

She decided to push her luck even further. *FLYBOY2: Do it now. If you feel as big as a monument, this is probably a good time.*

FLYBOY1: <g> Probably so, but you'll just have to take my word for it.

FLYBOY2: Why?

FLYBOY1: I don't have a ruler long enough.
:)

She lifted a grin in the direction of the webcam, amused, then posed the question that had just come to mind. *FLYBOY2: If you can see me, can you also hear me? Am I typing all this for nothing?* She was suddenly trying to remember if she'd moaned very much last night.

FLYBOY1: The camera captures sound, but it can be muffled, so typing is better.

Good. Maybe if she'd moaned, he hadn't heard.

FLYBOY1: Well, hot and sexy Laura, as much as I'd love to talk dirty with you all day, I have to sign off now.

FLYBOY2: Companies to take over? Empires to topple?

FLYBOY1: Something like that.

She couldn't help feeling vaguely disappointed that they were suddenly done. But then he IMed again.

FLYBOY1: Will I see more of you tonight?

She pulled in her breath at the loaded question. FLYBOY2: What do you mean?

FLYBOY1: Exactly what I asked. But let's make it earlier tonight. Ten, your time.

Ah, yes—it was an hour earlier in L.A. She considered the various ways she might respond, finally settling on simple clarification. FLYBOY2: Are you suggesting something similar to last night?

FLYBOY1: Yes, honey. That's EXACTLY what I'm suggesting. Except more.

FLYBOY2: More?

FLYBOY1: I want you to show me your pussy.

Laura pulled in her breath, forced back to reality. FLYBOY2: I can't.

FLYBOY1: Why not?

She hesitated, thought it through—then told him the truth. FLYBOY2: I thought I was alone last night. I don't think I could do that again—or more—knowing you were watching.

It was a slight lie, but last night had been more fantasy to her than anything else. Only just now had she truly discovered the fantasy had been reality—and she simply didn't think she was bold enough to do it again with the full knowledge that he was really watching her every naughty move. And to reveal herself even further? To show him the most intimate part of her, which only a handful of men had seen? And she had, at the very least, been *dating* those men. Never once had she fooled around with a stranger.

His reply took longer than usual. FLYBOY1: You don't know how much that disappoints me, Laura.

Her, too—in a way—if she was honest. But she knew herself too well. And the fact was, as much as she'd just let herself slip wholly into this hot conversation, when she drew back and looked at it sensibly, it still seemed . . . dangerous. FLYBOY2: I'm sorry.

FLYBOY1: No, honey, I'M sorry.

The statement could be read two different ways, but she knew he wasn't apologizing for having made her uncomfortable—he was bummed to hear the dirty fun was over.

She didn't answer, as there seemed nothing more to say.

Although it remained unnerving to know he was still watching her. A solution came to mind, given that she planned to spend the next ten days in his vacation home. FLYBOY2: Maybe I should move the camera, point it at the floor.

FLYBOY1: Don't bother. I can move the lens around no matter which way you aim it.

Her back went rigid. FLYBOY2: So you're saying you'll keep watching me, whether I want you to or not? Whether or not I'm even doing anything . . . naughty?

FLYBOY1: What can I say? I like watching you. You like it, too—I can tell. So just think of me like a fly on the wall. And who knows, if I'm patient, maybe I'll get lucky and you'll do something naughty for me anyway.

FLYBOY2: Don't bet on it. I know I just had a very dirty discussion with you, but I'm slowly coming back to my senses.

FLYBOY1: That's a shame. You do dirty very well.

Then an entirely new question hit her, the thought almost paralyzing her. FLYBOY2: Do you do this often? Watch women this way? Other people who come here?

She wasn't sure why the notion upset her so much, but it did. Maybe it made her feel less consequential to him than she wanted to—even if she *didn't* know him at all.

> FLYBOY1: No, I told you—this happened by accident. But now that I've seen you, I want to KEEP ON seeing you.

She bit her lip, torn between relief, flattery, and . . . what felt like a very sensible worry that prompted her next reply. *FLYBOY2: I suppose I could unhook the webcam from the computer.*

> FLYBOY1: You won't.

So confident.

> FLYBOY2: You don't think so?
>
> FLYBOY1: No.

And for some reason, she knew he was right. This was his home, and he'd been generous enough to lend it to someone he didn't know. Despite the circumstances, it seemed wrong to mess with his equipment and risk breaking something or somehow screwing up his expensive computer.

It would be daunting to sit here working, knowing he might be watching her at any time, but so long as she kept her clothes on, it was no big deal. Logically, anyway. In fact, before long, he'd probably get bored and stop watching her at all.

As she sat contemplating that, he sent another message.

> FLYBOY1: If you change your mind, I'll be here tonight at ten.

She drew in her breath, then simply lifted her gaze to the camera and quietly shook her head.

> FLYBOY1: By the way, assign yourself a new I.M. name other than mine. Flyboy2 just doesn't suit you. ;)

She felt a bit numb as she typed. *FLYBOY2: What does?*

FLYBOY1: Something sexy. Good-bye for
now, sexy.
FLYBOY2: Good-bye, Flyboy. Happy empire
toppling.
FLYBOY1: I'll see you tonight. ;)

* * *

The story finally took off—in leaps and bounds. By the time darkness fell around the mountainside home, Laura had written a chapter and a half and had outlined approximately a third of the book in her mind. Turned out the man Aunt Mimsey had seen lurking around the neighbors' guest-house had been a dark, handsome, rugged sort, full of mystery. Riley had confronted him—and been bowled over by his confident sex appeal.

Not a normal encounter for Riley Wainscott. Like Laura, Riley dated, sometimes had relationships that lasted a while, sometimes woke up happy after making love, but always behaved sensibly when it came to men and sex. So much so that it was almost a moot point in Riley's life, a subject that never really played into Laura's plots in any significant way—until today. For the first time, Laura had uncovered the sensual woman beneath Riley's staid exterior. She'd let Riley experience an unbidden pulse between her thighs, just as Laura had that morning. And she knew that pulse, that temptation, that forbidden instinct, would have real consequences for Riley and this case before the book was through.

She walked away from the computer with a familiar sense of satisfaction and progress—thank God, she was back on track!

Of course, walking away, leaving Riley and her enigmatic stranger behind, gave her time to begin pondering *other* things—like her online conversation with Monica's cousin this morning.

She *still* didn't know his name. They'd shared an intimate exchange about her pussy and his cock, but she didn't know the man's name. Ridiculous.

No, more than ridiculous. More like shocking. What had driven her to continue the conversation when she'd known good and well that the safe move was to ignore his suggestive comments and questions? *Watching the pleasure wash over your face while you worked your hot little pussy pushed me over the edge.* Okay, *way* more than suggestive. He'd been downright obscene. What she'd done this morning was so dangerous that she could scarcely believe she'd been so foolish, or so bold.

Moving into the kitchen, as spacious and lavish as the rest of the house, she dug in the refrigerator for the leftover spaghetti she'd cooked last night, trying desperately to ignore her physical response to the memory of this morning. Like it or not, thinking of him had her body humming again.

But then, hadn't her body been humming all day? She could tell herself it had been humming on *Riley's* behalf, for a shadowy stranger who might mean harm to Aunt Mimsey or her neighbors, but how could she deny to herself who that stranger *really* was? Her voyeur. Her companion in dirty message exchange. Her pussy tingled at the admission.

You need a shower—a nice, cool shower. Despite the deep snow outside, the house remained warm from afternoon sun having blasted in through all those enormous windows. So first she ate her spaghetti, hot from the microwave, accompanied by a glass of wine from the bottle she'd opened last night, then she placed her dirty dishes in the sink and headed toward the master suite, to the immense marble shower.

As she reached the oversize bedroom, complete with oversize bed, oversize Jacuzzi tub, and oversize closets with mirrored doors, she stopped and looked around. She'd slept in this bed last night, of course. And she'd showered here this morning. But all that had been before their online conversation, before she'd found out he'd watched her rub between her legs until she came, before he'd told her he wanted her to do it for him again.

Now she almost *felt* him here. She was sleeping in his bed, after all, on the same sheets, the same pillows. She would undoubtedly dry herself off with a towel that had dried *his* skin.

Suddenly, a shower didn't seem like such a great idea. It only stood to make her all the more aware of her body, how sensitive it was feeling since last night, how ready, how needy. "Fine," she murmured. "No shower."

TV. She would watch TV. Sitcoms. Or some twenty-four-hour news channel. Nothing sexy *there*.

As she moved back to the living room, she paused next to a set of tall oak bookshelves. She'd been meaning to inspect the books in the house since she'd arrived yesterday but hadn't gotten around to it. And it seemed as good a distraction as any.

She found mostly classics: *A Farewell to Arms, A Tale of Two Cities, The House of the Seven Gables, To Kill a Mockingbird*. And upon moving down to lower shelves, she was surprised—although instantly knew she shouldn't be—to find a small collection of classic erotica: *Story of O, The Pearl*, volumes by Anaïs Nin and the Marquis de Sade. Her breasts felt heavy just looking at the titles, thinking of her flyboy voyeur reading them, getting excited, getting off.

The gentle sensations in her cunt urged her to reach for one of them—but no.

Tonight was all about sitcoms and news and maybe something by Hemingway a little later. Tonight was about ignoring the tender throb in her pussy when she thought of the nameless, faceless man to whom the books belonged. In fact, it would be a good time to *stop* thinking of that part of herself as her pussy. *Time to be the staid, dependable, sensible you.*

Just then, her gaze fell on a small framed photo on the shelf above the erotica. She gasped at the sight. Two men dressed in cargo shorts held up a gigantic fish between them. One wore a T-shirt that said FLY ME, BABY! along with a graphic of what looked to be an old biplane with a big propeller in front. He was darkly handsome, as Monica had promised, his chin covered with a few days' stubble. Although in the photo he appeared lighthearted and casual, his dark eyes were piercing. And she couldn't help noticing that, despite his loose, baggy shorts, there was a nice bulge visible in front.

The other man was lighter in coloring—dark blond, wavy hair, with a classic ski bum look about him—and Laura knew without doubt that the first guy was *her* guy, the man who'd spied on her last night and talked nasty to her this morning. God, he was gorgeous. Her nipples tightened within her bra as she studied him, wishing the photo were closer up. Her crotch responded, as well, seeming to swell beneath her pants.

Finally, she set the picture back down and let out a sigh. Him being gorgeous really had nothing to do with her quandary. It made it no less frightening and dangerous to exchange dirty talk with a man she didn't know.

Nope, no less dangerous—but certainly even more of a turn-on now.

She let her eyes fall shut, feeling doomed.

But then she regained her strength and told herself to stick to her original plan. She padded to an easy chair that sat adjacent to the sofa where she'd sprawled so brazenly last night, then reached for the remote and flipped on the big-screen TV. She was in luck. World news.

Another glass of wine and maybe she'd get sleepy enough to go to bed early—as in before ten o'clock.

A few hours later, Laura lay in bed in her snowflake pajamas, tossing and turning. Like last night, the wine had left her more loopy than sleepy, but she'd gone to bed anyway. Of course, she'd taken a volume of Anaïs Nin with her and, before turning the lights out, had read about a woman having her "sex" shaved by two men. They'd touched the freshly smooth skin there, then teased her open with erotic brushes of a feather. Another story had featured a woman riding a large rocking horse with a knob built in to rub her clit.

God, what a stupid thing to have let herself read!

She couldn't resist shifting her gaze from the vaulted ceiling to the digital bedside clock. 9:54.

She tenderly bit her lip, trying madly to ignore the way her *own* sex pulsed, begging for her touch. Or *his* touch. *Any* touch.

Of course, she couldn't do what he'd asked of her. There was simply no way. Last night had been bad enough, but to know for sure he was watching? And to reveal herself to him—fully. She shook her head against her pillow. *You can't. For God's sake, you don't even know his name.*

Even so, she found her breath trembling and her belly clenching way down low as she reached to push back the covers.

Maybe she didn't know herself as well as she thought.

Chapter Three

It had been a damn long day.

Because unlike last night when he'd simply unzipped his pants, pulled out his aching cock, and jacked off, today he'd been stupid enough to wait, to want to hover on the edge of excitement all day, anticipating what might happen tonight. It was like a game he'd wanted to play with himself—with her, too.

Now his dick physically hurt. He'd floated somewhere between half-hard and full-blown erection all day, through meetings, phone calls, and lunch with a senior V.P. with whom he was doing some important negotiations.

The whole time he'd been fantasizing about Laura Watkins, mystery author, sex kitten. *She* didn't think she was a sex kitten, that was clear. But he knew she was—he'd seen the proof, and gotten off to it. Her hot little show, combined with their steamy conversation this morning, had excited him more than anything had in a very long time.

Now, as he sat in his Malibu home in a dark, quiet room lit only by his computer screen, a warm sea breeze wafting through an open window behind him, he found himself watching the clock, feeling as eager as a teenager getting his first peek at Internet porn. And he began to relive a few of the fantasies that had grown in his mind around lovely

Laura today at times when he most definitely should have been focusing on his work. Yep, millions of dollars at stake every hour, and he'd been fantasizing about a woman. But he'd felt powerless to stop—the images had simply kept invading his brain without his permission.

During a meeting with Cressler, Inc.'s entire board of directors, he'd imagined her in the Jacuzzi in the Vail house, soaping her luscious breasts, tweaking those hard, pretty nipples, then rising on her knees to run a soapy cloth between her thighs, sighing just like she had last night on the webcam.

Those visions alone were enough to keep him going for awhile, but by the time he got stuck on hold waiting for one of his investors around eleven, he'd imagined a sexy Laker girl he'd once dated walking into the master suite's bathroom, just as naked as Laura. Pam possessed a lush, curvy body, much like sexy Ms. Watkins', so envisioning the two of them together seemed a foregone conclusion for a guy who admittedly got off on the idea of women fooling around with each other. Pam's long blond hair had been swept up off her neck in a clip, her pussy waxed bare—and he knew from experience she kept it that way. Laura's hair had hung finer, a warm shade of chestnut, and fell just past her shoulders, but in the fantasy, Pam had moved behind her and pulled it up into another clip, as well.

Pam had stepped into the bathtub filled with bubble bath and whirling water, kneeling across from Laura, and the two of them had begun to wash each other's breasts. They giggled and cooed and made him all the harder as he waited on interminable hold. Thank God he'd had a suit jacket to cover his jutting cock since he'd been sitting in a large, open lobby.

Soon the two lovely women had begun kissing—gentle meetings of moist lips and warm tongues that made him think for a moment he might come in his pants like a schoolboy. They'd embraced softly, their plump, soapy breasts brushing together. He wondered if Laura had ever been with another girl *outside* of his fantasies. He doubted it, but it was nice to think about.

Finally, his investor had come back on the line, reclaiming his attention but not weakening his lust. It had been at lunch with the rambling comptroller of Ion Electronics that the fantasy had continued. He'd needed to hear what the man was saying—there was a pivotal merger on the horizon and he couldn't risk fucking it up—but he couldn't help himself. When he'd seen a pretty girl across the restaurant who, at a glance, made him think of Laura Watkins, he'd been taken back to that big bathtub and the two sensual women inside it.

As the Ion comptroller talked about recent acquisitions adding to the company's value, he'd seen Laura sitting on the edge of the tub, legs parted, Pam's face in between. Laura had caressed her breasts, just like last night, and she'd moaned and howled as Pam licked her pussy. God, how *he* wanted to lick that pussy. Hell, just *see* that pussy for starters.

And as the Ion comp droned about employee security and pension plans, he'd seen himself entering the picture, kneeling on the tile surrounding the Jacuzzi so that his cock was level with Laura's pretty mouth. She'd opened wide with a big smile and lowered her lips over him, moaning from still having her pussy eaten below.

Even reenvisioning it now had him sweating.

He shook his head to clear it and looked at the small gold clock on his desk. It read a few minutes past nine, which meant past ten in Colorado.

Damn—he'd quit paying attention and the computer had slipped into screensaver mode. He rushed to move the mouse and light back up the screen. Then he clicked on the icon for the webcam at the Vail house.

The room was empty, dark but for the pale illumination provided by the blanket of snow outside the wall of windows behind the computer.

His heart fell. His cock almost deflated. He'd been sure she would be there, putting on another sexy little show for him. After the way she'd responded to him this morning, he'd been sure she wouldn't be able to resist. After all, she was alone in that big house, just writing all day—surely she needed some kind of sexual release. And he'd given her a forbidden and exciting way to get it.

Even so, as he focused the camera, shifting the lens about the room, the space remained quiet, still, shadows of sofas and tables and nothing more. Apparently, he'd misjudged her enthusiasm. Apparently, she wasn't coming to the *last* meeting he'd set up for today, the one he'd waited for through all the rest with a raging hard-on. Looked like the forbidden aspect of their fun was, just as she'd intimated, *too* forbidden for her.

"Damn," he whispered in the dark. "I want more of you, honey."

Laura looked in the mirrored door on the closet, studying herself from head to toe. Her hair fell in loose waves around her face, which was made up with mascara and lipstick—same as she might apply for a night out clubbing with Monica and the girls. Around her neck, a beaded red choker. The scant lacy red push-up bra plumped her breasts nearly to her chin, making them look large and sexy. Below, she wore a matching red thong that clung so tightly to her mound that the fleshy rise already looked swollen with desire.

When she'd found the small shopping bag containing the bra and panties in her suitcase yesterday, she never dreamed she'd be so thankful her friend had snuck it in, with a note that said:

Just in case you decide to give up the solitude and find yourself some ski stud. Love, Monica.

Well, she hadn't given up the solitude, nor found a ski stud, but she had the next best thing—a stud with a webcam who wanted her. When all was said and done, she simply couldn't resist the same excitement she'd experienced last night upon just *pretending* someone was watching her. Try as she might, she couldn't seem to deny herself the real thing. She remained afraid, but also needy. That need pulsed through her veins as tangible as the flow of blood.

So she'd finally given in to the temptation. At least for now. She might have regrets later, but in this moment, it was show time. And there would be no cotton pj's tonight.

She took a deep breath and moved barefoot from the bedroom into the living room, then turned on the lights, but used the dimmer to keep them soft.

His eyes were on her, she could *feel* them—instantly.

The very knowledge made her nipples constrict within the scalloped edge of red lace that held her so snugly.

As she moved to the sofa, she felt like she was returning to the scene of a crime. Deliciously wicked. Her cunt vibrated against its lace confinement, the tender scratch of the fabric a further titillation.

Upon sitting down, she gently bit her lip, looked toward the webcam, and spoke quietly. "I wasn't going to do this, but here I am, for reasons I can't explain." Then she peered more intently at the green light, imagining she could see him, eye-to-sexy-eye. "Are you ready?"

She envisioned him—drawing the image from the photo on the bookshelves—sitting behind his desk, getting hard for her. The thought nearly took her breath—everything about this was utterly overwhelming. In fact, she feared if she thought too hard about what she was doing, she might get scared again and back out. So instead, she simply began, reaching both hands up to cup the lower halves of her breasts.

They were heavy, full and round in her palms. She imagined her flyboy groaning at the sight of her touching herself for him and wished she could hear it. Wished again that she could see him, just like he could see her.

She closed her eyes and gave her lower lip a small, sensual nibble, imagining how grand it would be if he sat right across the room from her. The camera *should* provide a sense of safety—and maybe it did, maybe the distance between herself and her voyeur was the one factor that allowed her to do this. Yet at the same time, she wanted him nearer, wanted him here.

Watch me, she thought as she tweaked her nipples through the lace that barely concealed them. She then massaged them fully, wishing for *his* hands, thinking of his cock doing what he'd said this morning—gliding between the plump mounds of flesh.

Watch me, she thought as she slipped her fingertips into both red cups, lowering them just enough to free the beaded pink peaks. Her face warmed at revealing them to him again. She remembered how "fucking beautiful" he thought they were and toyed with her hardened nipples, letting the sensation trickle through her, all the way to her lacy panties, making her pussy quiver.

Oh yes, watch me, baby, watch me. She ran her hands down over the smooth curves of her stomach, sliding them over the lace at her hips, letting her fingers splay onto her thighs. Moving slow but never stopping, she parted her legs, let her hands glide inward, both of them sweeping firmly over her crotch before drawing back to the panties' top edge.

Do you want to see me? See my pussy? She kept the words inside, but her own hunger to show him, to be this other entity, to release this other part of herself she was just now discovering with such shock, drove her. She'd never known she was such a dirty girl. She'd never known such forbidden fires burned inside her.

But burn they did—hotter and hotter with each passing second, she discovered—until she rose to her feet, squarely facing the camera, then smoothly lowered her panties over her hips, down her thighs, pulling damp lace from in between, then pushing the thong past her knees. The fabric fell to her ankles, allowing her to step free of it, at which point she turned around and bent at the waist, bracing her hands on the back of the sofa, letting him look at her from behind. Instinct led her to lift first one knee onto the couch, then the other, parting her legs slightly, arching her ass toward him.

You wanted to see me so badly—well, here I am, baby.

Look at me. Look at my pussy.

At that moment, it was the greatest part of her, filled with need and want and a raw hunger that knew no shame.

Oh God, she wanted him back there, behind her, wanted to feel his hands on her ass, his hard shaft pushing its way inside. Without forethought, she looked over her shoulder, into the camera, and said, "If you were here right now, I'd beg you to take me like this. To fuck me hard and deep."

A thousand miles away, he watched her, mesmerized—and spoke back to the screen even though he knew she couldn't hear. "Aw, baby— you're *so* fucking hot." His cock jutted from his open pants and his fist wrapped warm around it.

He'd spent a few sad, lonely minutes thinking she really *wasn't* going to show, that he'd really had all of her he was going to get—and then, when he'd been just about to give up and walk away, she'd appeared in that pretty and unexpected bra-and-panties set, her hair and face done up to make her into the sexual being he knew she was. A sizzling heat had burned from his chest to his dick at the sight of her. All that waiting hadn't been for nothing. And now Laura was showing him her pretty little cunt, telling him she wanted him to fuck her, and his whole existence in that moment became about good, hot, nasty sex.

He watched in pure amazement as she turned to sit on the couch, parting her thighs wide, draping one leg over the sofa's stuffed arm to put her pussy even more widely on display. He feasted on it with his eyes—so pink and open—wishing he could do so with his mouth. He heard the light sound of her breath, coming labored as she stroked one long, tapered finger through her wetness.

"Damn, honey," he murmured, pulling at his cock.

His own raspy breath joined hers, seeming to fill the darkened room.

"More," he urged her. "Touch it for me."

It was almost as if she'd heard, and he let a wicked smile take him as her middle finger began to twirl hard, rhythmic circles over her clit, now protruding so prettily from her slick folds.

"Oh yeah—rub that pretty pussy for me."

She did, thrusting lightly now as the first two fingers of her right hand extended down into her parted flesh. Her left hand rose to cup one breast, squeezing, raking her thumb across the taut mauve nipple pointing out over the uneven edging of her bra.

"So nice, baby," he breathed toward the screen, wishing she *could* hear, wishing all this fucking distance didn't lay between them. At first, that part had been exciting—but already, this fast, he wanted to do away with it and be with her, two bodies thrusting together, the way it was naturally supposed to be.

But on the other hand, who was he to complain? Laura Watkins had surrendered herself to him in a way she'd never planned and admittedly never thought she could, and his cock swelled further with dark, masculine pride at knowing this show was just for him, for his pleasure, and hers. If a few states separated them, hell, this was surely the next best thing to being there, and a damn hot treat to have grown from his innocent late-night peek into the house last night.

He gripped his hardened length tighter, wanting to give it to her so bad he could almost taste it. He kept his eyes glued to her gorgeous cunt, her bountiful breasts, the lost look of passion on her pretty face. She was getting close, he could tell, rubbing herself more intensely, gritting her teeth lightly, squeezing first one breast then the other with more ferocity than he'd yet seen from her. "That's right, honey," he said lowly, "keep going. Get yourself off for me. Get yourself off."

Her breath came heavier still, and so did his own. He tugged at his cock, matching her rhythm and knowing he couldn't hold back much longer. "Come, baby," he urged. "Come for me now."

The circles she rubbed over the top part of her pussy grew faster—and deeper, too. He could tell from the way she moved her hand, from the sweet agony reshaping her face. She was panting now, and then began to let out short, hot little sobs: "Oh . . . oh . . . oh . . ."

His chest rose and fell as desire tightened inside him, centering in his groin. His dick throbbed in his hand.

And then she released a high-pitched cry and he saw the ecstasy transform her expression—even with her eyes shut, her muscles relaxed, and any agony on her face softened to pure pleasure. She lifted herself in a harder, slower rhythm against her hand as she rode out the climax—and he said, "Ah, damn," since he knew he was going to come, too, no stopping it, and he exploded in long, intense bursts into the tissues he, thankfully, had already placed at his side.

The heated pulses forced his eyes shut and delivered the usual brief-but-blissful out-of-body experience before it all faded to exhaustion and let him refocus on the screen.

Laura sat on the couch, still now, but her legs remained prettily spread, like a centerfold picture on his computer. She licked her upper lip and looked straight at him, eyes glassy. In the aftermath of orgasm, her skin seemed to glow on the high-resolution screen, and she looked thoroughly satisfied . . . yet her expression made him wonder what *else* lurked inside her.

"This isn't me," she said quietly to the camera. Then gave her head a soft shake that made her hair bounce and her breasts jiggle lightly. "I don't know what you do to me."

His chest spasmed at her words. He hated that she didn't understand that this *was*, indeed, very clearly *her*. But he loved being the man getting to show her. And he continued to be all the more astonished to realize, once more, that it had happened completely by accident, and through a mere computer screen.

I know what I do to you, Laura. I get you hot. Hotter than anyone ever has.

And I'm going to get you even hotter.

Hold on tight, baby, because this ride is just starting, and before it's over, I'm going to make you do things you've never even thought about before.

Getting up and walking out of the room, stopping only to scoop up her sexy panties on the way, had felt no less than surreal. Laura had spent the next ten minutes fluctuating between embarrassment, disbelief, and the odd sense of exhilaration that had remained after so openly touching herself for her corporate-raider-flyboy-without-a-name.

She couldn't believe she'd done it. But she also couldn't believe how utterly incredible it had felt. *Knowing* his eyes had been on her—not just a fantasy—had excited her more than anything ever had. Starting out, of course, she hadn't been sure she could really do it—but oh, had she ever done it! And once she'd let go of her worries and fears, once she'd forgotten about everything else but his eyes and her body, it had been sinfully easy.

To her surprise, she didn't feel like changing into comfy pajamas afterward, so instead she'd slept naked. She woke up the next morning feeling freer and more energized just from remembering the previous night. She put on only a pair of white cotton panties and a strappy yellow cami to head down to the kitchen, wondering why she hadn't started wearing less here sooner. Despite the snow outside, the house stayed warm—overly so when the sun was out—so she'd probably be much more comfortable this way than she had the first night and through the day yesterday.

After consuming coffee and a bowl of cereal while looking out at the peaceful white setting—where she noticed the tracks of a rabbit or some other small animal—she headed straight for the computer, as anxious as Riley Wainscott probably was to find out what exactly the dark stranger was up to and if it had anything to do with the priceless antique broach that had turned up missing from Mrs. Dorchester's jewel box during her writing late yesterday. Aunt Mimsey certainly thought him suspicious, but Riley was holding her judgment for the time being—and planning to investigate him a *lot* more thoroughly before she made up her mind.

By noon, Riley had stumbled across the man pawing through the Dorchesters' toolshed behind the flower garden. But instead of making up some excuse when she opened the door and their eyes met across the dimly lit space, instead of trying to push past her and run away, he'd instead looked at her like a man who wanted to *possess* her. Her blood had run hot and Riley had been stunned, having never suffered such a visceral reaction to a guy before.

Then he'd kissed her.

Long and hard and passionate.

Riley felt the kiss everywhere—from the top of her head to the tips of her toes. She knew she should push him away— he was a suspect, not to mention a total stranger—yet she couldn't find the strength to end the most glorious kiss of her life. His mouth captured hers, leaving her no choice but to submit. The musky scent of him permeated her senses and he tasted vaguely of mint.

When finally the man pulled back—still holding her in his strong embrace but giving her the chance to peer up into his dark, commanding eyes—she thought of everything she should be doing right now: breaking free of his hold, asking him what the hell he was doing in here, finding out just exactly who he was. Yet his smoldering gaze made it hard to think of detective work at the moment, and when she opened her mouth to in- terrogate him, she instead found herself uttering one lone and telling word. "More."

The rumble of a large vehicle cut suddenly through Laura's concen- tration, forcing her to abandon Riley for the moment. Was someone arriving *here*? Must be, she presumed, given that the house was located at the end of a long driveway, several hundred feet off the winding moun- tain road. This was the first vehicle she'd heard since her arrival.

She hopped to her feet, rushed to the door, and glanced out the nar- row panel of glass beside it to see a standard-issue white delivery truck. The logo on the door said TRIXIE'S in a rather elaborate script. Trixie's?

She was waiting to see what on earth was coming to "Flyboy" from a place called "Trixie's" when she happened to glance down and no- tice her nipples pointing prominently through her little top. And damn it—she only had on panties below, which she'd totally forgotten about, so caught up had she become in Riley's sensual encounter.

She dashed for the stairs, jogging toward the master bedroom.

Unthinkingly, she shoved open the nearest mirrored closet door and—voilà!—spied a white terry-cloth robe like you sometimes found in hotels. Yanking it from the hanger, she thrust her arms inside.

When the doorbell rang, she started toward it, tying the robe in front on the way down the stairs. She opened the door to find the young man on the other side smiling at her as if they shared a private joke. "Laura Watkins?"

She flinched. She'd been sure this would be something for her voyeur. Who knew she was here?

Wait. Monica, of course. Which made the pieces fit. Trixie's must be exactly what it sounded like to Laura—some racy lingerie shop. And Monica of the red lace surprise had apparently taken it upon herself to send Laura something *else* slinky and sexy.

"Yes, that's me," she finally said.

He handed her a shiny black box sporting an even shinier thick black ribbon. Predictably, she blushed, since they clearly both knew something designed for sex was inside.

"Thanks," she murmured, embarrassment overriding any thoughts of a tip, then practically slammed the door in his face, turning the lock. After which she headed to the couch where she had so brazenly touched herself for her stranger last night.

Wow, apparently Monica was downright *determined* for Laura to see some action on this trip. Dear God, if her friend only knew about the unexpected—not to mention *bizarre*—action that *had* occurred.

Not that Monica would ever find out. They were best friends, but something about this felt so immeasurably *private* that she knew she'd never share it with another soul.

Although it flitted through her mind that another sexy outfit might actually come in handy, under the circumstances.

Maybe.

She let out a sigh. Was she really going to do it for him *again*? Going to *keep* doing it? Taking her clothes off and rubbing herself to orgasm for a stranger behind a camera? Put in those terms, it sounded absolutely horrifying.

If only it had *felt* that way, too, it would be a lot easier to resist the odd temptation.

As it was, well . . . she hadn't contemplated it yet today. She'd certainly *remembered* it. She'd certainly felt *alive* and *energetic*—and *creative!*—today. But she hadn't thought to the future, to what would happen now. Maybe she just hadn't let herself.

And now that she *was* mulling it over, she simply didn't know the answer.

Too hot from the robe, that fast, she untied the belt and let the terry cloth fall from her shoulders. Extracting her arms, she pulled at the black ribbon to untie the rather titillating package.

Inside, atop black tissue paper lay a white card.

For tonight. Ten o'clock. Don't be late, honey.

Oh God. It wasn't from Monica. It was from *him!*

Swallowing her shock, she cautiously folded back the tissue paper, gasping at what she saw inside. A black velvet corset. Black lace-top stockings. And a purple vibrator shaped like a penis, the likes of which she'd seen only on the one occasion Monica had dragged her into a sex shop. "Oh, dear God," she murmured.

Without another thought, she set the box aside, shot to her feet, and took the few short steps to the computer. Since he'd told her to change her screen name, she pulled up her usual IM identity—which she used mostly with Monica—*Riley*.

RILEY: Are you there? This is Laura, your houseguest.

She wasn't sure yet exactly what she was going to say to him, but it leaned toward letting him know he'd gone too far, and wondering how the hell he'd gotten the package to her so quickly, and telling him she was *not* going to . . . to . . . use a sexual device while he watched!

FLYBOY1: Good morning, snowflake.

What? RILEY: Snowflake?

*FLYBOY1: Just noticed them on your paja-
mas the other night, that's all. Before
you opened them, I mean. Then I quit noticing anything but you. ;) Who's Riley?*

RILEY: The main character in my books.

FLYBOY1: Are you her?

RILEY: No. Not really. But after a sigh, honesty
made her add: *Well, okay, yes, I guess we do
have a lot in common.*

*FLYBOY1: Then I'm sorry I've never read
your books. What are they about? I know
you write mysteries, but that's all.
What's Riley's story?*

Geez, of all the times for him to get inquisitive on a subject other
than sex. He'd managed to totally distract her from her purpose.

*RILEY: Riley is a part-time secretary at
a private investigations firm by day, but
an amateur sleuth by night. She wants
desperately to hang up her sensible pumps
and be a real detective, but no one in
her town takes her seriously or will give
her a chance. So she sets about solving
mysteries in order to prove herself, but
every time she solves one, someone else
gets the credit. Her Aunt Mimsey is the
only other person who realizes how smart
she is, but Aunt Mimsey is kind of dotty,
so no one believes her when she sings
Riley's detecting praises. Riley's only
real satisfaction comes from convincing
herself she's a good detective despite
what everyone thinks and looking forward
to trying to prove it to them next time.*

FLYBOY1: Wow. So does this mean you're a detective?

RILEY: No, that's not the part we have in common.

FLYBOY1: Then what DO you have in common?

Laura considered her answer. She'd never actually examined this before right now. RILEY: Well, Riley and I are both smart, sensible, and generally pretty conservative. Which brings me back to why I IMed you. I just got a delivery here.

FLYBOY1: Ah. That was quick.

She let out a heavy breath. That's all he had to say? Well, she'd just go with the flow, especially since that was one of her questions. RILEY: I'll say. How the hell did you DO that?

FLYBOY1: Simple, really. An online catalog for a place in Denver, and a phone call. It's called same-day delivery, honey.

RILEY: That usually costs an arm and a leg.

FLYBOY1: I have a lot of money. What did you think of the gift?

She hesitated. A minute ago she'd been overcome with a sense of urgency, ready to yell at him for this, but now, faced with the opportunity, she wasn't quite sure what she wanted to say. RILEY: I was . . . shocked.

FLYBOY1: Why?

RILEY: I've never . . .

I've never what? she asked herself. She didn't know how to say this. But she tried again anyway.

RILEY: I've never really done THAT before.

FLYBOY1: Really? You've never used a vibrator?

RILEY: No.

FLYBOY1: Damn, honey.

RILEY: What does THAT mean?

FLYBOY1: That now I'm EXTRA glad I got it
for you.

She let out a sigh. Was she so very odd? Did every other woman on
the planet own a wide array of such tools? RILEY: Why do you
consider a vibrator so vital to my existence?

FLYBOY1: Because you're a very sexual person.

She blinked at the computer, shocked and annoyed. RILEY: How
do YOU know?

FLYBOY1: <raising eyebrows> Are you serious?

Another sigh. RILEY: Okay, okay. But I told you
last night . . . I'm not usually like that. I
don't do those things.

FLYBOY1: You do now. And you're beautiful touching yourself, you know. I barely
managed to wait until you came before I
did. And that's not a problem I generally
have.

Time to get down to business. And she'd just made a decision. She'd
said it herself. She was smart, sensible, and conservative. Not a prim
goody-two-shoes who wore turtlenecks and insisted on dating a guy
forever before sleeping with him—not anything exorbitant or extreme.
But she was simply an even-keeled, middle-of-the-road woman who
didn't go to the *other* extreme, either. And last night had been inexplica-
bly extreme for her. It was time to get back to normal here. RILEY: I
can't keep doing this.

FLYBOY1: Why not?

RILEY: It's so . . . dirty. And I don't
even know you.

FLYBOY1: You're GETTING to know me.

RILEY: I don't even know your name.

FLYBOY1: Braden.

RILEY: Is that your first name or your last?

FLYBOY1: First. Braden Stone.

Laura hesitated. Braden. She liked it. Sounded strong. Rugged. Sexy. But that was hardly a reason to back down on what she was telling him.

RILEY: Well . . . I still don't know you.

FLYBOY1: And yet you want me.

True enough. Her pussy was pulsing again just from IMing with him like this. A guy she couldn't even see, or hear, let alone touch. And damn it, she'd just thought of that part of her body as her pussy again. If she really wanted this to end, that would be a good place to start. In fact, maybe she should just quit thinking about that part of herself *period.*

When she still hadn't replied to him a minute later, he sent another message. *FLYBOY1: I want you, too. I want to see you come again. I want to see you use the toy I sent you.*

Dear God. The very idea of that was . . . unfathomable.

Still, she didn't answer. Simply because she had no idea how to respond to such a raw, intimate request.

FLYBOY1: See you tonight, snowflake. Ten o'clock. I know you won't let me down.

Chapter Four

What arrogance. He was so sure of himself. So sure of her, too. She couldn't help rolling her eyes at the computer.

Well, he had another thing coming. *RILEY: Are you still there?*

She was going to tell him what she'd intended to in the first place, the part about him going too far.

Only no answer came. Drat. She tried again. *RILEY: Hey, are you there? Answer me.*

Damn it. He must really be gone—off to raid yet another corporation or fly an airplane or something.

"I hate you," she whispered to the computer screen, even knowing he could no longer see or hear her. Which was probably why she said it—since she didn't really hate him. Far from it. She was *intrigued* by him. Had a strange *crush* on him. Felt bizarrely *lured in* by him. It was the last one that scared her—how did this guy make her want to do these shockingly out-of-character things? Why did she want to please him, excite him, so much?

She glanced over her shoulder to the bookshelves where the photo of him sat. Was it just because he was hot? Admittedly, if he'd been twenty years older or twenty pounds heavier—or, frankly, just not attractive to her—she knew she wouldn't keep perpetuating this. In fact, she probably would have packed up and left by now, out of sheer horror over revealing so much of herself to someone she'd never even met. But there was a lot to be said for chemistry. And if it was possible to feel this much chemistry with someone so far away, that counted for something. Right?

You're just trying to justify this somehow, make yourself feel better about it.

She'd felt weird enough before the corset and vibrator had shown up. But opening that box to find them inside had somehow yanked her private nighttime sin out into the bright light of day in a whole new way. She eyed the gifts now, the velvet draped over the edge of the box still on the sofa, the fake purple penis jutting up from the tissue paper, as well. Why did it have to be *purple*, for God's sake? And shaped so realistically like a freaking *penis*? Somehow that made the gift all the more blunt, all the more in-your-face. She couldn't help it—she liked subtlety. So did Riley.

Of course, she thought, turning back to the computer, Riley wasn't getting subtlety anymore than Laura was at the moment, given that searing and unexpected kiss the dark stranger had just delivered before they'd all been interrupted by the deliveryman—and concentrating on Riley's situation seemed a lot more productive than continuing to stew over her voyeur and his so-called gift. She could deal with the reality of that later. For now—she'd come here to write, and she was going to write. Her deadline—and checking account—depended upon it. And besides, she was more than a little curious to see what happened next with Riley's handsome stranger.

Riley's lips tingled with the power of his kiss. Although, if she was honest, more than just her lips were left tingling—her entire body was getting into the act. When it ended, the handsome stranger pulled back and met her gaze. She'd never seen darker, more entrancing eyes, and merely looking into them made her want to melt onto the floor of the Dorchesters' toolshed. "Wha-what was that?" she asked.

One corner of his full mouth quirked into a hint of a grin. "It's called a kiss, honey."

Even his voice made her insides quiver, but she tried to stand strong. "I know what it's called, but who are you and what are you doing in the Dorchesters' shed?"

This time, a full-blown but utterly mysterious smile unfurled on the man's face just before he winked at her. "It's a secret," he said, then opened the door and walked out, leaving Riley in the shadowy heat, alone now but for the riding mower and a host of shovels and gardening hoes.

Feeling wholly unsteady, Riley eased back onto the mower's seat, letting her gaze drift toward the dirt floor. Her eyes dropped to an old broken brick that had fallen from the wall beneath a workbench. In a normal shed, she wouldn't have noticed such a thing, but the Dorchesters were unusually tidy, fastidious people, and that extended right down to their out-buildings. A chunk of brick on the floor of the Dorchesters' toolshed was the equivalent of a kitchen scattered with dirty pots and pans or a bedroom sporting an unmade bed strewn with hastily stripped off clothes and underwear.

Not that she was thinking about stripping off underwear—hers or anyone else's. She didn't even know the attractive stranger's name or what he was doing here, so she had zero interest in his underwear. Especially given that there was now a brand-new mystery to solve—who was he, and what had he been doing in here?

Riley stooped to look at the brick. Nothing unordinary about it—except that it had left an empty spot in the wall beneath the worktable. And Riley thought she must be insane to stick her hand into a dark hole that might contain mice or spiders or God only knew what else—*God, please don't let there be spiders; she hated spiders like she hated nothing else!*—but she was on a mission, and she would not be deterred.

Easing her fingers inside the space, she felt cautiously around—until she touched something that felt suspiciously like lush velvet! Grabbing on to the fabric, she extracted it to find it was a small black drawstring bag, so soft to the touch that it made her shiver in spite of the day's warmth. Hurrying to open the pouch, she spilled out into her palm—oh my!—Mrs. Dorchester's missing antique broach!

Riley immediately rushed home to share her discovery with Aunt Mimsey.

"Did that man have it?" her aunt asked. "Did you get it from that man I saw lurking about?"

Well, she'd certainly gotten *something* from "that man," but it hadn't been the missing piece of jewelry. "No, but maybe if we return this to Mrs. Dorchester, we can start putting the pieces together. We'll describe the man and see if Mrs. D. knows him. Surely, he's the culprit!"

"I've always said how much I admire that broach. I'm sure Winifred will be glad to get it back," Aunt Mimsey said.

Moments later, the two women strolled up the winding cobblestone walk to the Dorchesters' quaint-but-sprawling English Tudor home. Edna Barnes, the longtime housekeeper with her curling silver hair and a blue maid's uniform that made her look like a waitress, let them in, then fetched the lady of the house. "Mimsey and Riley have come for a visit," Edna told Mrs. D. with her usual smile as she led the regal older lady into the room.

Riley was about to explain why they were there—when a tall, dark, drop-dead-gorgeous man strode into the front parlor behind Mrs. Dorchester. Riley's mystery man! Her heartbeat kicked up at the mere sight of him as memories of their very recent kiss assaulted her senses.

"I'd like you two to meet my nephew, Sloane Bennett," Mrs. Dorchester said. "Sloane is a private investigator, visiting all the way from Los Angeles. He's come to hunt for my broach.

Sloane, meet my neighbors from the cottage next door—Mimsey and her niece, Riley Wainscott."

Riley's eyes locked on the so-called P.I., ignoring the introduction. "Well, he need not hunt any longer, because I *found* it." She opened her palm, cradling the velvet bag, the broach resting atop it.

Mrs. D. gasped. "Oh heavens! Wherever did you locate it?"

Riley still honed in on Sloane the mad kisser. "In your toolshed," she replied, then added accusingly, "right after I met your nephew there!"

"Damn, I must have overlooked it," Sloane Bennett said with arrogant ease.

"Sounds suspicious to *me*," Riley replied. "What were you even *doing* in the toolshed?"

"I could ask you the same question," he answered, appearing far too amused for her liking.

"I was responding to the report of a stranger sneaking around," she said smartly.

"And *I* was following footprints, probably left during the heavy rain my aunt tells me occurred a few evenings back."

"Oh." Well, so what? Riley could have found footprints, too, if she'd wanted to—she just hadn't officially taken up the missing broach case until a few short minutes ago.

Aunt Mimsey stepped forward to shake Sloane Bennett's hand. "How nice that you're a private eye. Riley here is a detective in her own right."

He gave his head a jovial tilt. "Is that so?"

She supposed she could understand his attitude—she'd probably seemed a lot more interested in kissing than detecting. But then again, so had he.

He snatched the broach and its black pouch out of her hand. "Well, you need not trouble yourself with this any longer, honey—I'll take care of it from here on out."

Like hell you will, Riley thought. Mr. Hotshot Private Eye Kisser might think he was the only one who could solve this peculiar little mystery, but Riley intended to prove differently. From now on, it would take more than a kiss to knock her off her game.

By the end of the day, Riley and Sloane had grudgingly agreed to work together to figure out who had taken the broach and why the thief had stashed it in Mrs. D.'s very own toolshed. Aunt Mimsey had suggested the partnership, and Mrs. Dorchester had thought it a grand idea, too. And Laura couldn't help being pleased that Riley was clearly going to have the opportunity to get intimate with her nemesis-slash-partner again, even if Riley wasn't yet a hundred percent sure the guy could even be trusted.

Maybe Riley, she thought, could use a little excitement in her love life. Passion had never been a part of Riley's mystery-solving, but now it had found its way onto the page as unexpectedly as Braden Stone had made his way into Laura's life via the computer. Fortunately, she was a lot more comfortable dealing with the fictional Sloane than the frighteningly real Braden.

Which, as dusk began to color the snow beyond the window a pale, flat gray, forced her mind back to Braden's gift, still on the couch all these hours later, taunting her. She turned in the rolling desk chair to look at it again, thinking what a nice, carefree day she'd had, having successfully banished it from her mind. Clearly, she'd been in denial.

Did he really think she was going to use that toy in front of him? Given that she'd never even used such a thing by *herself*, for heaven's sake? Even if she *wanted* to, trying out such a thing on camera just seemed like a bad idea.

So she'd ignore the gift, she decided.

And she'd ignore the clock tonight, too—ten would come and go without consequence, and her voyeur would be forced to see that she simply wasn't into this. She might have *seemed* into it the past two nights, but that shocking purple monstrosity had brought her back to her senses. Getting to her feet, she grabbed the box and took the whole thing up to the bedroom, just to get it out of her direct line of vision.

Having thawed a hamburger patty, Laura turned on a little music—a local pop station—then made herself a simple dinner, adding frozen crinkle fries to the burger. Flipping on the instant-but-still-cozy fire, she decided to settle in for an evening of reading after finishing her meal. No erotica tonight, though. Hemingway. Definitely Hemingway.

When she approached the bookshelf, extracting *A Farewell to Arms*, her eyes landed on the picture of her "flyboy" again. Of course, her stomach churned at the heat a mere photo managed to give off, yet she said aloud, "You might be hot, but this has gone far enough. It stops now."

Two hours later, she still sat on the sofa reading . . . or trying to. She let out a sigh at the realization that she'd just read two full pages without having any idea what they said. Drat. She *loved* this book and it had been years since she'd read it. She should have been completely drawn in by Lieutenant Henry and his English nurse, but instead she found herself—most unwittingly—thinking about much more tawdry liaisons.

Another sigh had her setting the book aside and slowly padding up the stairs into the bedroom. It was high time for that shower she'd put off all day. And as she shed her clothes and stepped under the warm, soothing spray, she ignored the fact that it was *his* shower and, in fact, reminded herself that the guy was hardly ever here. It wasn't nearly so much *his* shower as a place he'd showered *on occasion*.

So she tried not to envision *him* standing naked in this same spot in the huge marble shower as she rubbed soap over her body—and she tried desperately not to feel her own response to even *that* minor stimulation.

Would he like the way she looked soapy?

Biting her lip, she glanced down at her breasts decorated with bright white suds, the taut nipples peeking through, at her stomach and thighs, so slick and smooth-looking as bubbles clung to them, as well. Yes, he would definitely like it. He'd also like taking the round, spongy thing she was using and running it over her breasts, as she did now. He'd surely let his fingertips reach around the soft sponge to glide over her rounded flesh, and then the flat of her stomach. Her pussy tingled as she wished he could do just that—touch her in the shower.

Stop this.

Taking a deep breath, she banished the naughty thoughts from her mind for what seemed the fiftieth time since she'd arrived in the mountainside home, then rinsed hurriedly. She wrapped herself in a big plush bath sheet and stepped into the bedroom—where the corset lay on the bed.

She'd been so distressed over it earlier that she hadn't really *seen* it, hadn't let herself study the details, but now she couldn't help but admire how soft yet sophisticated it appeared. It came with miniscule velvet panties, too, sporting tiny rhinestones sewn in front. A dainty line of the same sparkling jewels outlined the top edge of the corset, designed to mold to her breasts. The back laced up with thick black satin ribbon, which meant, she supposed, that one size fit all.

She couldn't help wondering how she'd look in such a lush piece of lingerie. She owned plenty of pretty bras and panties and a baby-doll nightie or two, but she'd never worn anything that at once looked so glamorous yet sexual.

So maybe she'd just try it on.

Simply to see what she looked like.

For her own benefit—no one else's.

The lacings were already drawn and tied in back so that just fastening a row of invisible hooks in front closed her into it. It was on the verge of being too tight, but she decided not to tamper with the ribbons as she almost *liked* the confined, bound feeling the snug lingerie provided. It made it impossible to forget she was wearing something designed for sex—even *before* she turned toward the sliding glass mirror doors on the closet.

The view stunned her. The velvet molded to her curves deliciously and plumped her breasts even farther than the red lace bra had, making them look round and voluptuous. The press of the corset against them delivered the delightfully naughty sensation that they were about to bust free. The velvet G-string felt just as snug over her pussy and trailing down the center of her ass, and the black stockings made her legs look long and lean, even without heels. She'd never seen herself appear so utterly and wholly sexual—as if she were made for this, as if no other part of her existed. She couldn't help feeling that way, too. Like a good girl gone bad. Like a prim Victorian miss gone wild.

But the look wasn't quite complete. On impulse, she moved to the dresser where she'd just tossed the hair clip she'd worn in the shower, using it to gather her wavy locks back up atop her head, leaving only a few loose tendrils to curve around her face.

There, she thought, peering back in the mirror. That finished the image. The perfect prim lady ready for sex. A stark contrast that was making her cunt swell within the black velvet as she stood staring, amazed at her reflection.

She drew in her breath at the vague wish that Braden could see how she looked in the corset. He'd picked it out for her, after all. He'd shown her this vision of herself she'd never have seen otherwise.

Maybe she could show him. He'd already seen all of her there was to see, and this covered more than her bra and panties had last night, so where was the sin in that?

Of course, he'd expect her to take it off. And to use the toy. She glanced at the purple vibrator, lying by itself in the box now. She couldn't do it. She wouldn't even know how to go about it.

Yet curious after being somewhat afraid of it all day, Laura bit her lower lip and cautiously approached the fake cock. She made herself pick it up, scolding herself internally. *It's a chunk of rubber, not a real penis, for heaven's sake.*

Unfortunately, though, holding it in her hand gave the loose sensation of holding a real penis. Which made her pussy ripple. The vibrator was of medium size, nothing humongous—six inches or so—and the head was smooth and rounded, the shaft sturdy and thick, even sporting slightly raised veins along the length. She felt torn between thinking it ridiculous and realizing that it was making her want the real thing.

She gingerly twisted the knob on the end to start the buzzing vibrations—batteries had been included. Of course, her voyeur would have arranged for that. She found herself smiling at his bold confidence.

Maybe she would experiment with it. He seemed to think every woman should have such a gadget, and she knew Monica indulged in such toys. Maybe now, in the privacy of the bedroom, she'd see what it was all about. In fact, maybe having an orgasm *without* Braden involved would be just as satisfying—minus all the weirdness. Then she could go to sleep, get up tomorrow morning and write, write, write, just as productively as she had today, and continue this retreat more normally, more as she'd imagined it from the beginning. She'd come here to let a change of scenery inspire her creativity, not to let a strange man persuade her into hedonistic acts over the computer.

And *so what* if she'd found her muse over the last couple of days? Surely that had just happened naturally, and Braden Stone's bizarre entry into her life had, if anything, been more of a distraction than a help.

Well, okay, maybe he *had* inspired her to create a whole new character. A character who had driven the story up to this point and would probably *continue* to drive it.

But that didn't mean she needed Braden's presence to continue. If he'd inspired her to inject a little romantic excitement into Riley's life, then his job was done and she could move on without him.

Despite that fine lecture, however, she soon found herself exiting the bedroom, still in the corset and panties, still carrying the purple vibrator. She didn't know why and didn't ponder it. She walked downstairs, turned off the sound system—ready for some quiet time—and headed for the kitchen. She set the vibrator on the counter in order to pour herself a glass of wine. When she took a sip, her throat felt thick, as did her crotch. Every key part of her body had grown swollen and heavy. With desire, definitely. But also with temptation?

And why the hell was she carrying the damn penis around with her?

With a forlorn sigh, she transported the vibrator to the living room and tucked it between the couch cushions. An idea struck her—that maybe she'd just leave it there. And maybe sometime during a family gathering or some other inopportune moment, someone would find it, and wouldn't Mr. Stone feel silly then?

Ah hell, probably not. He'd probably laugh it off—he was likely so confident and charming that he could even find a graceful way out of having a purple penis turn up in his living room.

She returned to the kitchen for the bottle of wine and her glass, then settled on the couch. She peered out into the snow, although darkness now made it so that she could discern only a vague line between ground and sky. Given what she wore, she found herself envisioning a romantic evening here with a lover. A *normal* romantic evening. With a normal lover. The kind who was actually in the room with her. The attire was right. As was the low lighting and the fire. The wine, too. The only thing missing was the man.

She glanced at the crack between the couch cushions. Could she? And did she want to? She must, at least a little—or what was she doing dressed and in position like this?

Predictably nervous now, she drank more wine—two glasses. She listened to the silence. She lay back and closed her eyes and imagined the man in the fishing picture there with her, using strong hands to part her legs, then entering her with his thick, hard erection. *Mmm, yes. Fuck me, Braden. Fuck me now.* She was glad she'd found out his name.

Some time later, she opened her eyes to darkness. She'd fallen asleep. Her eyes focused immediately on the mantel clock in the still dimly lit room. Five 'til ten. She sighed. Sat up. Poured another glass of wine.

She could have slept right through the "appointment." She imagined Braden's reaction if he'd "tuned in" to see her asleep in her new corset and panties. He'd have thought she'd had every intention of performing for him but had just conked out from the alcohol. As it was, she still didn't have a plan—but she knew she needed more wine, so she swiftly drank the glass she'd just poured. And noticed that she wasn't racing away from the webcam.

At ten on the dot, she found herself looking over at the computer, the closest she could come to looking at *him*. As usual since getting here, the wine had her feeling drunker than it should have. Like a woman who knew how to go with the flow—even if her mind still fought against the extremes of what he'd asked her to do.

"Are you there?" she asked. But she somehow knew he was, could almost feel his presence, his eyes, from hundreds of miles away.

"I'm not sure why *I'm* here," she told him frankly. "Just like last night, I had no intention of doing this. This room was going to be dark and empty when you looked into it, and you were finally going to get the message that I'm not really that kind of girl, not really who you think.

"And yet . . . here I am." She swallowed at the realization, at the bluntness of their connection, distance be damned, and thought she should probably shut up now—but the wine kept her talking. "Does it make you feel powerful that I'm here, wearing this for you? Does it make you feel like I can't resist you even though I've never met you? Or does it just make you think I can't resist the lure of the forbidden?"

She sighed. "Maybe I can't resist *anything*. Or maybe I'm only here because I've been drinking—who knows? Monica says I miss sex. I told her she was crazy, but maybe I need it more than I thought.

"The thing is, Braden, if I'm going to fool around with you, well . . . I wish it was *you* I was fooling around with, not this camera. Maybe that made it easier at first—that distance. But now it feels *too* distant."

Too distant, and yet . . . just like the previous evening, she wanted to excite him. Whatever it took. Exciting *him* excited *her*. So she lifted her hands and smoothed them over the velvet that held her breasts. "I wish my hands were *your* hands," she said softly as pleasure from the touch echoed through her in gentle ripples. She squeezed her breasts fully, aware of the hot ache it created and that the move pushed their rounded curves even higher.

"Do you like the way I look in this?" she asked, then admitted, "I do. I don't think I've ever looked prettier in my life. I've never seen myself in something like this. Maybe *that's* why I'm here—because I wanted to show you." She lightly pinched her nipples through the velvet. "It feels so good on me, holds me so tight—just like you would if you were here.

"Would you run your hands all over my body?" she asked, gliding her palms down over her velvet-clad torso, her hips, then her thighs and the lace tops of her stockings.

"Would you part my legs?" She used her hands, splayed over her inner thighs, to spread them wide, wider.

"Would you touch my pussy?" She dragged one long middle finger up the velvet that enclosed her mound, then shivered from the sensation. Having his eyes on her heightened every little frisson of pleasure.

"You'd take off my pretty panties," she told him, growing more confident now, and leaned back on the couch, legs together, lifting her ass just enough to peel down the tiny swatch of velvet. She let it linger high on her thighs, her legs raised upright, remembering this was a show—all visual—so she had to make it slow, make it good. Leisurely, she hooked her thumbs into the elastic band and pushed it painstakingly toward her bent knees. When the thong dropped to her ankles, she gently kicked it off, then looked back to the camera.

"You want to see my pussy again," she said with surprising boldness. She bit her lower lip and peered darkly toward the camera. "And I want to show it to you."

Sitting back up on the sofa and lowering her feet to the floor, she parted her legs as widely as she could. She felt herself opening for him and knew he could see how excited she was to be on display for him again.

"You want to touch it," she whispered. "You want to touch me where I'm pink and wet for you." She raked two fingers through her folds to end up circling her clit, then sighed at the saturating delight and said, "God, I want it to be *your* hand on me, stroking me, rubbing me." She kept caressing herself—good, so good—heard her breath grow labored and wanted desperately to hear his, too. She loved knowing he studied her, but at the same time she yearned for much, much more. "Watch me," she said, her voice going deeper. "Watch me touch myself for you."

Her fingers grew wet with her desire, and she longed for something else. Him.

His hands—touching her.

His mouth—kissing her.

His cock—inside her.

Just like real sex, the touching was good, but there came a point in time when a woman needed to be filled—deeply.

She shut her eyes, still moving her fingers over the little nub that was the source of her pleasure. But she continued aching for more.

She knew, of course, that if she really wanted to be filled, she had the means to do it. It rested between the couch cushions.

She bit her lip and asked herself the same question she'd been asking all night. Could she?

She let out a sigh as her soul filled with yet more forbidden desires that she'd never known. What would she look like with the toy inside her? What would it feel like to pleasure herself like *that*—for him?

Her lips trembled, and her nether regions quaked with need.

Her fingers were no longer enough. She knew they weren't enough for Braden, either.

So with her free hand she reached down, digging between the soft cushions, until finally her fist closed around the thick vibrator. Her breath grew shaky as she extracted it, knowing he saw, knowing he knew what she was about to do.

Could she?

Yes. She could.

Chapter Five

Braden's lungs threatened to explode in his chest. As beautiful and hot and arousing as she was, he'd been starting to think she wasn't going to use the vibrator. And that would have been just fine—he loved watching her no matter what she was doing, and seeing her touch her lovely pink pussy was ample entertainment. But now that she held the toy in her dainty hand, it was all he could do not to come. "God, you're amazing, honey," he whispered raspily toward the computer screen, wishing she could hear him.

"I'm not sure how to do this," she said, her voice trembling as she leaned back on the couch, legs still parted, beginning to lightly drag the tip of the toy cock up the center of her cunt. Braden seldom felt particularly tender or emotional when it came to women or sex, yet her sweet honesty about her lack of such experience was almost enough to paralyze him. She'd made herself vulnerable on his account, laid her soul bare for him. And although everything she said sounded far away, muted, he heard the genuine emotion in her voice loud and clear.

"Just go easy," he prodded, even though she couldn't hear the instructions. "Go easy and make yourself feel good."

He listened to her breathing as she used the vibrator like a large finger, raking it through her slickness over and again.

"Yeah, baby," he growled. "That's right."

Her eyes fell shut, her lips parting in desire. He understood she was taking her time, getting acquainted with the way it felt against her flesh, and was more than happy to be patient, given the tantalizing vision she created. Yet if he didn't release his cock from his hand, he'd blow any second, and it was far too soon for that. He let go, letting his shaft plop hard against his lower abs.

He sat shirtless, in a pair of unzipped jeans, listening to the lull of the tide out the window behind him, yet still able to discern every soft sigh and moan from his cyber lover. Her breathing grew still heavier, deeper, as her strokes with the vibrator seemed to press deeper as well. He wanted to see her put it in her pussy so badly he could taste it. "Come on, baby, do it for me. Show me how brave and sexy you are."

Almost as if she'd heard his throaty pleas all the way in wintry Colorado, she bit her lower lip and, still keeping her eyes shut, began to ease the head of the toy cock against her opening. Braden almost couldn't breathe.

She moaned softly as the head gained entry, and so did he.

"Ohhh," she said as it began to slide deeper. "Oh God. Oh, I want this to be you."

Damn, he wanted that, too. Wanted to sink his shaft so deep inside her, feel her tight moisture encasing him. And she'd *be* tight—he knew instinctively. She was easily one of the most sexual women he'd ever encountered, but he also knew from her denials of such that she protected her sexuality closely, likely didn't sleep around, and maybe had, in fact, only taken a few lovers.

He watched, throat clogged with arousal, as she began to move the toy in and out of her beautiful cunt. "Oh yeah, that's so good," he said, his gaze riveted on her every move. Her body was fully open to it now and looked incredible taking it inside. He couldn't resist closing his fist around his own cock again, beginning to tug in firm, even strokes as he wished it were the one gliding so smoothly in and out of Laura's pussy.

"I'm imagining this is you," she said on a hot, high whimper of pleasure. "I'm imagining that you're fucking me, fucking me." The sex toy went in all the way now, right up to the fake balls, and he knew the little rise built in on the front—the one unrealistic part of the vibrator, added for her pleasure—was meeting her clit with every stroke.

She fucked herself harder now, and he worked his dick harder, too, matching the rhythm of her thrusts. "You're fucking me," she told him again, eyes still shut, face wrenched in passion. "You're fucking me, Braden."

"That's right, honey, I am. I'm fucking that perfect pink pussy, fucking you so hard."

He watched her mounting passion, listened to her high-pitched moans, let himself get lost in the sight, the sounds. *Yes, baby, don't stop. Keep going.* He kept stroking, and when he felt the blood gathering, felt his balls getting tighter and tighter, he said, "Come for me, honey."

On the computer screen, she worked the toy faster, and he knew the little nub on the front was pushing *her* little nub closer to climax with each thrust. *Come on, baby, come on.* He couldn't hold back much longer, but he sure as hell wasn't coming before her.

And then, like an answer to a dirty prayer, she let out a hot, thready breath and began to sob. The near-anguish on her face softened to pure ecstasy as she moaned her orgasm.

"Ah yeah, baby," he groaned, then let go to the obscenely beautiful sight of her, pumping his white hot semen into the tissues he'd kept ready ever since he'd started playing naughty computer games with Laura. The heat shot through him in hard, jagged pulses, and he wished like hell he was coming in *her*, in that tight, hot body, and that she could see his pleasure just the same as he saw hers.

He clenched his teeth to ride it out. Then came back to earth in time to watch her let the toy fall to the floor and slowly close her legs.

She peered into the camera, clearly stunned by her own actions.

No, baby, no. He longed, more than anything in that moment, for her to show him how thrilled she remained, for her to tell him how astounding it had been, or even just that she'd had fun. But he saw the regret washing over her, the embarrassment—and he hated it.

She shut her eyes, shook her head, drew her legs up under her on the couch. "This isn't me," she whispered, same as she kept telling him. "This isn't me."

Then she pushed to her feet and walked to the light switch, and the next thing he knew, the screen went black—first the lights extinguished, then the fireplace went dark. She'd run away from him merely by turning out the lights.

I want to hold you, Laura. I want to make you feel better. I want to make you know this is okay, better *than okay.*

Only he couldn't do that. All he could do was turn out his own lights and go to bed—alone. "I'm sorry I'm not there with you, baby," he said, then lifted one fingertip to the computer screen for just a short second before letting out a sigh and rising to leave the desk, and the girl, for the night.

Despite herself, Laura slept great, but still suffered the same sense of revulsion upon waking the next morning. She still couldn't believe she'd done it. She'd used the purple penis. In front of him.

Arousal was like drunkenness, she thought. The moment you got sober you couldn't make sense of what you'd done under the influence. And this, now, was the hangover.

As she lay in his bed staring up at the gently whirring ceiling fan, back in her safe-feeling snowflake pj's, a truly horrific thought struck her. What if . . . what if he hadn't been alone? Last night, or the night before, or both. What if he'd watched her with *friends?* What if he'd somehow made tapes of her? What if he was showing them all over the Internet this very moment, even as she lay here trying to rest? Thank God those brutal little musings hadn't hit last night or she wouldn't have slept at all.

As it was, they propelled her up and out of bed in a flash, down to the computer. It was just after eight, near the same time they'd chatted the first morning, so hopefully he would be there. She pulled up an IM box as fast as her fingers could click and type.

RILEY: Swear to me this is private.

A moment later, his answer arrived. *FLYBOY1: What are you talking about, honey?*

She took a deep breath and lectured herself. *Try to sound at least a little bit rational. Don't act like a total nutcase.*

RILEY: Okay, I just woke up with a ter-
rifying thought. That you're the sort of
creep who might . . . do something really
awful to me.

Yeah, that sounded really rational. She let out a sigh, her heart still beating too fast.

FLYBOY1: I still don't know what you're
getting at, but before we go on, I have
to tell you that you were beautiful and
hot and incredible last night, and I hate
that you felt badly afterward.

Laura sighed. Okay, hopefully this meant he wasn't out selling sex tapes of mystery novelist Laura Watkins. It provided enough reassurance to help her explain her hideous fears. *RILEY: I just had this*
horrible picture in my head—you sitting and
watching me . . . with a roomful of friends.

FLYBOY1: Are you crazy? I would never do
that to you. Why would you even think
that?

RILEY: Perhaps this would be an appro-
priate time for me to remind you that I
don't know you. At all.

FLYBOY1: Aw, come on, snowflake, I think
it's safe to say you know me at least a
little now. <g> And you can trust me,

I swear. This is just between you and me—completely private. I wish I could be there with you, so you could look in my eyes, and then you'd know I'm telling the truth. I also wished I could be there last night when you seemed upset at the end.

A true sense of relief rushed through Laura's body. It was hardly proof, but somehow she *felt* his earnest tone and believed in it. *RILEY: Okay, I feel better now. About it being private, I mean. The other part, though, not so much.*

FLYBOY1: Why?

Laura sighed in exasperation. She thought this was pretty simple, but he never seemed to grasp it. *RILEY: Let me make this as plain as I can. I have done things in front of you that I've never done in front of anyone. Extremely INTIMATE things. And I don't know you. A little maybe, but not much. This is not the kind of person I am.*

FLYBOY1: Don't tell me we're gonna go through that again. Honey, there's nothing wrong with letting your sexual side show a little.

A *little?* He thought she'd let it show a *little?* She nearly let out a mad cackle, but stopped, remembering that he was probably watching her right now. Instead of replying in some crazed, raving way—tempting since she currently felt pretty crazed and raving—she decided it would be smarter to go straight to the heart of the matter.

RILEY: I'm appalled at what I did last night, and I want you to leave me alone for the rest of my time here.

His answer took longer than normal, but when it came, was typical of him.

FLYBOY1: You didn't seem appalled while you were doing it.

She let out a sigh of disgust and didn't care if he heard her this time. *RILEY: Another bout of drunken insanity, that's all. I was DEEPLY appalled AFTERWARD, and that counts for a lot.*

FLYBOY1: Did you go to Catholic school or something?

Despite herself, she let out a short laugh, half-amused, half-hysterical. *RILEY: No. Afraid my conservatism is organic, all me.*

FLYBOY1: If I were there with you right now, do you know what I'd do?

She drew in her breath and her pussy fluttered, unbidden. *RILEY: No.*

FLYBOY1: I'd fuck the conservatism right out of you, honey.

She didn't type an answer. She had no idea how to respond. Because as much as she really thought it wise to banish him from her life and forget any of this had ever happened, she couldn't deny the hard jolt of arousal coursing its way through her conservative body at reading his words.

FLYBOY1: I'd think you were mad at me . . . except you don't LOOK mad. You look . . . excited. In fact, your cheeks are starting to flush, same as when you touch yourself.

Again, Laura considered her response. She hated being so easy to read. She hated that he could see her and she still couldn't see him.

RILEY: It's so unfair that this stupid camera only works one way. And for your information, I AM mad, at myself. Last night went too far, and it absolutely won't happen again.

FLYBOY1: *What size shoe do you wear?*

She blinked at the screen in utter disbelief. Here they were, discussing shared sexual depravities, and he was taking down sizes? *RILEY: Why on earth do you want to know?*

FLYBOY1: *Humor me.*

RILEY: *7½. But if you do anything stupid like have sexy shoes delivered to me because you want me to walk around naked in them or something, I will promptly throw them out into the snow.*

FLYBOY1: *You take the fun out of everything. <g> Bra size?*

She sighed. *RILEY: None of your business.*

FLYBOY1: *36C?*

She let out yet another irritated harrumph. *RILEY: 34, if you must know, but you got the C right.*

FLYBOY1: *Guess I'm a good judge of tits. And yours are beautiful, honey. Only problem with the present I sent you yesterday is that I didn't get to see them.*

She rolled her eyes. *RILEY: Poor planning on your part, I suppose.* Damn it, why was she letting herself be engaged this way? She was supposed to be putting a stop to this.

FLYBOY1: *Show me now.*

Laura sucked in her breath as she stared at the screen and tried to keep her expression neutral. No man had ever made her feel so torn between her real self and her inner bad girl.

To her surprise, part of her wanted to unbutton her pajama top right now, wanted to sit typing to him topless. But if she kept on with this, she feared she'd lose some precious part of herself. She'd come close to that last night, she thought—to giving away something she wasn't sure she wanted to give. At least not to a man she'd never meet in person.

RILEY: No. And you know what else? I'm done with this, Braden—REALLY done with it. As of right now, I want nothing more to do with you, got it?

She liked that his next answer took awhile. She liked having surprised him with her anger. And even though she sat in the desk chair, still aroused, still wanting—that anger was real. Last night *had* gone too far. She never should have done something so intimate with a stranger, and it had left her feeling ashamed. This had been mysterious and intriguing, and probably the most truly exciting thing she'd ever done— but the horror she'd felt last night, coming right on the heels of her orgasm, had made it clear to her that it had to stop.

FLYBOY1: Won't work, Laura. You won't turn the camera off.

Arrogant bastard. *RILEY: I don't have to turn it off to ignore you. And I'm going to start ignoring you right this instant. I came here to write a book, now I'm going to write it.*

FLYBOY1: How it's going, the book?

She didn't answer, instead pulling up the file she'd been writing in.

FLYBOY: Is your alter ego busy solving some heinous crime?

She swallowed, hard, because she found it difficult to ignore someone directly addressing her, even through the computer—but she still managed to. In fact, she started vigorously typing the next scene of the book. The writing was terrible, of course, but she could fix it later. For now, she mainly wanted to look busy and absorbed in her work.

FLYBOY1: Come on, honey—don't be like this.

I have to. To protect my sanity. It was tempting to tell him that, to let him persuade her back into conversation—but no, not this time. She had to stand strong. She kept typing—something about Sloane Bennett being hot, the hottest man Riley had ever laid eyes on, let alone kissed.

FLYBOY1: Talk to me.

Another sentence—this one about Sloane being the sort of man who could tempt Riley to do things she never had before, but how Riley *refused* to be tempted because she had a case to solve and she intended to show Sloane she was a good detective, and that having sex with him probably wouldn't do much to convince him of her mystery-solving prowess.

FLYBOY1: Please.

Drat—that almost got her. She felt guilty and mean.

But there was nothing mean about it. He was a big boy—he'd get by just fine without her company, she was sure of it. And for all she knew, he was dating twenty different women. And would have one of them in his bed tonight. Or maybe he was dating only *one* woman—a special one. And this was sort of like cheating on her. More than sort of—definitely cheating. She let out a sigh and kept typing, reminding herself that these were just more good examples of why it was a mistake to get intimately involved with someone she didn't know from Adam.

A few feet away on the desk, an antique black phone rang. She flinched—the phone hadn't rung since her arrival, and she'd thought this particular device only served as a decoration; she'd never dreamed the thing actually worked.

She knew almost certainly that it was Braden calling—*insisting* she talk to him. If she answered, she could finally hear his voice. She would definitely feel as if he were a little nearer, even if it was only an illusion. If only she dared.

Of course, it could also be Monica, or her mother, who also knew where she was—but they'd more likely call her cell.

Staring at the phone, then casting a slow glance back to the computer, she took a deep breath and reached for the phone. "Hello?"

"Hi, honey. It's me." As she'd suspected, his voice was deep and dark, flowing over her like thick, melted chocolate. Just hearing it made her breasts feel heavy and her inner thighs ache.

"Hi," she replied shortly. She glanced down, away from the screen. She couldn't let him see how just the very sound of him affected her.

"Don't be mad at me, okay?"

She suspected he'd used the persuasive tone on women before—and she also suspected it had always worked. "I never said I was mad." She swallowed back the nervous lump that had grown in her throat at this unexpected push closer to him. "I'm just . . . very uncomfortable."

"I don't want you to feel that way. I want you to love what we've been sharing as much as I do."

"Well, sure, that would be nice, but . . . I can't."

"Why do you think sex is wrong?"

She sighed. "I never said that, either. I don't think sex is wrong at all—I think sex is great. But I'm not comfortable doing weird things with a stranger. It might be different if we were together, in the same room, but we're not even in the same state, so . . . it's just a bizarre way to be intimate, that's all."

She heard him breathing on the other end of the line and, despite herself, couldn't help enjoying the continued illusion that he was somehow closer now. "I'd think most women might like it better this way—I mean, since you keep telling me I'm a stranger, I'd think you'd be glad I'm far away. That it would make you feel . . . safer or something."

"I'm not most women. I've told you, I'm conservative and sensible. Nothing about *this* is conservative and sensible."

"And if I asked you to meet me at the computer tonight at ten o'clock?"

"You'd find an empty room this time—I swear it." And she meant it—sexy phone voice or not. Because if there had been any safety through the anonymity provided by the computer, this kind of changed that, made him even more real than he'd been before. She simply didn't think she could muster another masturbation scene for him now that she'd heard his voice.

"So you'd really stand me up?" He sounded disappointed, but his voice also held a hint of teasing. "I hate to hear that, snowflake."

"Why?"

"You get me hotter than anyone has in a long time." No teasing this time. All serious, all heat.

"Why is that?" she asked frankly. "Why not find a *real* woman—one you can touch yourself? I hear they have attractive ones in California."

He laughed softly, although it held little humor. "You're real enough for me—trust me on that. More real than most women I know."

"Too much silicone and BOTOX in your world?"

"Maybe something like that. Just suffice it to say you're the woman I want right now."

She blinked slowly, then finally lifted her gaze to the camera, feeling she needed to face him if she were to get her point across. "Then I guess it's too bad I'm here and you're there. That's the only way this could go any further. I'm sorry, Braden."

With that, she hung up the phone, then pushed to her feet and walked away.

It took every ounce of strength she had to do that—really walk away from him, or as close as she could come to walking away given that he was actually three states away from her—but she meant it. She'd been reminded this morning of how little she really knew about him and just how intimate she'd become with him. It was too much. Too risky. Too strange.

His liquid voice still reverberated in her ear as she forced herself to eat a little breakfast—a bagel and coffee—then walk upstairs and get dressed.

And when she came back down, she gasped when she nearly tripped over last night's velvet panties and the purple vibrator, still lying on the floor in front of the couch.

Yes, this was too much, and it had simply gotten too *real*.

And that's why it had to end, once and for all.

Much to her surprise, Laura still managed to get some writing done, despite the morning upset with Braden. She'd waited to return to the computer until she felt certain he'd be busy doing other things, and as hoped, no IMs arrived. Outside the window, the sun shone brightly, the sky crisp and blue above a sparkling mantle of snow, and it somehow lifted her spirits and helped the words flow onto the page. Her only fear by day's end was that much of the afternoon's work might eventually have to be scrapped—for she was beginning to fear Riley was obsessed with Sloane Bennett ad nauseam.

That night, another hamburger, this one eaten in front of the TV—where sitcoms reigned. No reading, no thinking—just sitcoms. When ten o'clock rolled around, she felt predictably tense. And she even glanced at the computer once or twice, but she wasn't tempted. In fact, she didn't know if she was imagining it, but she had the oddest feeling that he wasn't even there—as if he'd finally really believed her when she'd said it was over.

Of course, just as Riley had thought of Sloane all day, so had Laura thought of Braden. She didn't regret her decision, but she supposed she wished things were somehow different—wished they'd met under more normal circumstances through Monica . . . heck, wished they'd really even *met*.

Then again, if they'd met through Monica at some family event, Braden Stone wouldn't even have noticed her. She wasn't the blond bombshell type she suspected could generally be found on his arm, not the type he probably would have categorized as even a *possibility*—if he'd not stumbled across her masturbating in the living room of his vacation home. As she shut off the TV a few minutes later, then headed upstairs, she shook her head once more, not quite able to believe she'd touched herself that way in the first place, let alone where it had led.

A few minutes later, she lay down to sleep in a pink cami and a pair of cheerfully striped flannel pants. She felt at once adrift, yet also settled, centered. The excitement with her voyeur had ended now—but that was okay. She would write her book, go home at the end of her re-treat, and life would get back to normal. And that's what Laura thrived on—normalcy.

Wasn't it?

She ignored the vague sense of loneliness she felt for the first time since arriving here—*writers like to be alone, remember?* she lectured herself— and tried to fall asleep peering out yet another enormous picture window at a bright, nearly full moon hanging low in the Colorado sky.

When blessed sleep came, it brought dreams. Of Braden. Of sex.

Only . . . when a kiss came on her cheek, waking her, she knew instantly it wasn't a dream, nor was the warm male body crawling into bed with her.

She should have panicked, but didn't. Somehow she knew it was him, and that this wasn't really over at all—even before he said low, near her ear, "Don't be scared, honey. It's just me."

Chapter Six

She still hovered on the edge of sleep, that place where everything was dreamy—yet there was no doubt in her mind that he was very real. She whispered his name. "Braden."

"I couldn't let it end," he breathed warm and wicked in her ear.

She lay facing away from him in the bed and could feel his erection—that quickly—pressing into the crack of her ass. One large hand curled around her waist, fingers splaying wide across her stomach through her top as he lowered a scintillating kiss to her neck. It set off explosions of pleasure inside her.

She never once thought of objecting, stopping him.

Having him here, next to her, touching her, after the things she'd longed for and the intimacies they'd already shared . . . there was no *hope* of stopping, no reason to *try*. She didn't have sex with strangers, but this was different. Maybe because he no longer *felt* so much like a stranger, having come to her like this. Or maybe just because he felt too overwhelmingly good, the sex dripping off of him and onto her like something tangible that instantly consumed her. Either way, she wanted it with her whole self.

He stroked and caressed her belly, his fingers finding the skin between cami and waistband and then flirting with the underside of her breast, all the while delivering more kisses to her neck, shoulder. Her whole body rippled with the supreme pleasure of finally having his hands on her, of having him in her bed.

When his palm closed over her breast, she moaned and instinctively arched into his touch. His breath grew heavy, hot, as he massaged her with a slow, intoxicating rhythm that quickly swallowed her, helping her forget to think and only to feel. His cock grew harder against her rear, and she found herself pushing back against it, wanting to feel even more. Braden growled softly in response, and the sound ran all through her, heightening her excitement.

Rolling to her back beneath him, she lifted her hands to his cheeks, studied his face. How strange to be in bed with a man whose eyes she'd never before looked into. Oh God, he was beautiful—even more than in the photo. Dark, thick hair framed strong features and expressive eyes, even seen only in the moonlight. She couldn't quite make out the color—brown, she thought. Deep and warm. Dark stubble covered his chin, and she grew aware that he wore a T-shirt and jeans, stretched out against her.

He peered boldly back at her the whole time, clearly taking in her face, as well, his look devouring her until finally he lowered a slow, passionate kiss to her lips. Her fingers threaded through his hair as she met his sensually prodding tongue with her own. Short French kisses mingled with longer, deeper meetings of mouths until she was lost in it—and utterly thunderstruck.

No man had ever kissed her this way, this . . . perfectly from the start. It was as if they'd been kissing each other for eons, as if they knew exactly how the other would respond, how lengthy or fleeting the kisses should be, how passionate or lingering. She felt strangely and suddenly like a schoolgirl, as if she could have kissed him all night and it would have been enough to satisfy her.

Until, of course, his palms returned to her breasts, capturing them both with unabashed possessiveness, massaging gently but thoroughly, and drawing a long, hard sigh from deep within her. His hands were skilled, confident—they owned her on contact—and, just as she'd somehow known, were way better at pleasuring her than even her own.

The kisses went on as he kneaded her and slipped his thigh between her legs beneath the sheets. His erection jutted rock-solid against her hip, and they moved together in rhythmic bliss as Braden pushed her top up over her breasts.

His strong hands molded to the outer curves as she peered down to see them within his grasp, the peaks taut and pink. He looked, too, then met her eyes only briefly before dropping down to capture one sensitive nipple in his mouth.

"Ohhh . . ." she moaned as the pleasure expanded through her with the pull of his lips. She curled her fingers into his hair and watched as he suckled deeply—*yes, yes*—then opened his eyes to lock them on hers. The connection was startlingly intimate—but they'd already been intimate in far more bizarre ways, so she didn't look away.

He released her from his mouth, still meeting her gaze, to drag his tongue up over the pointed pink tip. She saw the wetness he'd left, glistening in the moonlight. He moved his tongue in a slow circle around her nipple, ending with the leisurely licks one might give an ice cream cone.

She trembled at his ministrations, literally thought she'd come apart soon. But she didn't want to come yet—she wasn't a multiple orgasm sort of girl, so she needed to save it, needed to soak up more of him before she climaxed.

She said the words she'd been saying to him in her mind, without even an ounce of hesitation—although they came out breathy. "Fuck me, Braden. Fuck me." Like other certain words, she seldom used that one, but Braden had brought it out of her almost naturally, in front of the webcam, and now.

He kissed her again, heatedly, then leaned near her ear to whisper a promise. "I'm gonna fill you up, honey."

With that, he reached for the drawstring on her pants and pulled, then grabbed for the waistband, taking her panties as well when she lifted her ass. She shoved at his T-shirt as she kicked her pants off—

what had been slow and rhythmic up to now had just turned more urgent. She had to have him inside her. Her body ached for him. Her pussy pulsed with need.

Above her, Braden ripped his shirt off over his head, then unzipped his jeans and pushed them off with her help. His cock stretched naked now against her bare thigh, so utterly hard, and damp at the end, making her cunt surge yet again. The sheets concealed him from the waist down, but his chest appeared broad and his arms and shoulders sculpted in the shadowy light.

She watched as he reached for the jeans he'd just discarded, digging in a pocket, flipping open a wallet. She waited, trying to be patient, as he tore into a small packet. Unfortunately, the blankets blocked the moonlight from illuminating his erection as he rolled the condom on.

He pushed her legs apart with both hands, and she savored his masculine touch on her inner thighs. "Fuck me," she said again. Just letting that inner bad girl back out some more. Just to excite him.

"Soon," he replied, stunning her.

Soon? Before she could protest, though, Braden disappeared swiftly under the covers and, a few seconds later, dragged one long, luxurious lick up the center of her pussy. "Oh God!" she cried, the pleasure spiraling through her like electricity, leaving her astonished she didn't come just from that.

And then he was moving smoothly back up her body, positioning his hips over hers, pushing at her moisture, forcing his way inside, and—God, he *was* big! She pulled in her breath at the marvelous impact, adjusting to the sense of fullness, quite sure she'd never been with a man so large. He hadn't lied—about filling her up. Or the Washington Monument. She involuntarily curled her fingernails into his smooth shoulders, her teeth clenched.

"You okay?" he asked.

She nodded, tried to speak. "You're huge."

His grin shone with manly arrogance. "Told you."

"I've never . . . um . . . ." She couldn't form words.

"Does it hurt?"

She gave her head a shake against the pillow. "No, I'm just try-ing . . . to get used to . . ." She was squeezing the phrases out between heavy breaths.

"Does this help?" he asked and began to move, to thrust in slow, even drives.

Oh God, did it. "More," she whimpered.

Her eyes fell shut, but she sensed his conceited grin. "I'll give you more, all right, baby. I'll give you all you can handle."

She bit her lower lip as he increased his strokes, making them longer, deeper. Her legs wrapped instinctively around his waist, locking at the ankles. He groaned in response, his hands molding to her hips as he pumped into her. "I knew you'd be tight, baby, so wet and tight for me."

Laura had found his dirty talk arousing on the computer, but hear-ing it in that deep, seductive voice nearly stole her breath. This man knew exactly how to do something no other man ever had—make her forget all about being sensible and conservative. "Are you going to do what you promised?" she whispered up to him.

His hands slid to her breasts, his thumbs brushing across her beaded nipples. "What's that, honey?"

"Are you going to fuck the conservatism right out of me?"

A naughty grin accompanied the lecherous sparkle of his eyes. "Oh *yeah*, baby."

He plunged into her harder then, making her cry out with each firm thrust. She lifted her hands over her head, pressing them to the large wooden headboard for leverage. Her body was growing more used to him—less overwhelmed, allowing her to sink deeper into pure pleasure. Not only the physical pleasure of having him inside her, but the mental pleasure, too. The knowledge that she'd never done this before, slept with a man she didn't know very well, and that he was utter perfection and that it was exciting as hell. Everything she saw was like a visual assault: his dark, sexy eyes, his large hands massaging her breasts, their bodies moving together in a heated rush.

He went so long and hard in her that she was sure he'd come, and she didn't even care whether or not *she* did, because this was an entirely different kind of pleasure, unrelated to orgasm, about nothing but the way their bodies connected, the slick interlock, the powerful drives that reverberated all through her. She loved absorbing every hot stroke he delivered, loved the little cries they forced from her throat, the way she felt nearly out of her head with lusty joy, unable to think clearly, only to soak it in.

"I want to make you come," she heard herself say.

He softened his thrusts, took her face in his hands. "Not yet, baby."

She didn't argue. Now that she thought about it, she wasn't exactly ready for this to be over just yet, either. But she gasped when he eased back, drawing out of her. She'd never felt so abandoned and empty in her life. "What . . . ?" she heard herself utter in shock.

Rolling over, he pulled her on top of him until she straddled his thighs. Using two fingers, he plucked at one shoulder strap of her cami. "Take this off."

She obliged, removing it over her head.

He skimmed his hands slowly over her from hips to shoulders, then back again, gently tweaking her nipples along the way. She slid her palms up his firm stomach onto his chest, dusted with dark hair. Her eyes dropped to his penis, still rock-hard, arcing up his abdomen in the moonlight, past his navel. Dear God, he was as big as he'd felt.

"I've watched this beautiful body of yours on my computer screen, honey," he said, "and it's so good to finally have you in my arms." His hands splayed over the tops of her thighs before gliding slowly inward, inward, so close to her cunt she thought she'd scream from frustration. She heard her own breath, growing ragged again, and then—ah, God—he stroked one thumb up the center of her wet folds, then the other. She couldn't help pushing lightly at the touches, each ending with the slightest brush over her swollen clit.

"And I've seen this pretty body come so hot for me," he went on, still stroking her pussy, his thumbs moving gradually deeper, deeper into her open slit, "but now *I* want to make you come. Make you come hard and hot. Just for me."

Pulling in her breath, meeting his piercing eyes, she spoke her heart. "You made me come already. Every time. It was you—it was knowing you watched me. You must know that."

A sexy smile turned up the corners of his mouth. "But this is still different. You said you wanted my hands, my cock."

She let out a long, languid sigh, along with a nod, still shocked that she had said those things. "I did. I do." Her gaze dropped again to that phenomenal appendage.

"Well, now *they're* gonna make you come, baby. And I'm gonna watch it wash over you, watch you soar, watch you lose control."

She tilted her head, curled her fingertips into his chest. "Don't you know? I lost control the moment I realized you were watching me. And maybe I regained it, for a little while, but it's gone again—and I don't think it's coming back this time."

His smile widened. "That's what I want. You without any control. You just doing what feels good. You forgetting about everything except pleasure."

Like an answer, she let her hand go where it wanted, straying from his chest down to his shaft stretching so prominently between them. Her fingers curled lightly around it and he groaned.

"Ride me," he said.

And she couldn't think of anything she could possibly want more.

Rising to her knees, she hovered over him, enjoying the feel of his eyes still roaming her body. She'd never felt more wholly feminine or sexual. And though she'd never touched herself for anyone before Braden and no longer needed to since he was here to do it for her now, she followed a whim and let her palms glide up onto her breasts, squeezing sensually as she caught her nipples between thumb and forefinger to pinch lightly. Braden's hands played about her hips as he watched, his breath going shallow. And for the first time it dawned on her: through a loss of control over *herself*, she was *gaining* a certain measure of control—over him.

Situating herself directly over his erection, she wrapped her fist around it once more, positioning it upright, then lowered herself until the head met her swollen flesh. Needing him back inside her, she pushed her pelvis firmly downward, sheathing him in her slickness.

They both moaned at the reconnection, but Laura wondered at first if she could handle the position. She'd forgotten that being on top made her feel a guy's cock even more, and at the moment, Braden's felt incomprehensibly big in her. She instantly leaned forward, curving her body down over him, crushing her breasts into his chest. "How can you be so big?" she asked on impulse, her mouth near his ear.

He chuckled heatedly. "You don't like it?"

"I *love* it—I'm just not sure I can take it."

He turned his head to face her—their eyes, mouths, rested no more than an inch apart. "You can take it, honey," he said as if it were an absolute fact.

"How do you know?"

Certainty glimmered in his eyes. "I saw you take the one I sent to you."

The reminder almost embarrassed her, yet somehow that was passing. She was surprised, though, to hear herself laugh. "Did you have to pick a purple one?"

He grinned and she melted a little deeper into his chest. "I thought girls *liked* purple."

She returned the playful smile. "For a sweater, sure. But, my God, a purple penis?"

"I think, honey, that when they come in colors it's supposed to make them seem more fun."

She blinked, feeling a bit thick. "Oh. I guess I . . . wasn't thinking of it as *fun* then."

"And now?" He raised his eyebrows.

She bit her lip, thinking. "Now, *this* is fun. *Your* cock is fun."

The expression in his eyes said he liked her answer. "Then you must think you can take it."

She bit her lip and met his gaze, raising slightly, the move elevating her breasts just enough that her nipples abraded his skin. As he sighed his pleasure, she rose farther, sitting up, to realize her body had again magically adjusted to him. He still felt enormous in this position, but not so overwhelming that she couldn't enjoy it. "You're bigger than the toy, but you're right, I can take it," she assured him, her voice lower than she knew was possible. And then she began to move, to let her body guide her. "I can *definitely* take it."

She swiveled in small but potent circles atop him as she pressed her palms to his chest. She peered unabashedly into his hypnotic eyes. Her clit brushed against his body with each rotation, enough to lift her slowly higher, higher, toward the peak she sought.

"You're so hot, baby," he said, his voice dripping with a sensuality that seeped into her veins. His words fueled her, and so did his eyes. She supposed she'd grown accustomed to having them on her, even when she hadn't been able to see them, but now, she relished them even more.

Again, she found herself kneading her breasts while he watched.

"You look *so* good doing that."

"Do you want to kiss them?" she asked, her voice that of a sex nymph. She *never* said such things in bed—never, until this, until Braden. He'd clearly loosened something in her, and now that it was out, she wasn't sure it would ever go back in.

"Ah yeah, baby, bring me those pretty breasts."

Still moving on him in hot little circles that rubbed her clit just the right way, she bent to lower one nipple into Braden's waiting mouth. "Oh . . ." she purred when he sucked hard, the pleasure seeming to multiply the gathering pressure in her pussy. "Oh, that's good. Don't stop."

He suckled so intensely it almost hurt, but more than that, it increased her pleasure, driving her toward climax. She moved on him more roughly, too, clenched her teeth, felt the heat building, building. She shut her eyes and remembered the way he'd watched her, the shocking things she'd done to thrill them both, and that he was here now, truly here now, his huge cock thrusting up into her hungry, hungry body—and then she toppled, into the sweetest, most lingering orgasm she'd had in a long while. Her body convulsed at the start, then she found the waves and rode them out, letting them carry her until at last she collapsed, exhausted, back to his chest.

"Mmm, how was that?" he asked, his voice beaming with typical male pride.

She still couldn't believe she was pressed up against him, flesh to bare, perfect, hard flesh. "Amazing," she breathed, still limp and trying to recover.

And as she came back to herself, she realized how much she wanted to take him where she'd just been. He'd seen her climax over and over, yet she'd never seen *him* in ecstasy, and it seemed high time to change that. "I want to make you come now," she told him, her voice raspy. She began to move on him again, just a little.

"That won't be difficult," he said on a low laugh.

"What can I do?" she asked breathily, sitting up to peer down on his gorgeous face. "How can I make you come?"

"Tell me you want it," he said, staring up at her. "Talk to me the way you did before, over the webcam. Talk dirty."

Laura bit her lip. Right about now was when she generally went sullen and morose on him. After her orgasm. But—joyfully—having Braden here with her, inside her, changed everything. She'd never talked dirty in her life to a guy before Braden, and doing it in an essentially empty room hadn't felt quite as real as this did, but it still came shockingly easy. Proof, she supposed, of just how hot he got her.

"I want you to come in me, baby," she cooed, running her hands up his flat stomach onto his chest. "I want you to come so hard, want you to come deep in my pussy." She rocked on him then, more emphatically than before since this was about his pleasure, not hers. She felt the jiggle of her breasts and watched his eyes drop there and knew the plain, simple delight of being a boundless, brazen woman with no worries over what anyone thought of her. "I want you to fuck me, baby, fuck me with that big, hard cock until you can't hold back another second, and then I want you to come in me—so fucking hard."

"Ah, fuck, I am, honey—I am." His voice sounded strained as his hands pressed down on her hips, his erection thrusting hotly up inside her. The pressure was enormous and overwhelming, and she screamed, not with pain, but with the impossible fullness he delivered. One, two, three wild drives that each lifted them from the bed with brute force as he groaned deeply. She watched his teeth clench, his eyes fall shut, his face wrench in an agony she knew was actually joy, and she loved having made him feel something so brutal and severe.

Once again, she bent to rest against his chest, and his arms came around her, pulling her close. She thought they'd stay silent, thought maybe he'd drift off to sleep as guys so often did after sex, and she decided she wouldn't mind if that happened without him even pulling out of her since something about it struck her as bizarrely erotic. But instead he whispered in her ear. "Do you have any idea how breathtaking you are?"

The words sifted down through her like sweet powdered sugar, the supreme compliment, and it meant so much more now that their sex was real. "I know you make me do things I've never done before." For the first time, she said it without shame or regret.

"Do you know," he said, even more softly, seductively, "that we're only just getting started here? Do you know that, before this is over, you're going to do things with me you've never even imagined?"

She lifted her head to meet his gaze in the shadows. His words made her insides sizzle, but she wasn't surprised. Subconsciously, she must have known the moment he slipped into bed with her that he wouldn't have come all this way just for one simply lay. "Yes, I know. And I can't wait to see what they are."

He drew his head back deeper into the pillow, his look teasing.

"And you're not going to fight me, act outraged and offended, and tell me over and over that this isn't you?"

She blinked, then smiled gently into his eyes. "Probably, at some point," she replied, reaching up to cup his stubbled cheek. "But I guess you'll just have to persuade me."

With that, she kissed him, another stunning we've-been-kissing-each-other-forever kiss, and it shored up her resolve. This man had found something in her she hadn't known existed. Part of her wanted to cringe—it felt so foreign. But if she was honest, a bigger part of her was fascinated with her new self, and she wanted nothing more than to keep fascinating him, too.

Chapter Seven

The only bad thing about the marvelous floor-to-vaulted-ceiling windows in the bedroom was when the morning sun came blasting through. But Laura didn't really mind—since her arrival here, the sun had gotten her up and to the computer early, and now, today, it didn't bother her because she had such a nice view. Not of the vast wintry landscape outside, but of the man in her bed.

She turned to look, lifting slightly. It was like in a museum when a bright light shone upon a masterpiece. And in this case the masterpiece was Braden. High cheekbones and a patrician nose made him classically handsome, but the wayward lock of raven hair dipping over his forehead and the stubble dusting his chin that had grown even thicker overnight hinted at the bad boy inside. She'd been right—she didn't get guys like him. Only she *had* him now.

And even in the light of day, she harbored no regrets. Maybe she was conservative enough to need him here in order to be bad *with* him. But she was also free enough, suddenly hedonistic enough, now that he'd arrived, to keep *on* being bad—and to see this for what it was, a golden opportunity to indulge in the sort of affair she'd never experience at home, in her real world, her real life.

She bit her lip, studying his supreme male beauty, letting her gaze drop to his bare chest as her *thoughts* dropped even lower, beneath the covers. She drew in her breath, remembering what it had felt like to have him inside her.

Rolling to her back, she cast a little smile heavenward. She couldn't be completely sure God would approve, but she liked to think He wouldn't drop something like this in her lap if He didn't want her to enjoy it.

"Morning, snowflake."

She glanced to her lover as he pushed up on one elbow, wearing his own naughty little grin.

"Thinking about last night?" he asked, eyes teasing her.

"Guilty as charged."

"Then you're not sorry I came?"

She shook her head against the pillow. "Just the opposite. I told you that last night."

He shrugged. "Doesn't mean you couldn't have changed your mind by now."

"Let's just say having the real thing is a whole lot more persuasive than having just a camera."

He gave a short nod, devilishly arching one eyebrow. "So you liked my cock."

She was ready and willing to be bad, but in the bright morning sun, such talk still sent heat spreading through her cheeks.

He laughed softly and leaned in close. "Don't worry, honey—it likes you, too."

"I can't imagine what you must think of me by now," she said in a rush of honesty. "I guess I seem like I have a split personality. One minute I'm willing, the next I'm not. I probably seem like . . . someone in need of medication," she concluded with a giggle and wished she didn't sound so nervous.

But he stayed cool, sexy, his voice coming low. "You just seem like a woman in need of a healthy dose of *me*." Then he lowered a short kiss to her waiting lips.

Only it became a lengthier kiss, because kissing him was so easy—and so simply intimate. After having communicated with him through a computer for so long, just having his mouth move over hers was like the ultimate connection. Being naked with him in bed was, astonishingly, as comfortable and cozy as it was wanton and thrilling.

Before she knew it, Braden was reaching for another condom, parting her legs beneath the sheets, and nailing her to the mattress. Like the previous night, there was an adjustment period to being so very filled with him, and also like previously, she heard herself crying out with each thrust he so capably delivered. She wrapped her legs around him and held on tight as her body soaked up the glorious pummeling.

"Want to make you come," he told her and, in one smooth, sweeping move, slid his arms around her and scooped her upward until they both sat in the center of the bed in a close embrace—so close that it stole her breath. Adding that to the position that made him feel infinitely larger inside her, it was all she could do to maintain her composure.

She peered into his eyes—yes, they were brown, a rich, deep color like velvet—and saw him clearly for the first real time. Such passion brimmed in his gaze that it made it *easy* to be the bad girl he so clearly adored. She buried her fingers in his hair and kissed him wildly, then rocked against him, seeking her release. Her pussy locked tight around his incredible shaft, and she suffered the impression of his cock stretching up inside her to staggering lengths. "So big in me," she heard herself breathe over him. "So big."

His eyes glimmered wickedly. "Ride me, baby. Ride me hard. I want to watch you come for me again."

She didn't hesitate, yearning only to give him what he wanted. Somehow her cravings had become tied up in *his* desires. Nothing was more exciting to her than pleasing him. So she moved her body on his, gyrating in energetic circles that made her breasts jiggle against his chest. She arched, hard, harder, and leaned back to let him rain kisses across the sensitive skin of her neck. Inside her, the glorious fever rose, her breath coming in frantic rasps, and though she'd not often had sex in the bright daylight, she understood that—as always with Braden— having his eyes on her was the fuel, the impetus, that would take her to her final destination. It was as if his hot gaze physically pushed her—higher, higher.

Until she once again came tumbling down with shrieks of sheer pleasure as the harsh sensations of orgasm jolted her. She dug her finger-nails into his shoulders, crying out, "God, I'm coming! I'm coming!"

And then Braden joined her, thrusting up into her harder, deeper, and like last night, lifting her from the bed with his majestic cock. "Me, too, baby—ah yeah, me, too." She wafted down from the climax in time to watch the ecstasy sweep across his face, only she could see him so much clearer this morning, and it amazed her to know she'd made him feel so much.

As soon as he opened his eyes, she kissed him spontaneously, then smiled, leaning her forehead against his. "I love watching you come," she admitted.

He pulled back slightly to look at her. "Now you see why I enjoyed our little game so much."

She conceded with a shrug. "But this is better—because now I get to watch you, too."

Another short kiss, and Laura's eyes landed on a desk clock across the room, *this* sight delivering her unpleasantly back to reality. "And I wish I could *keep* watching you, but I'm afraid duty calls."

"Duty?"

"Books to write, deadlines to meet."

He lifted his chin lightly. "Ah." Then glanced down at their bodies, still joined, before raising his eyes back to hers. "So you're willing to give up *this* for *that*?"

"Not by choice. But if I don't turn in a book, I don't get paid. And not all of us own fabulous homes all over the map. Some of us only have one tiny apartment in Seattle, and the rent doesn't pay itself." With that, she reluctantly lifted off of him with a long sigh. She didn't like ending this, but she was determined to be practical, not let this man carry her *completely* away from real life.

"I hardly own houses all over the map. This is the only one besides my place in L.A."

"Which is where exactly? Beverly Hills or something?"

He smirked teasingly. "No, not Beverly Hills."

"Where then?"

"Malibu," he replied softly but didn't look even remotely sheepish.

She sighed longingly. "Right on the beach, I'm guessing."

He shrugged. "Hey, if you're gonna live in Malibu . . ."

She laughed, shocked that she'd ended up fucking such a wealthy playboy type. It *so* wasn't her. But then, she'd decided not to *be* her, hadn't she? Just for now, just for as long as he was here. And she didn't ask how long he planned to stay, not only because she didn't want to appear anxious, but because decadent, sexually-free-wheeling Laura didn't need to know. She'd take it as it came, for what it was worth. When it was over, no big deal. She'd just chalk it up as another life experience. A big one.

She dug beneath the covers, searching for the panties that had been shoved off with such abandon in the night.

"So how's the book going? You never told me."

She glanced over her shoulder to see him stretched out perfect and naked in the bed—the condom long since disposed of in a wastebasket nearby. She couldn't quite look away from him. "Good," she said simply. She didn't mention that his entry into her life had somehow kick-started her creativity.

"So your writer's block is gone?"

She nodded. "I guess this . . . change in scenery was just what I needed." Having found her discarded underwear, she slid the bikini panties on, still in bed.

"Glad I could help. By lending you the house, I mean." He added a wink, and she wondered if he somehow knew her success was about more than a new view out the window.

"So," she said, "I guess you high-roller investor types can just flit about the country whenever you feel like it?" She was actually wondering how it was possible for him to leave behind such high-profile work on a moment's notice.

"Nothing happening right now that I can't handle via phone or computer."

She pointed vaguely down toward the first floor. "If you need the computer I've been using, I can . . ." What *could* she do? Use the one in her back pocket? "Stop working." She'd hate to do that with her deadline pending and her story zooming along now, but she had to make the offer.

"No worries, snowflake. I brought a laptop. Anything I need to do can be accomplished from there."

"That was thoughtful of you," she said, probably too softly.

"What can I say? I'm a thoughtful kinda guy." They both laughed when she met his wicked gaze, since it seemed clear that his thoughtfulness definitely fell within the parameters of him also being deadly seductive and slightly domineering.

"So you'll spend your day toppling empires from here?"

He gave his head an easy shake. "Nah, I might have to do a little work, but this trip is mostly pleasure. When you're busy, I'll hit the slopes." She pictured him swooshing down a black diamond like a pro—he seemed like the kind of guy who was probably skilled at everything he did. "I'll give my friend Tommy a call and see if he can tear himself away from his work for a few hours. He lives here year-round in the next house up the mountain"—he motioned in that direction—"and the guy's always looking for an excuse to ski, so he won't turn me down."

It was good to hit the snow—and prime time, too, smack in the middle of February. A little cold—Braden sometimes preferred spring skiing more—but the day was bright and clear, the runs well groomed, and he felt full of energy as they boarded the Highline lift to the top of Vail Mountain.

"You're serious?" Tommy said as soon as the lift chair left the ground. "You came here to seduce some chick you never met before just because she's staying at your house?"

It was the last thing Braden had had a chance to tell him before heading down the Blue Ox run, a killer double-black that led straight back to the lift.

"And because she's hot," Braden clarified.

"How did you know she was hot?"

"Webcam."

"You watched her on the fucking webcam?"

Braden turned to face his friend. Tufts of Tommy's blond hair stuck out beneath his hat at different angles, framing an expression brimming with accusation. Put like that, it sounded pretty heinous.

He answered truthfully. Sort of. "I was just checking in to make sure she got there okay. You know I do that sometimes." He left out the part about her touching herself. Not so much because he was a nice guy, but because he thought it possible Tommy and Laura could meet before this little soiree came to an end, and he was *at least* nice enough not to embarrass her like that. Some girls he'd known wouldn't mind if Braden told another guy every detail of their sex, but Laura would *definitely* mind, and despite still wanting to draw her even further out of her conservative little shell, he could respect an unspoken desire for some privacy.

"And she was hot enough for you to get on a plane and come knocking on her door?" Tommy asked

"*My* door," he clarified again, this time leaving out that he hadn't knocked.

"Still, though, dude, you promised the girl your house and you just show up like that?"

Braden flashed him a look. "Since when did you become the morality police?" Usually, Tommy was all about good sex and would go to extreme lengths to get it.

His ski buddy shrugged in his parka. "Since I figured out I'm a jerk most of the time, I guess."

Braden blinked. What the hell? "What are you talking about?"

Tommy sighed. "You remember Marianne?"

A pretty little ski bunny Tommy had met on the slopes at Copper Mountain last winter. When Braden had come for a month in the summer, Tommy had still been dating her, but given how quickly he typically blew through women, Braden had actually forgotten about her. "Yeah, sure."

"I cheated on her." Tommy kept his eyes straight ahead as he spoke.

"Oh." He'd never condemn a friend for that, but he thought it a stupid move. As a rule, Braden *didn't* cheat. Because Braden also didn't commit. He'd figured out by the time he'd graduated from college that it wasn't for him—he didn't like feeling obligated to anyone, and he didn't especially believe in monogamy. He did believe that if you chose to be monogamous, you should damn well stay that way, but he'd never put himself in that particular position. "Let me guess. She found out."

"Yep. And it hurt her—bad." Tommy shook his head helplessly. "I don't even know why I did it—the other girl wasn't even all that hot. It was almost like . . . out of habit or something. Which was idiotic."

Braden had never heard Tommy be self-deprecating before—the guy was normally confident and carefree. He hardly knew what to make of it. "And the moral of the story is?"

"It was a huge mistake. I *loved* Marianne. I mean, I was really in love with her, dude."

Braden's jaw dropped. Like him, Tommy didn't "fall in love." "You? In love? With a girl?"

Tommy shrugged. "The end of an era, I know. But the point is—I fell for her, I did something dumb, and I lost her. And I regret it like hell. Happened six months ago, and I can't seem to shake it. Haven't looked at another woman since."

"You're kidding me." Ladies' man Tommy hadn't looked at a woman in six months? The sky should start falling any minute now.

"I wish. Sometimes chicks try to pick me up in bars, or if I'm hanging out in a lodge at the end of a ski day, and my dick wants me to pay attention, but I just feel too shitty about what I did to Marianne."

"And she won't forgive you? I mean, maybe if she knew you were still missing her six months later, it would change her mind."

Tommy gave his head a short, decisive shake. "She's moved on. Got a new guy. Engaged and everything. Ran into her sister at the Mexican restaurant down in Edwards last week, and she told me."

"Then she's over you, over the hurt. Doesn't that mean you can move on, too?"

"It *should* mean that, I guess. So far, though, I still feel shitty."

Braden let out a sigh. "Who *are* you? I don't even know you, man."

Tommy remained despondent. "I guess I just never realized how much a girl could hurt over something like that until I saw the way she reacted. And until I ended up getting hurt, too."

"And all this has *what* to do with me showing up here?" Braden asked. Shocked as he'd been by Tommy's confession, he'd been waiting to get to that particular point for the whole lift ride, which was nearing an end. The lift chair was fast approaching the departure point at the top of the hill.

"Well, it's none of my business, but . . . I guess I'm just thinking more about girls' feelings than I used to. And it seems pretty presumptuous to just show up unannounced when she came here for privacy. I mean, for Christ's sake, what did she do when she saw you?"

"She fucked my brains out," Braden said smoothly as he stood from the moving chair to glide down the exit ramp, ready for the next run.

Part of Laura wanted to kill herself for letting him go. She'd had him here, in bed with her, naked—the most physically perfect man she'd ever known—and she'd sent him away because she had a book to write? On the other hand, though, she couldn't be sorry, because the day flew by as quickly as her fingers over the keyboard, Riley and Sloane's story spilling out of her at record speed. She barely even had to think—the words simply flowed, as if they'd been trapped in a big bucket some-where inside her and it had finally tipped over.

As she'd suspected, Sloane was now a major part of the story. Riley remained completely in lust with him, but she still wasn't sure how much she trusted him. He was flirtatious and arrogant and thought he was God's gift to the world of private eyes—but when Riley and Sloane put their heads together, things started to happen.

The whole question of why someone would steal a valuable antique broach only to hide it in a toolshed lingered. But working together, the two had hit upon an idea: if someone had hidden the broach on the property, perhaps other missing items might be hidden there, too. For instance, just last week, they discovered, Mr. Dorchester had lost a dividend check before he could take it to the bank. A rare first edition of *A Farewell to Arms*, signed by Hemingway himself, had disappeared from the library, too. The Dorchesters hadn't mentioned either until Riley and Sloane had started prodding them—both Mr. and Mrs. D. had assumed they were just getting a little forgetful and had misplaced them. But now Riley and Sloane had set off on a treasure hunt of sorts. If they could turn up the other missing items, perhaps the pieces of the puzzle would begin to come together.

And, of course, he'd kissed her again, too.

She'd been climbing up on a step ladder, back searching the tool-shed, checking the top of a large old wooden cabinet. Sloane's hands had come warm at her hips, steadying her.

Riley feared there could have been a rattlesnake curled up atop the old armoire and she wouldn't have seen it—because all she could concentrate on at the moment were the two warm palms bracketing her hips. She'd been touched by other men before, but Sloane Bennett seemed to have an unusual hold on her—both literally and figuratively. She tried to tell herself it was simply because he'd kissed her before they'd even been introduced, that such powerful chemistry had been inevitable. Yet the explanation did nothing to dim her rather feral attraction to him.

"Anything up there?" he asked.

Focus. She saw some rusted pieces of steel that had probably once been attached to a cart or wagon, and a coiled garden hose. The hose seemed a likely hiding place, so she reached into the center, where she couldn't see, to feel around.

Something scurried across her fingertips! She screamed and leapt into the air.

She landed in Sloane Bennett's capable arms, her heart beating too fast as she peered up into his deep brown eyes. "Spider," she said on a quivery breath. "Or at least it felt like one."

"I've never heard of a detective afraid of a little bitty spider, Riley."

"Who said it was little?" she whispered, nearly breathless from being so close to him.

"But I'll be happy to take your mind off it," he said, then lowered his mouth fully onto hers.

It was the best encounter with a spider Riley Wainscott had ever had.

Of course, once the long and intoxicating kiss had ended, they bickered. Whereas Laura, prior to last night, had run from Braden every time she'd had an orgasm, Riley bickered with Sloane every time he kissed her. Riley simply wasn't used to feeling so consumed by a mere kiss, a mere man. She feared her overwhelming attraction to Sloane as much as she was drawn in by it.

As the writing day had gone on, the two sleuths had continued their search on the Dorchesters' grounds. Although Riley had lived next door with Aunt Mimsey for many years—since her parents had died in an auto accident when Riley was a teenager—she'd never really explored the Dorchesters' estate nor realized how vast it was. She'd attended teas in Mrs. D.'s parlor or the occasional Fourth of July picnic in the sprawl-ing backyard, but as she and Sloane searched for clues, she realized the picturesque lands stretched farther than she knew.

They'd searched around the tall shade trees dripping with bird-houses, the well-manicured shrubs and flowering bushes, the small vegetable garden where Edna and Mrs. D. worked together during the summer months—and then Sloane had spotted a path behind the gar-den that led back through the trees. He'd taken Riley's hand and they began to follow it together . . .

Until they found themselves standing in a beautiful park-like square of thick green grass dotted with colorful flower-beds, perfectly shaped pear trees—each sporting a bright red or blue birdhouse—and in the center, a stone bench clearly placed there so one could sit and soak in the tranquil beauty. A thick row of shrubbery—at least eight feet high—bordered the perimeter, so that it was impossible to see out and equally as impossible for anyone to see in. They'd discovered . . . a secret garden.

"I never knew this was here," Sloane said, clearly in awe.

"Me, neither, and I've lived next door for years."

"I stayed here during summers when I was a kid and roamed these grounds—but I guess I never ventured this far from the house."

"Why do you think it's here?" Riley asked. "Why do you think no one knows about it?" She lifted her gaze to Sloane's, realizing they still held hands. She made no effort to pull away, and neither did he.

He shook his head. "I can't imagine." Then he looked around, still taking in the wonder. "It feels like we're far away, though, doesn't it? From everything."

Riley nodded. The rest of the lovely estate was pristine and postcard-worthy, but something about this storybook patch of ground felt almost magical. The kind of place that could make you forget the rest of the world existed. The grass was greener, the flowers more vibrant. If she didn't know better, she'd swear the sky overhead was bluer.

As she stood there hand in hand with her dark-haired companion, she gazed about, soaking up every nuance of the place, feeling as if the garden somehow cocooned them and was, in some ethereal way, pushing them closer together.

That's when she spotted the sliver of paper poking from the round opening of a little red birdhouse shaped like a barn. Rather than release Sloane's strong hand from her grip, she pulled him along behind her, and he followed, for once letting her lead. The birdhouse hung too high for her to reach, but she pointed silently, and Sloane clearly saw what had caught her eye. He reached for it, extracting an oblong slip from the circular door.

As he stretched it between his hands, they both peered down to see Mr. Dorchester's missing check! "Uncle Howard's dividends," Sloane said as Riley gasped.

They, of course, had no idea what this might mean, but turning up another large clue felt like a supreme victory. On impulse, Riley threw her arms around Sloane's neck, and he closed her in a firm embrace. "Finally!" she said. "Another missing item hidden on the grounds!"

"Finally," he repeated, but his voice had gone lower, smokier, and his lids were shaded, his eyes half shut in what Riley could only decipher as pure desire. "Finally, I get to kiss you again."

It had only been a couple of hours since the last time, but it felt like forever to Riley, too. His mouth crushed hard on hers, the kiss swallowing her and making her forget everything else but this man and this secret space that felt so private, so perfectly isolated.

Riley had never made love to a man she barely knew, but

as the kisses deepened, she understood that was where they were leading, and she hadn't the faintest wish to stop them.

Of course, she supposed if she were serious about finally showing the world she could be a good detective, she should stay focused on solving this mystery. This might finally be the one that would lead to a career in investigations. And yet . . .

Sloane's kisses, as they dropped from her neck to her shoulder, made her whole body tingle. And when he unbuttoned her shirt, she couldn't help wanting him to see the pretty pink bra she'd just happened to put on this morning. Not that her choice of lingerie had anything to do with him—she might be madly attracted to the guy, but how could she have possibly known they would stumble upon a secret garden that would feel as seductive as Sloane himself?

Slowly, he stripped her free of her bra and sank his mouth to her aching breasts. Moments later, they dropped to their knees and Riley wanted nothing more than to lie down and feel the cool greenness against her back as he made love to her.

And that's exactly what happened. The carpet of grass cushioned her as sweet as any bed while Sloane moved inside her in slow, deep strokes that filled her senses. The rich scent of the grass mixed with the fragrance of roses nearby. The sun warmed her face. And Sloane made her feel every ounce a woman.

Perhaps she should have said no. Perhaps it was too soon, especially considering that she wasn't even sure yet if she really liked him. But she'd never met a man so tempting, and the lushness of their garden hideaway had seemed the final ingredient to something which—if she were honest—she'd been daydreaming about since the moment she'd laid eyes on him.

"I've never done this before," she told him. "Made love to a man I don't know very well."

He grinned heatedly down at her. "You know me *now*, honey."

If this was how they celebrated every time they found a clue, she had a feeling that solving this particular mystery was going to be a lot more fun than usual.

Laura smiled at the screen, having ended the chapter. She had no idea if her editor would let such a scene fly in what were generally quaint and family-friendly novels, but for now, she was following her muse, and her muse was definitely thinking about sex today. At the moment, she wasn't sure her muse would ever *stop* thinking about it. Since getting acquainted with Braden, she'd had sex on the brain, and now that he was here, she didn't expect that to change anytime soon.

Just then, the front door opened, letting in a small blast of brisk air. Another sunny day had filled the house with solar heat, so she wore only a cami and joggers. She looked up, wrapping her arms around herself to ward off the chill.

Braden appeared rugged and cold in his ski gear, like a man you wanted to wrap up with in a blanket next to the fire. "Fun skiing?" she asked, pushing to her feet to greet him.

"Yeah. Great day out there. I'm beat."

"Oh." Well, that was okay. She might have sex on the brain, but the blanket-and-fire idea appealed, too, so she'd make the best of it. She'd skied a little herself, and she remembered that a long day on the slopes could leave you exhausted.

She could only assume her disappointment was written all over her face when he said, "Don't worry, snowflake. I'm not *that* tired."

She practically felt her nipples harden at the deep promise in his voice. "Well, if you were, I'd understand. I mean, it's not like I need sex constantly or anything."

He chuckled. "Too bad, because that's how often I plan to give it to you."

She drew in her breath. "If you insist."

"I do. Right now, in fact. I want you in the shower."

A soft gasp escaped her. She'd envisioned them making dinner to-

gether, maybe talking a while, getting to know each other a little better—*then* having more sex.

"What's wrong?" He stripped off a sturdy pair of black ski gloves,
tossing them in the corner of the tiled foyer, then flung the baseball cap
with the Vail resort logo from his head, as well.

She bit her lip. "Nothing."

He stripped off his ski jacket and let it drop to the floor to reveal
a soft fleece pullover. "Did you go all sensible and conservative on me
again today?" he asked, moving toward her, down the two carpeted steps
into the sunken living room. He drew near, resting his hands on her
hips. "Is this where I have to convince you, persuade you?" He let his
palms glide upward to the sides of her breasts. She wore no bra, so her
nipples jutted prominently through her top as he stroked his thumbs
over them, and her pussy surged.

"I don't think," she said, her voice breathy as her hands curled into
the fleece at his chest, "you'll have to work too hard to get me where
you want me."

A slow grin spread over his face. "Good. Let's go get wet together."

Chapter Eight

They stood in the bedroom, outside the massive marble shower, Braden's eyes sparkling with mischief and sex. Part of Laura wondered again how she'd found herself in such a game—where she was willing to do whatever this man wanted and he knew it. Fortunately, she brimmed with more anticipation than trepidation.

"Pants," he said, pointing to hers, then the floor.

Pulling at the drawstring below her navel, she felt the fabric loosen, then pushed it down. The pants dropped, and she stepped smoothly out of them, leaving her in a pink cami and white cotton bikini undies. "Shirt," she said, following his lead and lifting one finger toward his fleece.

He took it off over his head and tossed it aside, but still wore a mock turtleneck and ski pants.

"That one, too," she added, nodding toward the turtleneck.

He smiled softly, then removed it, as well. "Top," he said.

Slowly, never taking her eyes off his, she pushed down one shoulder strap, carefully withdrawing her arm, then the other. Hooking her thumbs into the neckline, she peeled the fitted cami down, hotly aware that she enjoyed revealing her breasts for his hungry gaze. She pushed the little top past her waist, wiggling her hips to help its descent, until finally it dropped to her ankles. His eyes burned through her, making her feel wholly owned by him.

She had to swallow back her lust before she could speak the next words. "*Your* pants now," she said, watching intently as he lowered his ski pants and thermal underwear at the same time until he stood before her in sleek black boxer briefs that hugged his ass as well as the erection growing in front. She had to bite back a gasp at the sight of that arousing bulge.

"All that's left are the panties, snowflake." He gave his head a lecherous tilt, punctuating the words with a grin.

Laura's whole body pulsed with need now, so she didn't hesitate, pushing the cotton to her knees, then letting them fall the rest of the way. His gaze dropped unabashedly to her pussy.

"You now," she said. "Drop 'em."

He had to lift the elastic over his cock to lower his underwear, and she couldn't hold back her gasp this time, reminded anew of what a magnificent male organ he possessed.

"After you," he offered.

Laura stepped into the shower that was big enough to walk around with ease and sported a built in marble bench at one end as well as marble shelves at different heights. Braden followed, turning on the overhead nozzle. "Do you like it warm or do you like it hot?" he asked with a glance in her direction.

"Just warm, I'm afraid."

He winked. "No worries. I can get you hot in other ways."

She was *already* hot inside, her temperature climbing higher with each passing second. Her eyes were drawn back to Braden's enormous cock—it was difficult to believe she'd managed to handle it. But she wanted it again anyway, and soon.

"Come here, honey," he said from beneath the spray, and taking her hand, he drew her into the warm flow of water, letting it wet her breasts, belly, and lower. He slid his dampened palms from her hips upward to stroke her breasts, then bent to kiss her mouth.

Just like the previous night and this morning, Braden's kiss was at once easy and stunning, heightening every other sensation. She lifted her hands to his shoulders, let the kiss swallow her, let his tongue capture hers. When it finally ended, they both let out breathy sighs, and she couldn't help thinking that even Braden seemed affected. He'd probably kissed hundreds of women, so it imbued her with unexpected power to think hers might actually be special in some way.

"Mmm," he sighed. "You make it hard to go slow."

She tilted her head. "Do we have to? Go slow?"

He offered a solemn nod. "Yes."

"Why?" She bit her lip and felt heat rising to her cheeks with the realization that he'd gotten her in the mood for something hard and fast.

"Because I want to wash you."

"Oh . . ." The word left her in an airy sound, her body tingling from the promise as he reached to one of the shelves lining the dark marble walls.

He picked up a familiar sponge—the same she'd used—and squeezed her pink body wash onto it, filling the shower with the scent of fresh raspberries. He squished the sponge in his fist and white suds, sparkling like Colorado snow beneath the sun, oozed out.

With one strong hand, Braden drew her arm toward him to run the soapy sponge up its inner side. Somehow, her cunt rippled simply from that. He didn't stop there, though, gliding it onto her breast and around in a smooth circle that nearly stole her breath. "Oh," she said again, off balance from the heady sensation, and he steadied her with a palm at her hip. "You have a way with a sponge, Mr. Stone," she added with a slightly embarrassed laugh.

"You ain't seen nothin' yet," he teased, but his eyes were all fire as he drew the sponge slowly around the other breast, leaving a trail of thick white suds behind.

Next, he grazed her stomach, swiping slowly back and forth and making her yearn for it to go lower. Which is when it did—right between her thighs. She sucked in her breath, parted her legs, and watched as he moved the sponge up and down, every brush stimulating her swollen clitoris. "Mmm," she moaned, her eyes falling shut to the heavenly sensation.

"You look so good in soap suds, baby," he breathed over her hotly.

"Want to hear a confession?" she asked, peering up at him.

His eyes lit up. "Always."

"The first time I took a shower here, after we'd been . . . you know . . . talking on the computer . . . I got excited, thinking about you, and I wondered if you'd like seeing me this way, all wet and soapy."

"Unh—you just made me harder, honey," he said. "And I have a confession, too. I *fantasized* about you, all soaped up for me. But the real thing is even better." With that, he thrust the sponge back on the shelf and let his hands close over her soap-covered breasts. "So slick," he murmured, massaging them. "Slick and sudsy and beautiful." His erection pressed into her stomach, and she couldn't resist curling her hand around it. His groan filled her with the need to pleasure him more deeply.

On impulse, she reached for the sponge he'd abandoned and ran it up his rigid length. "Aw, baby," he growled. He still caressed her wet breasts, peered longingly into her eyes. But then his gaze dropped to the two soapy bodies touching amid the suds, and hers did, too.

She ran the sponge in a circle around his shaft, then slid it underneath to his balls. Yet another deep moan left him through clenched teeth, and she wondered if it was possible for her to come just from touching *him*. In addition to gliding the soft sponge between his legs, she swiped it over his chest, stomach, his muscular arms. Then she spun him around to wash his back and discovered as she moved lower that he possessed—not surprisingly—a fabulous round, firm ass, which also got cleaned.

The more she explored, the more she wanted him. The hell with chatting by the fire—she wanted him to fuck her hard and deep. "I want you," she heard herself murmur, leaning into him from behind. "I want your big, beautiful cock inside me." She reached around to caress it between sponge and hand.

His voice came deep, strained. "Not yet, baby."

She couldn't hide her frustration. "Why not?"

He spoke over his shoulder. "Because I want to do more."

She sucked in her breath, only half appeased, as her cunt ached with need.

"You'll get what you want eventually," he promised. "But first, we do things my way."

He sounded so sure, so confident—she didn't even think about protesting further. "Okay."

"Good girl," he whispered, then turned, lowering a kiss to her forehead.

Taking the sponge from her hand, he set it aside, then drew her halfway beneath the water. As soon as the spray had cleared the soap from the juncture of her thighs, he gently pushed her back against the cool marble wall.

He dropped to his knees and used one hand to part her legs, and she shivered with the realization of what was coming. "I want to taste this sweet pussy," he said, then sank his tongue eagerly into her slit.

"Unh!" she cried as the pleasure shot through her.

He licked her again, and again, tongue and mouth eagerly working at her folds.

"Oh God, yes," she whispered, "yes," because if she'd thought Braden's *hands* were skilled . . . well, his *tongue* almost put them to shame. He lapped deeply at her most intimate flesh before capturing her engorged clit between his tongue and the roof of his mouth. Her hands clutched at his head, and when she found the strength to glance down, he was peering heatedly up at her. "So good," she told him, her legs rapidly weakening beneath her. She wasn't sure she'd ever been eaten while standing up before.

Soon, he ran his tongue in languid circles around the hot little nub of flesh, almost as if he were French-kissing it, and Laura thought she'd collapse from the pure pleasure. She heard her breath coming heavier, felt her body nearing that crucial apex, gave one more thought to how mind-blowing it was that she had this man in this shower in this mountainside home so far away from her own, then tumbled into utter ecstasy. She cried out as the heat streamed down along with the water, the spasms making her clutch at his shoulders as they washed through her. "Oh God, baby, oh God!"

And then she *was* collapsing, her knees gently giving way—but Braden eased her down onto the marble floor, her legs bent in front of her.

Their eyes locked. His shone glassy. She was still busy trying to catch her breath, but she lifted her hands to his face and kissed him hard, thrusting her tongue between his lips. She shouldn't have been surprised to taste herself there, but she was—at once slightly put off but also aroused, deeply.

"I want you in my mouth," she said. She'd never felt hungrier in her life.

He only grunted in reply, clearly excited, and she said, still breathless, "Stand up."

Laura had never really minded going down on a guy as part of foreplay, but this was different. For the first time in her life, she truly wanted it. Had to have it. Had to have Braden's cock in her mouth.

He pushed to his feet, his eyes wild with anticipation now, and Laura moved to her knees. The water no longer hit either of them, but Braden's perfect shaft stood wetly at attention. She didn't hesitate to drag one long, slow lick from the base to the head, relishing how rock-hard he felt on her tongue. He moaned, his fingertips gently stroking her cheeks as he peered down at her.

Biting her lower lip, she looked back at him for a moment, but then dropped her gaze to the task before her. Curling one hand warmly around his glistening length, she slid her tongue around the head, lightly tasting the semen gathered there, then sank her mouth over him.

She held steady, testing, weighing—could she do this? Could she handle something so enormous in her mouth? Certainly, she couldn't take all of it—a physical impossibility—but she wanted to pleasure him as deeply as possible, so that meant swallowing as *much* of him as possible.

She lowered her lips, letting the thickness of him stretch her mouth, fill her. Above her, he moaned, and it encouraged her to take more, a little more, and then even a little more.

His breath rained down heavy, labored, and he whispered, "Baby . . . oh baby . . . so fucking good . . . so deep . . . so deep."

Maybe other women didn't try this hard, and it pleased her immensely that he thought her a skilled lover. It also persuaded her to press herself a bit farther, until the tip of his cock touched the back of her throat. She worked hard to relax the muscles there—and then she began to move. Up and down. Taking him in and out. Never as deep as that first, slow, still descent, yet as far as she comfortably could, continuing to push herself with each stroke.

"Oh yeah, honey, suck me. Suck my cock. You suck it so good."

She'd never particularly enjoyed such talk before, but from Braden she did. Perhaps since they'd met through sex, since everything they'd shared was *about* sex, it made it okay for this to be about nothing more than animal impulses, carnal desires, raw, unadorned, and dirty. She'd never known dirty could be so good.

She continued working over his erection, caressing his balls with her hand, listening to his sounds of hot delight from above. She couldn't remember a time when she'd felt so energetic, so unfettered, free to follow urges without worrying what anyone would think or how she would feel afterward. Her experiences with Braden and the webcam had been a difficult initiation to such feelings, but knowing it had brought her here made it worthwhile.

"Baby," he growled lowly, his hands in her hair. "Baby, stop now."

When she ignored him, he gently lifted her head until she was forced to release him. She peered up, wondering why he'd stopped her, and wondering if her lips looked as stretched and swollen as they felt.

"I don't want to come yet," he said, his voice dark with passion. "I want to lick your hot little cunt again."

She felt her face flush with heat. "But I already came. *So* good," she said, remembering the force of the orgasm. "I want to make *you* come now."

But above her, Braden simply shook his head, silently reminding her that he was calling the shots here, and that she'd agreed to let him do so.

"I want to lick you again," he repeated, "because this time it's going to be different."

She blinked up at him. "Different how?"

"I want to really *see* your cunt, honey. Want to really *feel* it. I want you to shave your pussy for me, Laura."

Laura swallowed, hard.

She knew some women did that—women in porn magazines, and in the erotic story she'd read the other night. But she'd certainly never thought about doing it herself. Something about it seemed . . . beyond risqué. But then again, everything about this trip had gone beyond risqué, days ago.

She pushed slowly to her feet, finally forgetting about his cock for a minute, so that they were face to face. "It would be more arousing to you . . . bare?"

He gave a short, simple nod. "I want to see all of you."

She tried to swallow back the various sorts of nervousness suddenly striking her. "I've never . . . shaved there before."

"Then you'd better be careful," he said, voice deep, commanding. He stepped up close to her and slipped his hand between her legs to cup her. "I want you to be as slick and smooth as a peeled peach."

Laura drew in a deep, fortifying breath. Part of her was scared to death. But she tried to tell herself that was the old, conservative her—not the new, wild, sensual her that Braden had unleashed.

"Wh-where should I . . . ?" she began brokenly.

He pointed toward the marble bench. Two disposable razors and a can of shaving cream sat in the corner. She'd noticed the small mirror near the nozzle, and that Braden had left for skiing this morning clean-shaven, so obviously he shaved in the shower.

As she walked toward the built-in bench, situated at the opposite end from the flow of water, she asked herself if she could really make herself do this. The last time she'd asked that question had been right before she'd used the vibrator for him. In comparison, this actually seemed . . . not as extreme.

She tried to approach it practically. She lifted one leg up beside her on the bench, knee bent—although as she did it, it was impossible not to be aware that she was putting her pussy fully on display. Braden stood at the other end of the shower, water streaming over his back, watching.

Spraying shaving cream into her hand, she smoothed it over the flesh between her thighs. She drew in her breath at the light flutter that wafted through her, then took up one of the plastic razors and cautiously began to swipe the hair away. The sensation of moving the razor over such a sensitive area while Braden watched added to her growing arousal. Damn—she'd expected the task to excite *him*, not her—and yet her breath grew shallow as she saw the dark hair disappear, leaving soft, smooth skin in its place. Something about revealing this final hidden part of herself—to him, and also to herself—left her feeling alive, vibrant, brave, and gloriously brazen.

Across the shower, Braden's eyes were glued to her pussy, making it feel so swollen that she couldn't imagine what it looked like in such a state, now without even pubic hair to conceal it. She worked carefully, steadily, trying to remain calm and ignore her own ragged breathing, until she'd finished, leaving only a small tuft of pale curls at the top. "Good?" she asked, lifting her eyes to him.

His dark gaze shone with masculine pleasure as he answered with only a short nod, then bent one finger toward himself, summoning her. He stepped out of the spray so that she could move under it, and they both watched as the water washed away the remains of shaving cream.

The second it was gone, Braden's hand slipped between her legs. They both moaned at the touch.

"Just like I wanted you," he said. "Soft and slick." Then he pulled his hand away. "Feel it," he instructed.

Given that she'd touched herself for him before, she didn't hesitate. Yet she sucked in her breath when she discovered just how incredibly smooth she'd left herself.

"Beautiful," he whispered over her, leaning in for a lingering kiss.

"I can't really see it," she admitted.

Reaching behind him for the shaving mirror, hung on a small hook, he held it in front of her at just the right angle—and she gasped. Men were used to having their sex organs on display—women, not so much. The vision was at once startling yet . . . lovely. Lovely to see what *he* saw and to know it turned him on. Lovely, too, to see what she really *was* down there, how she really *looked*.

Then she remembered what had prompted this. He'd told her he wanted to lick her some more. She'd already been very satisfied when he'd offered, but now she ached for stimulation to the flesh she'd just spent long minutes teasing in so many ways. "Do you want to kiss it now?" she whispered, peering up into those dark eyes, hoping he could see the lust in hers.

An expression of supreme gratification washed over his face—as if maybe he'd just figured out that he'd truly begun to change her, change her into what he wanted her to be.

He never answered, just pressed his palms to her hips and began walking her slowly backward until she bumped lightly into the bench. He eased her down onto it and issued a simple command. "Spread for me."

Pulse racing, she parted her thighs, and it felt like she was opening herself to him in a whole new way.

He dropped to his knees, slid his hands up her thighs, and peered intently at her face. "Do you know how beautiful you are, Laura?"

She didn't answer for a long moment, not sure how to. On an average day, she'd probably call herself a six. She wasn't a stunner—she knew that and was okay with it. But with him, she *felt* beautiful, more desirable than ever before. "You *make* me beautiful," she finally said.

The words brought a small smile to his mouth just before he bent to lick her. Same searing pleasure as before, yet even more intimate now, somehow. Because she'd bared this last private part of herself. She'd had no idea when he'd asked her to do it that it would feel like such a monumental change, yet it did. So much that she parted her legs even farther, as wide as she could, until she was lifting them both onto the bench on either side of her. She sighed and moaned with each tantalizing lick he swept through her wetness and felt every graze of his fingers where he stroked her outer flesh, the skin now soft and bare.

Even when she let her eyes fall shut, she knew his gaze shifted from her pink folds to her face and back again. She could feel those dark eyes as tangible as a touch—it seemed she'd always been able to, even when he'd been all the way in California.

Her breath grew labored with his ministrations, each stroke of his tongue lifting her higher. She moaned, sighed, lightly massaged his scalp. *Yes, yes, so good, baby.* She kept the words inside now, though, because so much emotion combined with so much sensation was weakening her all over again.

Suddenly he raised his head and said, "I need to be inside you," so firmly she would have thought his life depended on it. It made her want him there, too.

"God, yes," she agreed.

Grabbing her wrist, he yanked her to her feet, turned her body, and used his hands to plant her palms flat against the shower wall. Mist from the warm spray floated over them as Braden gripped her hips and plunged inside her.

Oh God—so big, so deep! Her legs nearly dropped out from under her as she released a hot sob.

"You okay?" His breath came warm on her ear.

"Mmm" was all she could manage. Then, with a Herculean effort, "Big. Good."

He growled a response. "You're so tight around my cock."

She sobbed again, lightly this time, overcome by the whole encounter.

When he first began to thrust, she had to fight to keep her footing, keep her knees steady. He anchored one strong arm around her waist to help her stand. Every hard stroke pulsated all the way to the tips of her fingers and toes and made her cry out from the intensity.

But before long, she was instinctually arching her ass toward him, wanting to somehow take him even deeper. His hands snaked around to grasp her wet breasts, massaging in time with each drive of his stiff shaft, then one dipped down to stroke through her moisture in front. Only then did she realize he was no longer holding her up, that she'd found the strength to take what he had to give.

She felt out of her mind with pleasure, letting it envelop her. She could no longer think or reason, only absorb him—his cock, his hands, the mouth that occasionally rained kisses across her shoulders, neck. She heard her own voice—she sounded like someone in pain, nearly crying, but they both knew it was pleasure that consumed her.

His big fingers turned in perfect circles over her clit, and thrusting against his cock in one direction brought a sweeter, hotter pressure in front when she moved back the other way. She'd never had multiple orgasms before—but maybe that was just because her other lovers had quit trying after one? She'd thought she might climax a few minutes ago, when he'd started licking her again, and now, as he touched her, moved in her so powerfully, she knew she would come a second time.

It broke over her in waves of light and heat, and like before, she started to go down—too weak to keep standing—but the hand at her breast dropped to her waist to support her as she screamed out her pleasure. "I've got you, baby, I've got you," he cooed in her ear as the final vibrations echoed through her.

And it struck her that she felt safe with him.

How the hell had *that* happened? She barely knew him, after all— they'd done nothing together besides have sex.

Yet she trusted him. Trusted him to take her to these new, hedonistic places without letting her fall. Figuratively or literally.

But then there was no more time for thinking or examining, because he was still pumping into her, hard and fast, and she knew he was getting close, too. Each stroke still filled her, thrilled her, beyond comprehension. "I'm gonna come soon, honey," he rasped. "I'm gonna come so hard. I'm gonna come on your ass."

Whoa. That caught her off guard and she looked over her shoulder.

"Let me" was all he said, voice low, sure, persuasive. As if he knew with all certainty that she'd agree, but just wanted to hear her say it.

It wasn't, she thought, as if she had much choice anyway, if that's what he wanted to do, but as always with Braden, she wanted to excite him. "Yes," she said.

And it was only as he pulled out of her, growling the word "Now" through clenched teeth, only as she felt the hot liquid evidence of his orgasm arc across her rounded flesh, once, twice, thrice, that she discovered yet another new, searing pleasure. Feeling his semen this way made it more real, more like a vital part of him that she'd brought forth, that he was giving to her. Instantly wanting to feel it even deeper, she followed the urge to reach behind her and begin rubbing it into her skin.

"Oh God, honey," Braden murmured, breathless. "That's so hot, I could almost come again." And then he began to *help* her rub it in, which was so hot she almost thought *she* could come again, too.

They stood that way, silent, hands meshing with the moisture, massaging it into her ass, until she peered once more over her shoulder. "I never come twice," she said.

His gaze twinkled darkly. "You do now."

Chapter Nine

When they stepped from the shower and Laura reached for her discarded cami, Braden's voice sounded behind her. "Don't get dressed."

She looked over her shoulder, surprised—and exhausted. "I thought you were tired from skiing."

He chuckled. "Don't worry. I am." Then his eyes warmed on her. "But I still don't want you to get dressed. I want to be able to see you."

With that, he walked to a closet, slid open the mirrored door, and pulled from a hanger a black see-through kimono, holding it out to her.

Laura drew in her breath. "How many women have worn this?"

He gave her a soft, playful smile. "None, snowflake—I bought it just for you. Before I came up here."

Suddenly wondering if she could catch a glimpse of other feminine-type things in the closet, she leaned past him, trying to look. "What else did you buy for me?"

"Naughty, naughty," he said, sliding the door closed. "You'll find out when I give them to you, and if I catch you peeking, I'll have to give you a spanking."

She bit her lip and spoke unguardedly. "That makes it even more tempting."

"Why, Laura, I didn't know you liked to play that way." He raised his eyebrows, looking heatedly amused.

She dropped her gaze, feeling only a tad sheepish. "Neither did I."

His dark eyes pinned her in place. "Well, we'll explore that another time. For now, put this on and we'll go make dinner."

"I'm supposed to make dinner in this?" She let out a short, sarcastic laugh. "*Only* this?"

"I want to be able to see you whenever I glance over. I want to see that pretty, smooth pussy, and I want to be able to touch it if I feel the urge."

Oh. Well. As a fresh frisson of heat skittered down her spine, she decided to quit arguing. The Laura of old would think this preposterous. But Braden's Laura couldn't help being aroused and intrigued by the notion.

So she slipped on the barely-there robe as Braden stepped into fresh black boxer briefs that hugged him deliciously. He put on nothing more, either, so she had a nice view, as well.

Together, they headed down to the kitchen where Braden found a frozen lasagna and a loaf of garlic bread in the freezer, mentioning they were from his last visit a couple of months ago. Laura had seen them, too, but had bought her own food for the stay back before her voyeur had arrived. They worked together in the kitchen, opening another bottle of wine, getting the lasagna in the oven, finding plates and utensils, and Laura offered up the salad she'd assembled at the local grocery store. At first, she felt weird walking around in the robe, but slowly, she began to feel . . . more sensual, knowing that even as their dinner preparations weren't about sex, they *were*.

She also stayed unerringly aware that they strolled about in what one could almost think of as a glass house. Floor-to-ceiling windows covered the entire rear of the dwelling, which included the kitchen and dining area as well as the living room and Braden's master bedroom upstairs.

As they sat down at the table with their salads, he on one end and she at the side so that their knees touched underneath, she motioned toward the nearest panes with her fork. Outside, all was black with night, but inside bright lights shone. "You realize that anyone on any other hillside nearby who happens to have binoculars or a telescope like yours could see us right now." She'd noticed the expensive telescope by the window, near the computer, upon her arrival.

Braden cast a devilish grin. "But we'll never know, so what's the harm?"

She glanced again to the telescope. "Do *you* look at people through *your* telescope?"

He gave his head a matter-of-fact tilt. "No, snowflake. I look at *stars* through my telescope. But it's not a bad idea, now that you mention it." He winked.

"So you haven't always been such a voyeur?"

She watched him consider the question. "I guess I've always had tendencies toward watching, always been turned on by the visual aspect of sex. But I've never been as into it as I am right now, with you."

Why did that warm her heart? She supposed, even if it was silly, it made her feel a little bit special to him in some way—different from all the other women he'd surely been with.

"I love being able to look over and see your gorgeous tits through that sheer fabric right now, honey, love the way your nipples poke against it to make those dark little points. And I loved being able to see you in the kitchen, too. You might think I was busy opening up the lasagna and pouring the wine, but in between I was looking at your beautiful naked pussy and your nice little ass."

She pulled in her breath and knew instinctively that her nipples jutted even *more* prominently at the transparent fabric now.

"By the way," he added, "as much as I liked coming on your ass, I should probably mention I did it for a practical reason, too. I forgot a condom." For the first time since they'd met, guilt laced his expression.

Laura gasped—she hadn't even realized! How incredibly irresponsible of her!

"The good news is," he said, "I've never forgotten *before.*"

She lowered her chin in doubt. "Never?"

He shrugged those strong, sexy shoulders she'd dug her fingernails into earlier. "Okay, when I was young a few times. But long enough ago that if anything was wrong, I'd probably know it by now. Anyway, I remembered about halfway through, and I know it's not foolproof or anything, but figured pulling out couldn't hurt—and as it turned out, it was pretty damn fun."

She let out a sigh of relief. "Well, I'm notoriously careful, so no worries from me. Notoriously careful until now, that is," she added, letting her brows knit. "And I'm on the pill, too."

"Good to know," he said with a hint of a grin, then glanced to a large wall clock. "Time to check the lasagna."

Laura cleared their salad plates as Braden opened the oven to send the scent of Italian spices wafting through the air. "Mmm, think it's ready," he said, and she wasn't sure she'd ever seen a sexier or more endearing sight than Braden in his black boxer briefs, wearing two big oven mitts as he extracted the tray. Maybe it was about sex and food—two primal needs being met by the same handsome source.

As he started cutting the lasagna, Laura asked, "So how old are you, flyboy?"

"Thirty-five," he said with a quick glance.

And they said men reached their sexual peak at eighteen? She wasn't buying it. She also found herself liking that he was older than her—his age somehow fit the sophisticated man-of-the-world image she held of him.

"You, snowflake?"

"Twenty-nine."

He grinned, scooping squares of lasagna onto two plates. "Big three-o coming up."

"You look like you survived it okay." Boy, did he ever.

"But I hear that particular milestone is a lot harder on women."

"For most maybe," she said, "but I'm kind of looking forward to it.

To me, thirty is like . . . real adulthood. A last leap into true maturity. All grown up."

His lids lowered, darkening his eyes. "Oh, you're all grown up already, honey—trust me on that." And then he smoothly reached out, beneath her kimono, to swipe his middle finger through the moisture between her legs. She sighed at the flash of pleasure and wasn't sorry she'd agreed to wear only the skimpy robe. In the end, it seemed, everything he asked her to do brought her far more pleasure than regret.

"So tell me about being a corporate raider," she said a moment later as they sat down to dinner and Braden poured them both a second glass of wine. "Are all your takeovers *hostile?*" She raised her eyebrows, half teasing but truly curious.

Braden smiled at her playfulness. "Most are friendly, actually," he admitted, much as he might have enjoyed making himself out to be some bad-ass rocking the corporate world. "I look for companies in trouble, find investors to go in with me, and arrange a buyout. Then I restructure the company—sometimes selling off parts of it, other times just reorganizing it to be more cost-effective. When a company is seriously in trouble, I can be doing them a big favor and they usually know it. Hence the lack of hostility," he said with a grin.

"So you own all these companies, huh?" she asked, clearly impressed.

"Well, I own *pieces* of a lot of companies. Sometimes I sell the pieces off after I've made a good profit, and I use the money to orchestrate the next takeover."

She tilted her head. "How does a guy get into this line of work, anyway? Did you tell your mother you wanted to be a corporate raider when you grew up?"

He chuckled. He loved her intelligent sense of humor and couldn't remember the last time he'd found that particular element in a woman he was dating. "Actually, I started as a stockbroker fresh out of college. I was into deep analyzing companies and discovered I was good at it. Made a bundle for my clients—and for myself, too. Enough that I was able to start dabbling with small buyouts and, soon, enough that I didn't need the broker's commissions anymore."

"You must be very good at what you do to make that much money at it."

"The best," he said, eyes on hers. He'd never seen any point in being modest.

"And you're a pilot, too?"

"That's just a hobby. I keep a little Cessna at the airport in Long Beach. Best feeling in the world, flying. Second only to sex."

"I'll stick with the sex," she said, casting a flirtatious grin.

Under the table, he grazed his palm up her thigh. "I'll help you with that."

She let out a soft giggle. "You're too kind."

"And you're too hot . . . for me to resist." He found himself smiling, too, now, stretching farther, wanting to feel that perfectly smooth cunt again—but he couldn't quite reach.

"You're such a silver-tongued devil," she teased.

"Hey, gotta keep up with my lover the writer." He finally withdrew his touch, deciding he'd definitely be getting more of her later, and dug into his lasagna. "Speaking of which, the book still going well?"

She gave another nod. "Shockingly so."

"Why is it shocking?"

"Well, I was completely without a story when I got here. Now it's zipping along. And I'm not even sure where it's headed—which is not the norm for me—but I'm just trusting the story to keep finding its way, and so far, it's working like a charm. The last few days have been the kind writers dream of—where the words just flow without thought. Totally amazing."

He listened to her pretty sigh, and said, "Maybe it's like flying."

She tilted her head, gave him a slow smile. "Yeah. Maybe it is."

The pleasurable silence hung between them—perhaps a beat too long. At least too long for his comfort. He liked her, a lot, but he'd never been into relationships, so even thinking about how pretty her eyes were or how in sync their thoughts felt at this moment seemed like a bad idea. Time for a new topic. "You don't seem much like Monica."

She didn't look surprised. "Opposites attract, I guess, even in friendship sometimes. Now, you, on the other hand, seem *exactly* like Monica."

He raised his eyebrows. "Oh?"

"Confident. Take charge. Sex-crazy."

He blinked. "Monica is sex-crazy?"

And she flinched. "Oh, I guess maybe you didn't know that about her."

He gave a shrug. "We're cousins, not best friends. I see her once or twice a year, generally around the holidays. I never realized she had a wild side."

Laura looked sheepish. "Well, now you know. Just don't tell her I accidentally let that out. But she's the whole reason I had that sexy bra and panties I wore for you over the webcam. She wanted me to come here and get laid. I just don't think she meant by you."

He laughed softly. "Will you tell her?"

"Would you mind?"

He gave his head a short shake. "I'm a big boy. I'm sure my family knows I have sex with women."

She bit her lip, looking all too bashful. "I won't be giving her the details, though. I don't think I could."

He leaned closer, peering into her eyes, and reached back under the table to gently squeeze her knee. "All right then, honey—it'll all be our secret."

Normally, he probably would have told Tommy once it ended. Maybe another buddy or two at home with whom conquests were sometimes shared on the golf course. Not to degrade her in any way, but because she'd be out of his life, someone they'd never know, a nameless, faceless woman who would never matter again. Yet he understood how big this was for Laura—he understood, from every reaction she'd had, and every single persuasion, that she'd been giving him an unspoken trust that she'd never given anyone before. So he could be quiet about it for her afterward, even if the guys *would* never meet her and it *wouldn't* really matter. He could keep the details of their mountainside affair secret.

"Thank you," she said, her voice still, soft.

And without quite planning it, he found himself tenderly caressing the inside of her knee, just rubbing his fingers in small circles. She bit her lip, looking incredibly innocent yet ready as she sat there in that sexy, see-through robe that showed off every private part of her so well.

He smiled into her eyes as an idea came to mind. "Want to see some stars, snowflake?"

"See it?" he asked, having just relinquished the telescope to her. He'd shown her Orion and was now helping her locate Canis Major, explaining the latter was supposed to be Orion's hunting dog.

"I think so."

"That bright star at the dog's neck is Sirius—it's the brightest visible from Earth besides the sun."

"Oh, I see it now," she said, her lithe body flinching in delight at finding it. "I see the dog shape." She took her eye from the telescope to glance up at him from her partially bent position. "Although those astronomers had a vivid imagination to think that was a dog."

"This from the writer," he said cynically, teasing her. "Okay, now let's try another one. I'd show you Lepus, the rabbit that Orion and his dog are hunting, but if you can't buy the dog shape, seeing the rabbit is hopeless for you. So let's look for Gemini, the twins."

Taking back control of the telescope, he moved it until he found the large constellation he sought. Then, stepping back so Laura could look, he explained how to find it among the stars he'd focused on. "The twins are like stick figures," he concluded, rubbing his hand lightly over her ass through the filmy fabric that covered it, "tilted heavily to the left. Although mythologically, they weren't really twins—just half brothers."

Slowly, she looked up at him, her eyes filled with question. "How do you know about this stuff?"

"Another hobby," he said. "I wanted to be an astronaut when I was little, but I guess this and my pilot's license are as close as I ever got. Now get back to looking for the twins."

As she turned around, he wondered why he felt a little sheepish about what he'd just told her. He supposed he didn't go around telling women things from his childhood—or how much he happened to know about the stars, either. Laura was so genuine, so sweet, that she made it easy to let out sides of himself that didn't always make it to the surface.

"See 'em?" he asked, placing his hands gingerly at her hips.

"No."

He sighed. "Then you're not looking in the right place." He leaned in behind her, arms closing comfortably around her waist, and said, "Let me look." When she did, he adjusted the telescope slightly, centering Gemini more. "Now, try again. They're right in the middle of the lens."

A moment later she said, "Does one of them have knee joints and the other one doesn't?"

He'd never thought about it like that before, but he laughed lightly and said, "Yeah, the guy on the left has knees."

"Got 'em," she said triumphantly.

"Good girl," he said, following the urge to slide one hand up to caress her breast.

"Mmm," she purred in response, still looking at the constellation. "I didn't realize astronomy could be so much fun."

"It's about to get even *more* fun," he promised hotly in her ear, aware that his cock was growing hard against her lovely ass now. He'd been half hard through dinner, slowly growing more aroused by the mere sight of her and, admittedly, by the sweet, trusting control she let him have *over* her. Her breast was full and weighty in his hand through the fabric, and he massaged lightly, catching the taut nipple between thumb and forefinger. She whimpered gently, rubbing her sweet bottom against his increasing erection and eliciting a soft moan from him as the sexy moves stiffened him more.

"Are you still looking at the stars?" he asked, dropping his other hand from her slender waist to stroke into her denuded pussy.

"Oh . . ." she sighed, then said, "Yes, I'm still looking." But her voice had gone beautifully breathy.

"You're so wet for me already, honey," he rasped, raking his fingers through the welcoming moisture—deep, deeper.

"Although," she said, her words coming between weak breaths now, "I don't think . . . the twins . . . are both guys. I think one of them . . . is a girl."

He relished her sweet dewiness as his fingers made longer, stronger strokes through her slit. "Yeah?" His breath came hard, too. "Which one is she?"

"The one with the knees. I think she has knees . . . so she can do this." With those words, she turned in his grasp and knelt before him, eagerly extracting his raging erection from his underwear to go down on him.

"Jesus God," he breathed as she took him deep into the recesses of her pretty, wet mouth. "Oh God, yeah."

His sweet Laura moved her lips up and down his shaft while he watched every glorious second of her enthusiastic affections. He'd noted she was particularly good at this in the shower, but this was a very pleasant reminder, far sooner than he'd expected.

"Oh yeah, baby, suck it," he prodded her, as turned on by the sight of her head moving over him as he was by the sensations her mouth so skillfully delivered.

He slid his hands to her face, ran the tips of his fingers down around her lips where they encased him. "Look at me," he said, lifting her face toward him.

She raised her gaze, and when their eyes locked it was all he could do not to come. He'd told her to look at him, but he suddenly couldn't return the favor, letting his head drop back with a deep groan. "Oh God, baby, good," he managed through clenched teeth.

He'd gotten blow jobs from countless women in his thirty-five years, some of them damn good ones. But something about this one, from this girl, in this place, this isolated moment in time, was different, better, exciting him more, hurtling him closer to orgasm quicker than he could ever remember.

So much that he forced himself to gently push her away, until his drenched cock sprung back against his stomach. "Much more of that sweet mouth and I'll explode in it."

"I wouldn't mind," she said, still kneeling before him, peering up, that black kimono casting only a pale shadow over her perfect body.

"Have you ever?" he asked, curious. "Swallowed?"

She shook her head. "But I would. For you. If you wanted me to."

His whole body went weak. From another woman, the sentiment wouldn't have mattered so much, but from Laura, spoken so solemnly, so surely, the gesture overwhelmed him.

He took her hands and helped her to her feet. He lifted his palms to her face and kissed her, brisk but deep, and even *that* left him feeling light-headed. He leaned his forehead over to meet hers, fingers still lingering on her cheeks. "You are so sweet, baby. But when I come . . . I need you to feel me. Inside you. In your hot, beautiful pussy. I need you to feel every last thrust deep inside." He concluded with another kiss, slanted across her mouth, tongue dipping inside to find hers, drinking in the simple pleasure of having her arms twine about his neck. One kiss became two, then more, each getting him hotter, his cock now aching for her tight cunt.

Ending the kisses, he prodded her past the telescope, toward the window, until her back pressed against it. Yanking at the sash of the little robe, he jerked the fabric apart and let his gaze fall on her every curve. "Fucking beautiful," he whispered.

"Take me," she breathed, drawing his eyes back to her face. "Take me hard, Braden. Fuck me."

Nothing excited him more than hearing her talk dirty, and the more he got to know her, the more he understood how out of character it was, and that it was for him alone. "Say it again. Tell me."

"Fuck me hard and deep. Make me scream."

Damn, he even got off on watching her mouth form the words, just seeing them come from sweet little Laura, who had been bold enough to masturbate in the dark and start this wild affair that he never really wanted to end.

Curling his hands possessively over her ass, he picked her up and nailed her to the window with his cock—hard, just like she wanted. She cried out, then leaned her head back against the glass in a huge sigh. "So unbelievably big in me," she whispered, their faces mere inches apart.

"Oh God," he said, her words continuing to excite him, now propelling him to drive into her in long, hard strokes designed to make her feel every inch of him in her moist passageway. When his balls bounced against her, he felt her bareness there and it escalated his passion.

Her legs locked around his back, scissoring to pull him into her, help him thrust, and her breasts brushed against his chest as she met each drive. When she began to set a slower, hotter rhythm, he had no choice but to follow. She was gorgeous when nearing orgasm, and he knew that's what this slower tempo meant. She was taking him in, riding his cock, letting her clit rub against him with every hot little gyration she made.

He wanted to suck her pretty pink nipples, but holding her as he was, he couldn't get the right angle. So he kissed her mouth instead, more of those sweeping, lingering kisses that were almost as good as the sex itself, then she leaned back her head and he sprinkled more kisses across her long, slender neck.

When she lowered her gaze to him, she said on heavy, heated breaths, "You know someone really *could* be watching us right now."

She was right—it would be easy. Two people fucking in the middle of an enormous, lit-up window. Only a few other houses could be seen in the distance from his—the view was mostly pristine mountain and sky—but he knew he wasn't the only mountain-dweller with a telescope. "Does that excite you?" he asked.

She hesitated only briefly. "Yes." Another heated breath as she continued to move on him. "It shouldn't . . . but it does."

"Baby, good sex isn't about should or shouldn't." He still moved with her, his cock still buried deep, easing her toward climax. "It's about what is. What excites you. Don't think. Just feel."

"*You* excite me," she breathed. "More than any man ever has."

The words shouldn't have surprised him, all things considered, but they still sent a hot shock of pleasure through his veins. "God, I want to make you come, honey," he told her. "So, so much."

She thrust against him, still working her pussy in those hot little circles. "Soon," she murmured. "So soon."

"Imagine someone is watching us," he said.

Her voice came soft, light. "Who?"

"No face, no name. Just someone. Feel their eyes on us. Feel them watching, just like I watched you touch yourself, just like I watched you fuck yourself with the vibrator."

"Oh . . ." she moaned, arching against him, again, again.

"Do you feel it? Do you feel their eyes? Do you want them to see you come?"

She nodded, breath still ragged, eyes glazed with passion. "But mostly . . . I want *you*. You to see me. You to watch me." Her undulations were changing, becoming more pronounced—her breath grew still more audible.

"Well, I'm watching, baby. I'm watching you fuck me slow and sweet. I'm looking at your beautiful body, the way it moves against me. Come for me, honey. Come for me. Come for me."

She drew in her breath, deep, seeming to hold it—and then the climax broke over her with a high sob as she pushed her cunt harder against him, thrusting, thrusting, crying out, and in that moment, Braden thought she was the most extraordinary woman he'd ever known.

She clung to him when it ended and he hugged her tighter, closer. Then whispered. "I love watching you get off."

She lifted a small, sensual tongue kiss to his mouth. "Just like when we first met, your eyes alone are enough to make me come."

"Was it good?"

Her gaze lit up. "Beyond magnificent."

He spoke lower. "Want more?"

She nodded eagerly, so Braden finally lowered her to the floor but quickly shifted her to face the window. Now it was he who imagined the eyes out there somewhere watching them, getting to see her beautiful body full frontal—her perfect round tits and smooth pussy. He imagined the voyeur's colossal jealousy—because they could look, but he got to *have*. All of her.

He pressed her palms flat to the cool window, same as he had in the shower.

He slid his damp cock through the crack of her ass, teasing her beneath the robe still draping her shoulders and back, loving the way she arched toward him, offering herself.

It was an offer he couldn't resist, so he plunged back inside her without delay. "Oh!" she cried, and he loved even *that* now, the mere power to make her cry out, make her feel so much.

He bent to breathe in her ear. "Do you love my big cock in your tight little pussy, honey?"

She moaned as he drove deeper. "Oh yes, baby. Yes!"

Dragging his hands over her plump breasts, he settled them on her hips and proceeded to fuck her in earnest, hard and fast, pleased to hear her moan at every thrust.

Moving in her, he let his gaze travel out the window, not thinking of the eyes anymore, but of the stars, of the sensation of the two of them almost being outside. He wanted to fuck her *there*. He wanted them to be part of nature together, just enjoying each other beneath the sun or the moon or the falling snow.

Next his hand dipped to that sweet, nude mound. He thought he could spend hours just touching it, stroking his fingers over the bare skin, and of course, the pink folds resting between. Her cries increased as he let his middle finger linger over her swollen clit. Swollen even after she'd just come for him. He was going to make her come again.

He stroked her slit with each drive of his cock, moving his fingertips in rhythmic circles over that hot little nub protruding so prominently. "You're so open for me," he breathed over her.

"I love . . . when you touch me." Her voice was but an echo of its usual self.

"You're going to come for me again, lover," he promised her. "Your sweet pussy is going to feel like it's exploding in my hand."

She responded with only a thready moan, but he kept caressing her as he moved inside her, plunging deep, making her take every inch, listening to her cries of pleasure as his tempo increased. "Gonna come hard," he said through clenched teeth, not even sure if he was talking about her or himself now.

"Oooh yes, oooh yes," she cooed, swiveling against both his cock and his hand.

"Come, baby. Come." And then, to help her along, he lifted his free hand from her hip and brushed his thumb across the tiny fissure of her ass.

"Oh!" she burst out, hands still braced on the glass.

He stroked her there again, gently, making her jolt.

"Come for me *now*," he said, his voice more commanding as he raked his thumb deeper over her anal opening—and then she erupted with deep, jagged cries, her whole body trembling with the force of the climax.

"Oh! Oh baby, oh baby! Oh . . ." Her hot moans trailed off only when her body ceased quaking, and Braden needed to hold her, so he closed his arms about her from behind, leaned in close, and kissed her shoulder.

But then his own tension began to build, from watching her come— twice—from having his cock buried in her hot warmth for so long, from the imagined eyes out the window, from the stars overhead, from everything he'd shared with her.

He pumped into her furiously, his body taking over. He knew nothing but the force of wanting to pummel her hard, drive into her as deeply as possible. She still arched toward him, that sweet offering, and he took it, never slowing his strokes, never easing up, thinking only of how much he wanted to make her feel him, feel his cock, feel his desire. Her cries increased his excitement, as did the sight of her body before him through the naughty transparent black and the reflection of her breasts in the window.

"I'm gonna come, honey!" he yelled.

"Oh yes," she purred, and the very sound of her voice pushed him over that steep edge into the abyss of pure, pulsating pleasure. It swallowed him, and nothing existed but the heaven she delivered—and he closed his eyes, seeing a whole new sky of twinkling stars.

He slowly started to collapse afterward, so he slid his arms back around her to ease her to the floor with him. And as he turned her to look into her eyes, he knew a second's worth of fear—because sex like that, he figured, could be just the thing to make Laura revert, feel that awful regret she'd suffered back in the beginning. Yet to his relief, her eyes were filled with nothing but joy. "Still with me?" he asked.

Her grin said she knew exactly what he meant. "All the way, flyboy."

He smiled in return, too exhausted to do or say more.

"And just so you know," she said, her voice soft as the night, "that was the most exhilarating sex I've ever had."

Me, too.

But besides being too tired to get the words out, that was simply something she didn't need to know. It would be giving too much away—from a man who seldom gave anything other than his body and a little charm when it came to women. "I'm glad, snowflake."

"And I came twice again." She sounded girlish and delighted.

"Get used to it."

"What were you doing at the end there, right before I came the second time? Whatever it was . . ." she trailed off, voice as breathy as during sex. "It was fabulous."

"I was rubbing my thumb on your ass."

It took her a moment to make sense of that, at which point she raised her eyebrows. "You mean on my, um . . ."

He cast a tired grin. "It's called an anus, honey."

"Really? You were rubbing me *there*?" She sounded sincerely shocked.

He gave a short nod, not surprised to learn she'd never experimented with that particular area. "We'll file that with spankings," he told her, "under 'things to examine later.'"

Chapter Ten

R iley Wainscott's story continued to fly with ease, just as Laura had told Braden last night. Riley's romance was zipping along quite speedily, too. As Laura herself had just learned, having sex early in a relationship really seemed to *up* the zip factor.

Not that she was having a *relationship* with Braden. She wasn't—she knew that. No matter how intense their sex had been last night, no matter how close to him she'd felt. A *new* closeness. But that still made this nothing more than an affair. And heck, if all affairs were like this, she was beginning to understand why people had them, even if they went nowhere.

Of course, she wasn't sure Riley was really having a relationship, either. She and Sloane Bennett mainly talked about the case, the clues, what it all might mean—and then they had sex. Usually in the secret garden. They never planned it—it just happened. Something about that garden was intoxicating to them, turning them both passionate and uninhibited—kind of like Braden Stone had turned Laura last night. She couldn't believe some of the things she'd said. That the idea of strangers watching them turned her on? Yikes. And yet, in that moment, it had been the truth.

She lifted her gaze from the white computer screen to the white blanket of snow beyond the window and remembered being pressed against that very glass last night, yipping and yowling her head off. Then she caught her breath, her pussy tingling beneath her jogging pants.

Get back to work, she told herself. Riley and Sloane had just had spectacular orgasms beneath one of the pear trees in the garden—and not only that, but Sloane had, while still lying prone atop Riley, spotted something shiny in a rosebush a few yards away, and they'd discovered it to be Mr. Dorchester's gold cuff links!

As Riley pulled her top back into place, she said, "I didn't know Mr. D.'s cuff links were even among the missing items."

Sloane lifted his gaze from the links to her face, looking rumpled and sexy from their romp in the grass. "Neither did I."

"Does this mean we're now finding stolen items even your aunt and uncle don't yet *know* about?"

Five minutes later, after straightening their clothes and exchanging a few last kisses, Riley and Sloane walked hand in hand back up the path, through the spacious backyard and into the Dorchesters' house. Riley would have enjoyed more cuddling time with Sloane, but the truth was, she didn't know where this was leading. Sloane was only in town temporarily, until the mystery was solved, so perhaps it was wise not to get too attached. For Riley, sex had always been part of a healthy relationship, so this was something new . . . and potentially frightening. She could only hope the affair wouldn't leave her too emotionally scarred.

"Aunt Winifred," Sloane addressed his aunt when they found her in the front parlor, "we need to talk to you for a minute."

"Well, sit down, you two, and let's chat. Any new clues?"

"Yes," Sloane replied, opening his palm to reveal the gold links. "These. We found them in . . ." He glanced over at Riley.

They'd not yet told anyone about discovering the garden, although they'd never discussed why. Riley couldn't help thinking it had started to seem like their own special place, though neither had used such words to describe it. Finally, Sloane went on. "We found them in a garden, back on the grounds beyond the vegetable patch. Someplace I'd never seen before. A beautiful little garden with a wall of high shrubbery around it."

Mrs. Dorchester's face flushed noticeably. "Oh my. Well then, I guess now you know our little secret."

Riley leaned forward slightly. "Little secret?"

Mrs. D. shifted her glance back and forth between them, then spoke confidingly. "Many years ago, when Mr. Dorchester and I were young, we . . . well, we wished to have a private place, all our own. Oh, I know what you're thinking—we have this lovely house and the rest of the estate, yet . . ." She stopped, sighed. "Sloane, you may be surprised to hear this, but your uncle Howard was one romantic devil when we were first wed. And what with the servants and other visitors running hither and thither around this house, well . . . he wanted us to have our own private sanctuary, someplace we could be alone without . . . well, without fear of interruptions, if you know what I mean. That garden was our private love nest for many years, and I'll tell you another secret, too. Had God ever blessed us with children, that's probably where the blessing would have taken place."

Both Sloane and Riley flinched. Sometimes when Mrs. D. got on a roll, she forgot to shut up, and this seemed to be one of those times.

"We had many a romantic interlude there, and I remember one particular time," she went on, starting to say more—until Sloane held up his hand.

"Aunt Winnie, stop. Too much information."

The older woman covered her mouth with her hand and

giggled. "Oh me, I suppose I did get a bit carried away with myself, didn't I?"

Neither answered, and Sloane said, "Do you, uh, still go back there with Uncle Howard?" Riley could feel the wheels turning in Sloane's head—he didn't want to find out they'd all been rolling around in the same grass, and neither did she.

"Oh no, not for a long while now," she said, and Riley mentally wiped her brow.

"But you still keep the garden the same as it was?" Sloane asked.

Mrs. D. cast a merry little smile. "It's a sentimental place for us," she explained. "Well worth the time it takes Hawthorne to keep it groomed and tidy."

Riley and Sloane immediately exchanged glances. Mr. Hawthorne had been the gardener for many years, and finding out he knew about the garden meant that, finally, they had a suspect.

"Does anyone else know of the garden?" Riley asked.

Mrs. D. tilted her head first one way, then the other, thinking. "No, I don't believe so. It's not so much that it's a secret we try to keep, you understand, but we've simply never mentioned it to anyone. On the occasions we stroll to the garden, well . . . knowing it's ours alone makes the visit somehow a little sweeter."

Riley could certainly understand that, given her own recent experiences in the garden.

"Of course, now you two know about it," Mrs. D. said, but then she smiled. "Not that I mind. I've always been fond of you both, and who knows, perhaps our little love nest will hold the same magical romance for the two of you, as well."

Riley practically leapt to the end of the couch, away from Sloane. They'd let no one in on their affair and hadn't planned to, having decided there was no need to get their relatives involved in something that was just between them. "Why on earth would you think *that*?" Riley asked, trying not to sound flustered.

Mrs. D. looked uncharacteristically dour, again switching her gaze back and forth between them. "I guess you two think the rest of us around here are blind, but it's been clear you have the hots for each other since the moment you walked in that door, Riley Wainscott." Mrs. Dorchester pointed toward the foyer, and Riley shrunk back into the sofa.

So they knew. About her and Sloane.

Yet for some reason Riley couldn't quite explain, even to herself, she still wasn't ready to admit the truth, even if the cat *was* out of the bag. Because Sloane's stay here was so very *temporary*. As was their relationship. She had to remember that, and to protect her heart.

Before Sloane could do anything stupid like confess, she spoke up. "I'm afraid you're mistaken, Mrs. Dorchester. Sloane and I have a purely professional relationship and intend to keep it that way."

Sloane propped his elbow on the arm of the sofa, perched his chin comfortably on top, and flashed an utterly dry look in her direction. "That's too bad."

She swallowed nervously. "Why's that?"

"Because you don't know what you're missing."

At the end of the last scene, Laura stopped to freshen her coffee, then returned to the computer. Outside, the first snow to fall since her arrival began to waft down in soft, pretty flakes. She thought of Braden's silly pet name for her—snowflake—and smiled.

That's when she heard his footsteps on the stairs. He'd slept in this morning, but she'd refused to let herself stay in bed with him. She'd been burning to write—and thinking that snuggling too much with her lover could only lead to her doom, just like Riley with Sloane.

"Hey, snowflake, what's shakin'?"

She turned to find his hair mussed, and the lower half of his body clad in flannel pants dotted with miniature beer mugs, which she thought cute. His bare chest, however, far *surpassed* cute.

"My book's shakin'," she said, getting to her feet. "Sleepyhead."

He cast a lazy grin. "You wore me out last night."

She met him halfway across the room in a comfy embrace. "Try having four orgasms in one night, buddy," she teased.

He tilted his head, peering wistfully off into the distance. "I did that once. Many years ago, back when I was a young stud."

"What are you now?"

"A more mature stud," he said with one arched brow, "who's only good for a mere two or three." He concluded with a wink.

Her breasts practically swelled as she remembered their shower, and their sex in the window. "Mmm, last night's two were heavenly." She lifted a small kiss to his sumptuous mouth.

"I was thinking," he said slowly, "that we could make today fun, too—in a different way."

"Oh?"

"Why don't you let me steal you away from your work for an afternoon on the slopes."

Laura pulled in her breath, weighing the invitation. Part of her was thrilled, and dying to accept. She hadn't skied in ages and knew she'd enjoy spending a snowy day with Braden, even if he had to give her a refresher course on the finer points of the sport.

"Fresh powder coming down," he said, motioning toward the window in an attempt to sway her.

And she was just about to say yes—when she stopped herself. "I can't, Braden."

He looked sincerely disappointed. "Really?"

"I've backed myself into a corner with this book," she explained. Which was the truth. "I have a looming deadline, and if I stay on my current pace, I *might* be able to keep paying my rent. But if I stop writing now, even for a day, there's a chance I'll lose my rhythm—I'll get too far away from the story and won't be able to get back into it with the same speed." She pressed her palms to his sexy, muscular chest. "I would *love* to ski with you, but I really can't. Forgive me?"

She couldn't quite read his eyes when he stayed silent for a minute, but he finally said, "Make it up to me later?"

"Any way you want." She dropped her hands to his ass and squeezed.

Of course, she'd left out all the *other* practical reasons she was turning him down. Besides having a book to write and bills to pay, she also had a heart to protect. This was all about sex, her and him, and if she let it become about anything more, she feared she'd start getting too attached to him. Hell, maybe she already was—she doubted she could share such intense intimacy and not feel a sense of loss when it ended.

But she could at least try to keep from making it worse. She'd gotten her wish of getting to know him a little last night, and it was just enough to worry her, to make her feel that pang of warmth in her heart that went beyond the connection of their bodies. Just seeing his smile now affected her a bit deeper. And Lord, how she'd let go of her inhibitions last night in a way she never had before! All because of him, because he'd willed it, wanted it.

So turning down a day of fun in the snow with him was torturous— but wise.

"Guess I'll have to fall back on Tommy again. I'll let you get back to work, and I'll be out of your hair soon, snowflake." He said it all very dramatically, as if he were greatly put upon, and she tossed him a playful smirk just before he disappeared back up the stairs.

Twenty minutes later, as Riley was making up lies to Sloane about why she'd denied their involvement even when his aunt had figured it out, Braden came trotting back down, looking rugged and hot in blue jeans and a gray cable-knit sweater with the sleeves pushed up. "I'm gonna hang at Tom's for awhile, then head down the mountain to pick up a few more groceries. Any special requests?"

"Just a kiss good-bye." She wanted to smack herself as soon as the words left her—it sounded romantic, like something a girlfriend would say.

She relaxed, though, when he strode easily to the desk and bent to give her a soft, sweet kiss that curled her toes.

"So, your friend," she said, "what does he do that he can just ski or hang out whenever he feels like it?"

"He designs computer games. Sets his own schedule. Which reminds me," he added with a tilt of his handsome head, "would you mind if I invited Tommy to dinner tonight?"

Laura hoped the surprise didn't show on her face. She couldn't help suffering some disappointment that he'd want dinner with a friend to interrupt their hot and heavy sex, since—as last night had proven—even dinner could be foreplay. But she said, "Sure, that's fine."

"Tommy didn't seem quite himself yesterday. Apparently he had an ugly breakup last fall and hasn't really recovered. I figure maybe he could use the company, a change in routine or something."

"Oh." Guilt for her selfishness instantly reamed her. "Well, yes, definitely invite him." She supposed, now that it was sinking in a little, she was also touched that Braden would allow her into his personal life this way, since having his friend over to dinner with them made her feel almost relevant in his life, not like someone he was keeping under wraps. "What does Tommy know about me?" the musing prompted her to ask.

"Just the basics. That you're a writer here on retreat. That I saw you through the webcam and thought you were hot so came up to meet you."

She sucked in her breath. "Whoa, he knows you watched me?"

"Relax, snowflake. He has no idea what I watched you *doing*. I promised you that was just between us, remember? He thinks I just saw you walking around the house or working at the computer. Clothes *on*." He winked. "And he thinks I then rudely shoved my way into your retreat with no regard for your privacy."

She smiled with relief, then uttered her next thought. "Though I guess he knows we're sleeping together now."

Braden shrugged with his usual confidence. "Wouldn't make sense for me to still be here barging in on your retreat if we weren't. But it's no big deal."

Ah, the statement reminded her—these were playboy types who had lots of girlfriends, lots of wild affairs. It eased her mind about meeting Tommy, under the circumstances, but also forced her to remember she was one of many. So it was a darn good thing she wasn't getting attached to Braden, and a good reason to keep making sure she didn't.

As she watched her lover walk out the door, it occurred to her she'd been in this house not quite a week yet. But in that time, she'd written half a book and had the most outrageous, scintillating affair that she ever—or *never*—could have imagined.

"So what's the deal with this girl at your house?" Tommy asked as they sat watching the snow fall out the window and sharing a couple of beers.

Braden was surprised Tommy hadn't asked more about Laura yesterday, but skiing had kept interrupting talking. He wasn't quite sure how to answer, given the promise he'd made Laura about keeping the specifics just between them. "Let's just say," he began, "that I'm . . . expanding her sexual horizons."

Tommy's curiosity was clearly piqued. "Details?"

Ah, just what Braden couldn't provide. Maybe he'd said too much already—so he'd at least try to keep it simple. "Don't get me wrong, I think she liked sex before, but"—he grinned—"she likes it better *now*. She's . . . losing her inhibitions."

Tommy laughed. "Under your expert tutelage, right?"

"Something like that." And Braden knew he should shut up if he really wanted to keep his promise, but thinking about those inhibitions that had been dropping away from her, falling as smooth and effortless as the snow outside, he felt compelled to add, "I like watching it happen, watching her let herself go. I think I'm coaxing something out of her that no other guy has ever bothered to look for in her before."

Tommy's expression dripped with disbelief. "If you tell me she's like a butterfly bursting free of her cocoon, dude, I'll throw up."

Braden just laughed. He'd apparently gotten a little too insightful there. But if it changed the topic, that was probably a good idea. "You're just sour on women right now," he told his buddy. "You need to snap out of it."

"You're right. I do." Tommy took a swig from his longneck. "But something about the same old snow bunnies isn't working for me. It's not that I want another big relationship—I don't, not for a long time anyway—but I seem to attract such . . . total airheads."

Braden raised his eyebrows. "This is news to you?" Braden had skied with Tommy enough in the eight years since they'd become neighbors and friends—and gone with Tommy to enough bars, too—to know the girls who generally approached him. He was right—he drew rich little ski bunnies without a thought in their pretty heads beyond what was hot in skiwear this season and how much they wanted to get laid. It wasn't that a girl needed to be a rocket scientist, but even Braden could see where the chicks Tommy drew would get old fast.

"I guess I never cared about that before. But now, even if it's just a one-nighter, I'd like a woman I could at least have a decent conversation with before we fuck—know what I mean?"

"You need to make a change of some kind, dude," Braden advised him.

"Like what?"

Braden shrugged. "I don't know. Take a trip. Go to different bars—or slopes. Just do something to shake things up a little so you can get back on the horse and get on with your life. Which reminds me—you want to come down tonight, eat some pizza, meet Laura?"

Tommy drew back, clearly shocked. "You want me to meet this girl? This is *that* kind of thing?"

Braden blinked. "*What* kind of thing?"

"Dude," Tommy said, lowering his chin to flash a knowing expression, "we've been hanging out for a long time now, but you've never asked me to meet a girl."

True enough. Yet it wasn't like Tommy thought. "Look, it's pizza. And beer. She just happens to be there. I'd invite you down either way."

Tommy tilted his head. "She doesn't mind trading in a night of sex for a night of hanging out with your buddy up the hill? Hell, *you* don't mind that?"

Braden tipped his bottle to his mouth, then grinned. "I didn't say you were staying *long*."

By the time Braden returned home, Laura was glad to see him. But damn, that was a bad sign—it meant she was starting to miss him when he wasn't around.

She offered to help with the groceries, yet he declined, telling her to keep working. "But, uh, if you're close to a good stopping point for the day, get there."

She looked up. "Why's that?"

He sent her a suggestive smile from the kitchen. "Tommy's not coming 'til eight, so we've got a few hours. I'll take care of putting this stuff away, but then I'm running a bubble bath in the Jacuzzi."

On one hand, she really hated to stop working this early. She'd done so well resisting him this morning, and she'd had a great day writing, but she hadn't reached her daily goal yet. On the other hand, though, her breasts ached and her pussy rippled at the thought of getting in a bathtub with Braden. "Like bubble baths, do you?" she teased.

"When they come complete with sexy girls." He was unpacking canned goods from a brown paper bag.

"Oh, does yours have some of those in it already?"

He glanced up. "Only one. I call her snowflake. But I can round up some more if you're interested in that type of experimentation."

She let out a slightly startled laugh. "For your information, you don't have time for more than one—I'm going to keep you busy enough on my own."

Fifteen minutes later, Laura closed the file containing her novel and padded up the stairs and into the bedroom. But she wasn't prepared for the staggering sight that met her gaze.

Braden sat on the edge of the bubbling, sudsy Jacuzzi, naked and gorgeous, cock erect, a glass of wine in his hand. Another rested on the tile enclosure next to him, and he'd even lit a couple of candles to glow in the shadowy light of the afternoon. She nearly lost her breath.

The corners of his mouth quirked into a sexy grin. "Come keep me busy, baby."

Laura didn't waste time—she was ready to get wet with Braden again. She pushed down her jogging pants, then shimmied from her cami and panties, aware of his eyes glimmering on her.

Once naked, she stepped carefully into the tub, kneeling down into the bubbles as the warm, gurgling water began to massage her body beneath the surface. Braden moved to join her, putting down his wine, until she said, "Stay where you are."

He stilled in place and she positioned herself between his well-muscled legs, then ran one wet palm up the length of his massive cock. She followed the same path with her tongue and he hissed in his breath. After lowering a gentle kiss to the tip of his shaft, she smiled naughtily up at him. "Is this busy enough?"

He gave only a short nod, eyes dark on her. Then he whispered, "Suck me, honey."

He didn't have to ask twice, as Laura had quickly learned that taking Braden in her mouth was among her deepest pleasures. She lowered her lips over his hardness, as always amazed at the incredible way he filled her mouth. She loved the low moans echoing from his throat, loved his hand in her hair, raking through the tousled tresses since she'd forgotten to put it up in a clip, too anxious to join him.

"So good, baby," he breathed over her.

When she eased up, letting his cock slip from her lips to peer up at him as she licked her way around the darkly engorged head, he said, "Trade places with me."

As he lowered into the water, she stood, suds clinging to her skin when she sat up on the tile and spread her legs wide, no longer the slightest bit hesitant to offer herself.

"Take a drink of your wine and look out the window," he told her, then leaned in to lick a soft path across her clit.

She sighed at the heavenly sensation, then sipped the wine. She glanced out the large window above the tub, wondering what he wanted her to see since the snow had stopped.

"Look down at the house through the trees," he said, voice low.

Laura searched, finding the house nestled among the snow-covered pines, closer than she'd even realized another home was situated. And just as Braden dragged another long lick up her center—she spotted two people fucking in the window.

Just like *they* were, she realized, gasping at the sight.

Suddenly, she was a voyeur, too.

Chapter Eleven

"My neighbors, Stan and Candy," he said from between her legs. She studied the couple as they stood in profile right inside the wide, uncurtained window, Candy holding on to the back of a kitchen chair with both hands, naked, while Stan slammed into her from behind. Stan was classically handsome, light-haired, in his mid-forties. Candy looked closer to Laura's age—a stacked brunette with large breasts that bounced with each thrust.

Braden French-kissed Laura's clit as she watched what took place in the window, and the sensation spread through her with even more intensity than usual.

"Stan went to Vegas on business a few years back," Braden said, blowing on her clit and forcing a shiver. "He came home married to Candy, and she's been here ever since." He dragged another hot lick up her pussy, making her moan as she continued observing the two strangers having sex.

"Showgirl?" she managed, her voice thready.

"Stripper," Braden replied lowly. "Stan mentioned it over a beer with Tommy and me last summer."

Laura had grown breathless. Down through the trees, Candy's perfect body arched against her husband's, her face wrenched with hot desire. She wore thigh-high fishnet stockings with black ruffled edges. "Do they do it in the window often?"

"Yeah, actually." Braden's voice came even lower now and a glance down revealed him studying her parted cunt. She watched *him* instead of Stan and Candy as he pushed two fingers inside her and lowered another kiss to her clit.

"Mmm," she purred in response.

"Not sure if that's by accident," Braden went on, "or if maybe they want me to see. Of course, I'm not here all the time, but I guess they can tell when there's an SUV—or, in this case, two—in the driveway."

"And you watch them?" she asked, her heart beating harder and pulsing in her crotch where he now laved her. She looked back at the couple through the window as Stan's hands rose from Candy's hips to her plump breasts, squeezing, kneading.

Braden peered up at her, his look pointed when she drew her gaze back inside. "*You're* watching them."

"Oh God, you're right." She took a nervous sip of her wine.

"No, baby—you don't get it," Braden said, gently massaging her slick inner thighs with wet hands. "I *want* you to watch them—while I get you off."

Laura drew in her breath. Braden had such a way of making things she'd always considered extreme or even perverse seem completely normal.

"Watch them, Laura," he said again—because she was still looking at *him*. "Watch them."

"Maybe I want to watch *you*." She was learning what a powerful aphrodisiac one's eyes could be, and she couldn't deny she loved the sight of him working his mouth between her thighs.

"*Think* of me instead," he said. "And this time—just this time— watch *them*. For *me*."

She let out a sigh. *Watch them for me.*

For Braden, she would.

So as he thrust his fingers into her cunt and delivered rhythmic licks to the folds of flesh above, she peered back out the window, down through the trees, and became what she'd briefly thought of herself as moments earlier. A voyeur.

She watched as Stan withdrew from Candy, his penis shining with wetness even this far away. Candy turned and sat back on the dining room table, spreading her legs as wide for her husband as Laura spread for Braden now. Each of Braden's licks echoed through her strong enough to make her moan, and she began to thrust at him, lifting against his mouth.

When she glanced down at the arousing sight of Braden tonguing her pinkness, he stopped just long enough to say, "Watch them. In fact, tell me what they're doing since I can't see."

Laura drew in another deep breath, then tried to describe what she witnessed in the house next door. "She's sitting on the table now. She has on black stockings, and sexy, high heeled shoes. He's . . . he's leaning over her, kissing her breasts, and now . . . now he's sliding into her, all the way."

For the first real time, Laura began to worry briefly that the neighbors could easily look up and see *her* through the window, especially if they really had sex in that particular spot hoping Braden would watch. But when, below, Braden latched on to her swollen clit, somehow both licking and sucking at the same time, she quit worrying and just let herself go.

"He's . . . he's fucking her now," she went on, "and her legs are wrapped around his back, and her heels are digging into his skin. He's . . . doing it hard, really hard. She's lying back on the table, and she looks . . . like she's screaming. And now she's . . ." She swallowed, overcome with mounting pleasure from Braden's mouth combined with what she was watching—and saying. "She's touching herself, rubbing herself while he fucks her." Laura's own hands rose to her breasts without planning it, the nipples jutting into her palms. She continued pushing her own cunt at Braden's skilled mouth and knew she was rapidly approaching climax. "She's . . . still rubbing herself, rubbing really frantically now, and she's . . ." Oh God, there it was—orgasm, breaking over her hard. "Oh, oh God, baby. Oh, I'm coming! I'm coming!" She stopped watching Candy and Stan as her eyes fell shut, her head dropping back. The climax rushed through her rough and jagged, her pussy feeling as if it were the biggest part of her.

When finally she came back down to feel the tile beneath her again—along with Braden's final sweet kiss on her clit—she found him wearing the most wicked grin ever to grace his face. "Damn, honey, that was hot."

She bit her lip, her body still pulsing with the aftershocks. "*What* was hot?"

"Telling me what you saw, all while you touched your pretty breasts. You made me so damn hard."

She cast a playful grin. "You were already hard."

His eyes shone glassy with lust. "Trust me, baby, you made me harder." His hand closed back over her thigh. "Now come down here into the water with me so I can get my cock inside you where it belongs."

The promise made Laura moan with joy inside, but she held it in. Just in case it was the "where it belongs" part that was filling her with such gratification. She eased down into the warm, gurgling water and kissed him, no longer even fazed that she could taste her juices on his mouth. She wrapped her arms around his neck as he curled his hands over her breasts, freshly covered with suds, to rake his thumbs across her erect nipples. "So damn pretty, baby," he growled in her ear when the kisses ended. "Mmm, I need to fuck you."

She simply nodded her agreement.

And was surprised when he turned her on her knees to face the window—since the pane extended nearly to the tile enclosing the tub, which meant they could see Stan and Candy in this position. She'd nearly *forgotten* about Stan and Candy already, but now Candy had dropped to her knees, visible only from her breasts up as she sucked Stan's cock. Laura focused on them as Braden pushed slowly into her from behind, and she yelped with the deep pleasure of that initial intrusion.

"Ah, baby, so snug around me," he moaned.

She sighed. "You fill me up."

Braden moved in her—slow, deep, thorough strokes that seemed to reach to unbelievable lengths inside her. She felt every single inch of him and let out a soft moan at each drive, still watching Candy deliver a vigorous blow job through the trees.

When Braden reached in front of her, pressing here and there on the wall of the tub, she wasn't sure why, until he used his other hand to shift her body a bit. "Move over, just a little."

As she slid to the right a few inches, the Jacuzzi jet shot hard against her mound, and she let out a high whimper before looking over her shoulder in shock.

"Lean closer," he said, wearing a devilish smile.

"I've already come once—"

"I said lean closer," he interrupted, using his body to shove her forward, flush against the streaming jet.

"Oh!" The impact on her clit, and from his cock ramming into her, was powerful enough to make her grip the top rim of the tub with both hands.

He continued his slow, deep plunges into her pussy, each pressing her to the stimulating jet. His hands rose to caress her breasts—the massage slow and deep to match the rhythm of the sex.

"Unh . . ." The sound left her involuntarily. It all felt too good.

In the window below theirs, Candy released Stan's shaft from her mouth, then rose and turned to lay facedown across the table, bent at the waist. Stan massaged her ass for a minute, sawing his cock back and forth in the center. Laura saw Candy's mouth move. *Fuck me.*

When Stan entered her, both Laura and Braden released a low moan. Below the water, Laura's pussy felt utterly pummeled and she knew another orgasm was coming fast. Braden's breath echoed slow, labored, in her ear. She never took her eyes from Stan, now pounding into Candy with wild abandon. She could see Candy crying out in passion, eyes shut, fingers curled around the table's edge. Braden's strokes grew more intense, and Laura met them, her clit worked by the jet on the other side until she said, "Oh God, here I go again."

This time she erupted with a series of high-pitched cries, the waves of orgasm more brutal than usual, her body jerking. She'd not even come down yet when Braden said, "Ah, God—me, too," and shoved his cock into her hard, hard, hard, rocking her body so wildly that water splashed over the sides of the tub.

Below them, Laura could tell Stan had just come, too, as he lay resting across Candy's back, both of them still now and smiling.

She peered over her shoulder at her lover. "And they say it's hard to have an orgasm at the same time."

He let out a short laugh, his arms closing around her, and Laura thought she could get used to this. The Braden part, not necessarily the Stan and Candy part. But just as quickly, she reminded herself that she *wouldn't* be getting used to it, so she banished the thought from her mind as quickly as it entered.

"Aren't you going to tell me you came twice?" he asked, his voice holding just a hint of teasing.

"I guess I'm getting used to it."

"Damn straight," he said with a definite injection of masculine pride.

Multiple orgasms, she thought, sighing. One more thing she'd better not get too used to, because she'd probably never have them again once she left Braden behind.

They'd stayed in the bath awhile—Braden had offered to wash her hair, so she'd returned the favor. She'd almost regretted it, though, for she discovered there was something so personal, so intimate, about massaging shampoo through a guy's hair that when it was done, she felt worrisomely clingy to him. It had been about silence, and touching.

She'd never have dreamed the mere act of touching could make her feel so close to a man—but maybe it was the *man*, maybe it was the *way* he touched, maybe it was the way he encouraged *her* to touch. Her emotions were deepening by the moment, and she was suddenly glad Tommy was coming to dinner—a distraction from sex, a distraction from Braden's large, singular presence in her life at the moment.

She'd packed for comfort, so she donned the jeans and fitted baby blue sweater she'd traveled in, punctuating the simple outfit with a fun pair of socks: the same shade of blue, sprinkled with white snowflakes. She didn't bother putting on the only shoes she'd brought—lace-up hiking boots for trudging through the snow—and Braden noticed her socks as soon as she joined him downstairs.

Reaching out to where she'd pulled her feet up onto the couch, he grabbed on to her toes, wiggling them. "See why I call you snowflake, snowflake?"

It was only a few minutes later that they heard a truck rumble up the snowy driveway and both rose to greet Tommy. Braden told her Tommy had volunteered to drive down the mountain on pizza detail, and he showed up with two large, flat boxes and a dimpled smile.

Although it was his eyes that captured Laura as Braden introduced them. He'd looked cute enough in the fishing picture, but his gaze, in person, shone blue and dazzling, and she could only imagine how many girls he'd seduced with that particular asset. His blond hair was a little messy, befitting his ski-bum image, and his face tan for February, which Laura figured was a testament to exactly how often he hit the slopes. Like Braden, he was muscular but lean and clearly didn't shave every day, as a thick stubble covered his chin beneath a dark blond mustache. She couldn't help thinking of a young Robert Redford as the Sundance Kid in one of her mother's favorite old movies.

"Wait a minute," Tommy said as they all stood in the foyer, "you're Laura *Watkins*? As in *the* Laura Watkins? The mystery writer?"

Laura felt herself flush with delight. Despite her success, it was rare that anyone outside the writing community recognized her name. "Um, yes," she said, smiling.

"My mom *loves* you," he informed her, handing the pizzas off to

Braden. "She asks for your newest book every Christmas. Riley Wain-scott, right?"

Wow, he even knew her series. "Right," she said, duly flattered.

"Braden mentioned your first name and that you were a writer, but I had no idea. My mom will be thrilled when I tell her I met you."

They sat down at the table and doled out pizza, Braden supplementing it with beer he'd picked up on his trip to the grocery.

"Braden tells me you design computer games for a living," Laura said to Tommy. "He already explained to me how a guy becomes a corporate raider—so, tell me, how does a guy become a computer game designer?"

"I've always been the techie type," he began, surprising her. Up to this moment, Laura had generally equated techie type with geeky type, but Tommy was about as far from the latter as a man could get. "Around twelve years ago, when the Internet was really starting to take off, I formed a game company. I got lucky—the timing was right, and within a few years, we'd hit it big. I had the most popular online game site with millions of visitors every day playing free demos and then paying to download the games.

"After awhile, though, I got tired of the commute to Denver, even when I had put enough dependable people in place that I only made the trip a few times a week. Guess I just wanted to make a change—I'd been there, done that. So I sold the company at a nice profit, and I'm a freelancer now."

"I'm seeing a trend here," she said with a smile, glancing back and forth between Tommy and Braden. "You guys build companies, then sell them. What does that mean? That you get bored easily?"

Tommy swallowed a bite of pizza, then said, "It's probably more like we have trouble with commitment."

Both guys laughed, and Laura got a little more insight into the friendship, and the men themselves. It wasn't surprising to hear Braden was commitment-phobic, but still a little saddening. *Stop getting attached to him—now.* A few more days and she'd be heading home and all this would be just a memory, so she had to turn off her emotions surrounding him this very minute.

"So what kind of games do you design?"

"Anything you can think of. Puzzle games, word games, casino-type games, sports games, racing games—all over the board."

"Don't forget my favorites," Braden said, reaching for a slice of sausage and bacon pizza.

Laura switched her gaze to him. "What's that?"

He grinned. "Sex games."

"Sex games?" She raised her eyebrows, feeling a little thick since she didn't quite know what he was talking about. "What . . . kind of sex games?" She forced her gaze back to Tommy so she wouldn't seem embarrassed to discuss it with him.

He shrugged. "I wasn't going to mention those, but since old Braden here did . . . they're basically just games to entertain horny guys. If you reach certain levels, your reward might be pictures of naked girls or maybe a girl who strips off a piece of clothing each time you reach a certain score."

"But some games," Braden said, clearly forgetting his pizza for the moment, "are really more *about* sex. There's one where the player has certain tools he uses to try to give an animated girl an orgasm. There's another that's more like an action game, sort of like the old Super Mario, but the setting is a party district and the goal is to seduce as many girls as you can. You get points for grabbing condoms out of the air, and beer mugs give you an extra life. You have to avoid big bouncers and boyfriends with baseball bats, and when you finally get to a girl, there are some good graphics." He chuckled. "It's actually my favorite game Tommy's ever come up with."

Laura thought it actually sounded fun, and because of that, she forgot to be embarrassed. "I'm intrigued. What's it called?"

"Babe Quest," Tommy replied.

"Sounds pretty entertaining," she said, proud of herself. The old Laura would probably have turned up her nose or rolled her eyes or turned bright red by now, just over a game—but she wasn't doing any of those things.

As they continued eating and drinking, Laura mentioned the picture of the two guys on the bookshelf, with the fish. They told her they took a fishing or hiking trip at least once a summer. "More if Braden can get his ass up here," Tommy added. "But in winter, we're just total ski bums. Which is good, because I can be *that* with or without him."

Somewhere along the way, an invisible layer of sensuality had begun to settle over the room. Laura wasn't sure if it had started with talk of Tommy's sex games or if maybe she just liked sharing dinner with two rugged, sexy men—but she couldn't help being aware of it. For all she knew, it had started with the beer—as usual since arriving on the mountain, a little alcohol had her feeling loopier than it would have at home. As the three of them talked and her gaze moved back and forth from Braden to Tommy, she drank in their good looks and well-muscled physiques, she soaked up their easy masculine laughter, and she realized she liked the odd sense of being isolated with two hot guys. Stan and Candy might be only a stone's throw away, but the setting made it easy to forget that as quickly as she'd learned it, giving her the sexy impression of being all alone in the middle of nowhere with Braden, and now also with his friend.

Before she knew it, the two guys were debating who worked out more. Apparently Braden went to a health club four times a week, but Tommy thought mountain life in general—skiing, chopping wood for the fire, dealing with general upkeep on his house—added up to just as much exercise. Which had Braden lifting up his sweater to reveal the six-pack on his torso. And, mmm, after not seeing him naked for even just a couple of hours, that torso looked very fine.

"Afraid you got nothin' on *me*, dude," Tommy protested, raising up his long-sleeved cotton pullover to reveal similarly hard abs, which Laura couldn't help admiring, as well.

"How about you, Laura?" Tommy asked. "Work out? Want to get into the ab contest?"

"Oh, I do crunches in front of the television, and I try to take walks when the weather's nice—but I'm not a hardcore exercise chick, I'm afraid."

"Crunches count," Braden said. "And if all it takes to get that body are some crunches and walking, just keep doing what you're doing, honey."

"Well, I don't have anything chiseled-looking like you guys do—no six-pack or anything."

Braden tilted his head skeptically. "Come on, you've got a *great* tummy."

She shook her head, not to be self-deprecating, but because she really thought it was just average. "Well, I'm glad you like it, but it's hardly a *workout* tummy."

Tommy gave her a chiding look. "Why don't you let me be the judge?"

Bold from the beer, Laura obliged without hesitation, raising the hem of her sweater up over her stomach. Tommy leaned forward across the table to look, lifting his hand to gently pat her belly. "Ah, now, you sold yourself short. I see at least the hint of a four-pack there."

She raised her eyebrows, laughing, even as her pussy tingled lightly— the result of his touch. "A four-pack?"

"Sure," he answered easily. "Next best thing to six. Trust me—it's very sexy." He added a wink. "Most women would give their right arms for a pretty stomach like that."

She couldn't help feeling flattered—and utterly feminine.

"She has great tits, too," Braden said.

She gasped, letting her eyes go wide on him as heat filled her cheeks. *"Braden!"*

But her lover only grinned. "Sorry, honey—that just came out. Tommy here happens to be a connoisseur of fine breasts, so I figured he'd be interested."

"Is that so?" Laura shifted her gaze to her other dinner companion, drunk enough to have forgotten her embarrassment that quickly.

Tommy flashed a mischievous smile. "I just have a habit of . . . noticing that about women. More than other guys, I've been told. But hell, what can I say—I like boobs." His grin was so endearing that Laura didn't feel the least bit uncomfortable with the conversation, and she couldn't help thinking both Tommy and Braden were getting a little drunk themselves—each having downed several beers over the pizza.

"Let me guess," Laura said. "The bigger the better."

Tommy spread his hands and shrugged, admitting it. "But," he added, "I'm getting tired of fake ones that are *too* big. If a girl wants a little enhancement, cool—but they go overboard sometimes." He didn't bother with subtlety as he dropped his gaze to Laura's chest. "I can tell yours are real—and pretty damn perfect, too. Am I right?"

Braden answered before she could concoct a reply. "Damn straight, they're perfect."

She cast him a sexy smile, her breasts feeling heavy, achy now, and her cunt rippling with sensation. Not only did she like being with them both—she liked being the center of their attention, and liked knowing they both found her body attractive. With Braden, it was nothing new, but Tommy's added presence seemed to somehow amplify her sensuality.

After dinner, they moved to the living room, all settling on the sofa as the adjacent chair was piled with towels Braden had run through the washing machine earlier but hadn't yet folded. She couldn't help recalling it was the same sofa where she'd touched herself for Braden.

He sat at one end and Laura leaned her head back against his chest. His arms came around her in a cozy, easy embrace, and his thumb hooked into the top of her jeans, his fingers caressing just below, overtop the denim. A couple of inches lower and his caress would have been a fondle. Tommy sat opposite them, and she was tempted to remind Braden they had company—yet she didn't, for reasons she couldn't explain to herself.

"Laura got to see Stan and Candy going at it earlier," Braden tossed out.

She supposed it should have embarrassed her, but *nothing* seemed to at this point.

"Ah. What did you think of their little show?" Tommy asked on a deep laugh.

Intoxication made her unflinchingly honest. "He's pretty hot for an older guy. And she had great breasts."

"Definitely fake," Tommy pointed out, one finger in the air, "but as fake ones go, yeah, they're pretty nice."

Laura let her gaze widen on him. "You've seen them, too?" Was there anyone who *hadn't* seen Stan and Candy having sex?

Tommy nodded, chuckling as he shifted sideways to pull one knee up beside him on the couch, and Laura became aware that her sock-covered foot, stretched out along the cushions, now touched his jean-clad thigh. Normally, she would have pulled her foot back, but neither of them made the effort to move. His leg felt thick and warm. "I keep an eye on Braden's place in between his visits," he explained. "Came down one day last winter to spend a few hours just running water through the pipes, turning on the gas fireplace for a while, that sort of thing, and sure enough—as soon as my truck shows up, I glance out the window and see Stan and Candy bouncing around in the window."

The tips of Braden's large fingers skimmed back and forth across the front of Laura's jeans, his sexy touches now officially setting her pussy on fire. She'd never been in a situation like this—having one man excite her while she looked into the eyes of another.

But look she did, since Tommy kept talking. "So how long are you staying here with Braden?"

"Just a few more days." She didn't like thinking about that, her "retreat" coming to an end—and so far, she'd chosen *not* to think about it. For the moment, she remained very much in the present, with Braden's fingers stroking just above her mound as her foot touched Tommy's muscular thigh and she looked into his very blue eyes.

Silence pervaded then—Tommy said no more, and neither did she. She wasn't sure if she could have kept conversing anyway—her throat began to feel clogged, as if that layer of sensuality she'd noticed earlier was pressing down now, almost smothering her. Her breasts felt tight within the cups of her bra—her pussy swollen against the denim that covered it.

"Well," Tommy said, his voice lower than usual and sounding a bit thick, "I think it's time for me to go."

Laura didn't answer, and neither did Braden. She wanted to get naked with Braden—fast—but also didn't really want Tommy to leave just yet since she was enjoying his company. And enjoying having her foot against his thigh. Outrageous a realization as it was, she couldn't deny it. A long, quiet moment passed, that sensuality almost tangible, weighting the air. Until finally, Braden said, "Uh, yeah, I guess so."

Laura let out the breath she hadn't realized she was holding.

As they all got to their feet, Tommy thanked them for the invitation, and Braden said, "You bought the pizza, man—*I* should be thanking *you*," and Laura tried to examine what had just happened. Why had they all hesitated when Tommy announced his departure? Were Braden and Tommy feeling what she felt—some confusing sensual chemistry between them all that defied definition? Or was it only her, half-intoxicated and completely misreading it, seeing something that wasn't there, except maybe in her own mind?

As they moved to the door and Tommy put on a brown leather jacket, he shook Braden's hand, then lifted one palm to Laura's cheek, leaning in to kiss the other. Like every sensation that had struck her in the last hour or so, she felt the kiss down below, her vaginal muscles flexing as he pulled away.

"Good night," he said, then exited out into the dark.

Both she and Braden turned to look at each other. "Great guy, huh?" he asked, but his eyes were glassy with the same emotions currently buffeting her.

She nodded. "Yeah. Very . . . pleasant. Easy to be around." *And he has nice thighs.* "I was afraid you were going to rub my pussy right in front of him." She raised her gaze to his, gauging his reaction.

"I was tempted," he replied. "You felt too good, baby."

She slid her arms up around his neck, leaning in to press her body to his. "Well, now we're alone so you can indulge yourself."

They lay in Braden's big bed, the snow cover outside combining with the moonlight to cast a glow over the room. His head rested between her legs and hers between his, and for the first time in her life she understood the true thrill of the sixty-nine position. As Braden rhythmically laved her most sensitive flesh, she sucked his cock deeply, at times releasing it to let it fall between her breasts.

His moans as she cradled his length between the two mounds of flesh reminded her that he'd mentioned wanting to slide between them in one of those early instant message exchanges that seemed so long ago now. This position made it easy, almost natural, and the feel of his hard shaft between her soft breasts filled her with more pleasure than she could have imagined. But then *everything* was different with Braden—every kiss, every look, every sexual encounter was more intense and, in turn, more satisfying than anything she'd known up to now.

As she lifted his wet shaft from between her breasts to wrap her lips back around the head, he delivered a sudden and incredible pressure to her cunt. Oh God, what *was* that? She cried out—then realized he'd pushed their old friend the vibrator inside her when she'd least expected it.

Her body's natural response was to meet the slow, firm thrusts he now delivered, although she let his cock fall from her mouth to breathe, "Where did that come from?" She didn't even know the last time she'd seen it. Not that she was complaining. It made for a very welcome intrusion. His moist tongue on her clit and the toy inside her at the same time brought on a whole new sumptuous pleasure.

"Found it under the bed," he rasped.

"Oh God," she sighed, meeting another thrust, taking the sex toy deeper.

"Feel good, honey?"

"Mmm" was all she could say.

And all she even *wanted* to say—because she had better things to do with her mouth. She suddenly wanted it back around his penis—badly—and didn't hesitate to wrap her fist around his length and pull his powerful erection back between her eager lips.

She sucked him vigorously, even more than before, as he drove the vibrator into her below. Oh God, the waves of delight that shook her, consumed her—not orgasm, but a marvelous feeling of such fullness that she couldn't have conceived of it before experiencing it. His shaft in her mouth and another in her pussy. Being filled in both openings somehow delivered more than just twice the pleasure—just like having the attention of two men earlier.

Of course, this was more intense. This was hot, raw, swallowing sex. She let it do that—swallow her. She quit thinking and only responded. His mouth worked just above the toy—she couldn't see but thought he was sucking her clit. She sobbed her pleasure around the erection between her lips, stunned and amazed and as deep into pleasure as she'd ever been.

She'd always enjoyed going down on Braden—way more than with other men—but now even *that* was different. She wanted him to fuck her mouth, actively fill it as he filled her below. She knew a desire for hardness, for maleness, that she'd never known before this moment, an almost blinding lust to be overtaken in every way, to have her whole body filled with him.

She pulled him to her mouth, silently urging him to thrust. *Yes, yes.* He drove in firm, short lunges. And below, the marvelous vibrator fucked her and his sweet tongue laved her. Frantic cries erupted from her throat, around his length. Her whole body felt pleasantly pummeled with hard male shafts, and she moved against both, maddened by the glorious sensations stretching through her.

The orgasm struck with little warning, forcing her to release his cock as she screamed her joy. "Oh God, baby, oh God!" The pulses of heat racked her from head to toe, over and over, almost violent in their intensity, to leave her thoroughly spent when it was done.

Opening her eyes to see his majestic erection still only a few inches away, glistening from her ministrations, she gently kissed the tip, a tiny thank you for such overwhelming pleasure.

Below, he slowly extracted the vibrator, then shifted in bed to come face to face with her in the shadowy room. His eyes gleamed wickedly. "Was that as good as it sounded?"

She drew in her breath. "Completely mind-blowing."

Once upon a time she would have said, *This isn't me, this isn't me.* But she'd long since stopped that. Because, now, it *was* her.

Chapter Twelve

"Wake up, snowflake. It's a beautiful day and you need to get outside."

Laura opened bleary eyes, surprised to see her lover standing over her, fully dressed in jeans, a flannel shirt open over a dark green T-shirt, and sturdy outdoor boots. He looked as rugged and handsome as ever, one lock of dark hair dipping recklessly over his forehead, his chin dusted with stubble.

"You know I need to write," she said. Just like yesterday, spending the day with him would be delicious, but she had to protect herself. This was now officially more about her heart than the book—she was just growing way too close to him the last couple of days.

"Don't worry. I'm not trying to drag you away from your work—but it occurred to me that you literally haven't set foot outside this house since you got here, and it's a sunny day, so we're having breakfast on the deck."

She blinked her surprise. "Um, isn't the deck covered with snow?"

"Not since I just shoveled it. Now come on, get up. I've got eggs ready to fry and English muffins ready to toast. Just pull on a pair of sweats, shoes, and your coat while I cook, and I'll meet you at the back door in ten minutes."

As Braden turned and walked away, Laura simply stared after him, blinking yet again. Oddly, it felt almost as if he were . . . wooing her or something. Or, at the very least, caring about her a little, concerned to see her get outdoors. She hadn't thought about that—how confined she'd been here. As she'd recognized before, she rather enjoyed the strange sense of isolation, given that it came with a sexy, commanding lover. And she couldn't help but think it would be freezing outside. But if Braden had cleared the deck and was making her breakfast, she wasn't inclined to refuse.

After locating panties and a pair of black jogging pants, she tossed on last night's sweater, then found a thick pair of socks and laced her boots up over them. It was only as she walked into the kitchen, saying, "Hey," that it occurred to her what an awful outfit it made.

He didn't seem to notice, merely turning from the stove with a smile on his face and a spatula in his hand. "Grab me a couple of plates from the cabinet, snowflake?" Then he expertly flipped an egg in the skillet.

"Sure," she murmured, falling a little more in love with him. He was her perfect lover, she thought, standing there staring at his flannel-clad back. He pushed and persuaded her past her normal boundaries to bring her unfathomable pleasure—and yet, at the same time, he was so easy to be with, like right now. Her perfect man. And she was leaving him in a few short days.

"Plates?" he asked.

"Oh. Yeah. Sorry." She scurried to get them, then watched as he plopped flawless eggs onto each just as four muffin halves popped from the toaster.

She rushed to grab her winter jacket from the foyer closet and a moment later, they were sitting down at a wooden picnic table built into the deck. Although the sun had already dried away most of the wetness left by the now, she noticed Braden had brought out thick towels for them to sit on.

"This is nice," she said, smiling over at him as she forked up a bite of her eggs. To her surprise, the sun was so bright that it made the cold manageable, more brisk and refreshing than bitter. The view of snow-covered mountains as far as the eye could see was gorgeous, maybe even more than usual because she could feel the mountain air and see just how far the expanse of blue stretched overhead.

It was as if he read her mind. "Nothing like a clear Colorado morning."

"How did you come to buy a house here anyway?"

"I used to take ski trips to the area with friends back in college. Over time, I fell in love with the place—and with the stark contrast from L.A.—so when I had enough money for a second home, Vail seemed a natural choice."

"I'm . . . glad you made that choice," she ventured, a bit timidly. "If you hadn't, I would never have met you, never have had this time with you."

"Good point," he said, chin perched in his fist, elbow balanced on the table. "I'm glad I made that choice, too, snowflake."

For some reason, it was a sobering moment for Laura. Because as sweet as he was being, she knew it meant more to her than to him. He didn't say it—nor did his voice or his eyes—it was just something she knew inherently. He was a man of the world, a man who took lovers, had affairs. It *had* to mean more to her than to him, was undoubtedly more of an unprecedented event in her life—something *life altering*, in fact, she had to admit.

Not so for him.

Just take it for what it is. Soak it up. Enjoy the sex. Enjoy him.

And try not to worry that this span of time with him will be the defining period of your entire life. Try not to worry that it will never be this good, this utterly grand, again.

"You were right," she said, ready to return to a normal, easy topic. "It's good to get out in the sun for a little while."

He nodded, a sexy yet superior look gracing his face. "The *smart* little snowflake would take a *bigger* break, let me take her skiing. Or we could drive over to Breckenridge. Cute little ski town with lots of cafes and shops you'd probably like."

Tempting, oh so tempting. But . . . "No, the smart little snowflake has a book to finish. So as nice as this breakfast is, I have to go back inside and get to work soon."

He let out a groan of frustration. "You know, honey, I'm about as much of a workaholic as there is, but even *I* know it's wise to take a break and refuel every now and then."

She gave her head a knowing tilt. "And I'm willing to bet that if you had some big deal on the table right now that was time-sensitive, you'd be working at it night and day until it was done instead of wanting to play in the snow."

He lowered his chin, narrowed his gaze on her, and let out a sigh. "Point taken." Then, popping the last bite of a buttery English muffin into his mouth, he wiped his hands on a napkin and pushed to his feet. "Before you go, though . . ."

"What?"

"Stand up."

She flashed a speculative look in his direction, thinking his expression had just shifted to a darker and oh-so-familiar one, even beneath the bright morning sun. "Why?"

Without answering, he rounded the table and took her hand, leading her across the large deck until she faced that same striking view of Vail and beyond. He stood behind her, hands pushing up under her coat to close warm on her hips. He leaned into her from behind, and even through the jacket, she could feel his hard-on. "Thought I'd give you a little morning treat before you go inside," he breathed near her ear.

She looked over her shoulder into seductive brown eyes, offering her sexiest grin. "One problem—*that's* not little."

He returned the smile. "Your fault."

"I guess you should make me pay then."

He leaned closer, pulling back her messy hair to lower a kiss to her neck. "I intend to."

As Braden's hands gently began to push down her pants, just over her ass, the brisk air hit her and her pussy trembled with a mixture of sensations. She reflected on the fact that she stood on a snowy mountainside, her private parts exposed. She thought of Stan and Candy, and of Tommy, and of all those eyes she'd envisioned upon them in the dark the other night. She drew in her breath as Braden's warm middle finger stroked into her, pleasure echoing through her from the touch.

"You realize," she breathed, voice gone thready this quickly, "that someone somewhere could be watching us right now." She could see neither Tommy's house up above or Stan and Candy's below from this angle, but the sudden "appearance" of Stan's house through the trees yesterday had proven Braden's place wasn't truly as isolated as it felt.

His voice warmed her ear. "Unlikely—but possible."

"Is that why we're doing this?" she asked. "Because someone could see us?" Behind her, she was aware of him unzipping his jeans just before she felt his hard cock press warm into the center of her ass, flesh to flesh, his arms closing around her. She shivered—not from the cold, but the heat.

"You liked the idea that someone could see us the other night," he reminded her.

"I think I was drunk," she admitted quietly.

He laughed softly. "That had nothing to do with it." Lowering his grasp back to her hip, he slowly slid his whole length into her, making her gasp at the sudden fullness. "Because you like the idea right now, too."

And as he began to move in her, and as she began to meet his slow, firm strokes, her hands clamping to the railing for support as she arched her ass toward him, she couldn't deny it. The knowledge that somewhere, hidden within the trees, someone could be watching them, watching her take his cock, watching the passion etch itself across both their faces, added to her excitement. The brisk winter air all around them, the realization that they were outside, doing it on the slope of a snowy mountain like two animals—just part of nature—exhilarated her.

He said nothing more as he thrust deep into her—only their hot moans filled the silence—and she knew they both understood that his last words had been true. She liked the notion of being watched. He'd taught her to. He felt it *with* her. And it enhanced every hard drive of his length into her softness until finally he said, "God, baby, I'm gonna come," then filled her in a whole different way.

A moment later, still inside her with his arms wrapped warm around her waist, he said something she'd never imagined Braden Stone would say. "I fucked up."

She turned her head to look at him. "What?"

Uncharacteristic guilt shrouded his face. "I didn't give you an orgasm."

She blinked, then smiled. "Believe it or not, I'm not in it just for the orgasm."

He looked at her as if she'd just announced she was from Mars.

"Seriously," she said. "Don't get me wrong, I love 'em—but I don't have to have them every time. It feels good enough just to have your perfect cock in me, just to have you fuck me so thoroughly."

Withdrawing, he turned her in his arms, his eyes lighting with what looked like awe. "Have I mentioned that you're incredible?" He kissed her forehead, and she feared she might crumble beneath the weight of the emotion that filled her.

Stop. Don't feel this. Don't let yourself. Only madness that way lies.

But instead of answering him, of coming up with some flip remark that would ease the tension in her heart, she simply responded by kissing him, another of those soul-searing kisses that they'd shared from the beginning, those kisses that were almost as good as sex itself.

"Mmm," he sighed when it ended, their foreheads pressed together. "How do you do that?"

"Do what?"

"Make me crazy with just a kiss. All the stuff we've done, and still your kisses make me feel like I'm sixteen."

It was like a starburst inside her to know he felt it, too—all that magic, all that power, just from a kiss. She lifted her mouth back to his, wishing she could tell him everything she felt, how much she'd loved his kisses from the very first moment he'd climbed into bed with her, how changed and new he made her feel. But she stopped herself—again—and just teased him. "Guess I'm just that good."

He chuckled softly. "That you are, snowflake."

Then he began looking around them, at the mantle of white across the backyard and the hillside below.

Laura peeked over her shoulder, in case there was something she was missing, but saw only the glitter of the sun on the pristine, untouched snow.

"Since we're out here," he said, "why *don't* we play in the snow for a little while?"

She laughed, thinking he was getting relentless about keeping her from her work. "Define play."

He tilted his head, looking deadly serious. "I build a killer snowman."

Laura smiled. She hadn't made a snowman since she was a young girl. As simple as it sounded, the idea appealed immensely. Only . . . "We don't have on snow pants."

Braden did a dramatic eye roll, leaning his head back. "You're right—it would be a tragedy of epic proportions if we actually built a snowman without snow pants."

She grinned at his sarcasm, conceding. "We *will* get wet, though. And cold."

"I own towels, snowflake. And blankets. And a fireplace. I promise it'll all be okay," he added with an indulgent wink.

By the time they were done, they were both soaked and cold, but to show for their efforts, they had a perfect three-tiered snowman complete with scarf, wool cap, and carrot nose, all nabbed from inside, and eyes of dark gray stones dug from beneath the snow in the landscaping by the front porch. The only consolation Braden had made to her worries over their attire was ski gloves, which he'd retrieved from the closet by the front door, and he'd also grabbed one of his ski caps for Laura.

Upon coming inside, they both stripped down, dried off, and climbed into cozy dry sweats. Braden made mugs of hot chocolate, which they drank by the fire, discussing the attributes of good snowman-building. He'd had more fun with her out in the snow than he could easily understand.

Now, he'd finally gone upstairs to let her work, deciding he could stand to do a little of that himself. At the very least, he needed to check his e-mail. He couldn't remember a time since the advent of the Internet that he'd gone this long without checking it. God only knew what fires might need to be put out by now.

But after hooking up the laptop to the Internet connection in the master bedroom, he was pleasantly surprised to see nothing too urgent had arisen. So he took his time answering messages, then closed the computer and retreated to the upholstered window seat where the sun still blasted in full force. Propping up the overstuffed throw pillows at one end, he reclined and thought he might let the sun lull him into a nap. Spying the snowman he and Laura had built brought a small smile to his face as he let his eyes fall shut.

He was still horny, though. Damn, no matter how much sex he had with this woman, she *still* kept him in a constant state of arousal.

His mind drifted to what she'd said out on the deck about how it was enough just to be fucked by him. Understanding the woman who lay at Laura's core still made such talk more exciting than it would be from any other girl. Like everything with her, he never quite got used to it—it excited him as much each time as if it were brand-new.

Before long, he found himself pondering Tommy's visit last night, which had turned out much differently than he'd imagined. He'd issued the invitation in all innocence—he enjoyed the guy's company, valued his friendship, so it had seemed natural to have him down for a meal, even if he did have a lover on the premises. What Braden hadn't expected was the sense that something heavier was developing throughout the evening. There'd definitely been very sexual vibes in the air, and it wasn't just from talking about Tommy's sex games. Braden knew he'd proliferated it—he'd been just intoxicated enough to go with the flow. So he hadn't held back on saying Laura had great tits, and he hadn't hesitated to bring up Stan and Candy, nor to let his touch drift dangerously near to Laura's crotch while Tommy watched.

The odd truth was—he'd felt a certain unfamiliar pull, found himself imagining Laura being with *both* of them, him and Tommy. He'd found himself envisioning her letting go that much more—opening herself up that much deeper. And he found himself *wanting* it. Wanting to see her that way, with another man, with *two* men.

He also couldn't help remembering how much she'd obviously liked having two cocks last night in bed—even if one had been only a toy. She'd wanted it, too—wanted him and Tommy, together. He doubted she *knew* she'd wanted it—but she had.

The sun finally made him sleepy enough that he began to drift off. But as drowsiness meshed with his arousal, a question edged his mind. Would she do that for him if he asked her to? Would she let herself indulge her true desires in a ménage à trois?

She'd done everything else he'd wanted—*everything*. So very perfectly, so very passionately. This would be a big step further, for all of them. He'd never shared a woman with another guy before, either, let alone a good friend. But damn, he wanted her to know that ultimate pleasure, and he wanted *himself* to know the satisfaction of giving it to her, of knowing she did it because he asked it of her.

Riley and Sloane continued to turn up still more items concealed on the grounds—some were hidden in the backyard and outbuildings, but most appeared in the secret garden. Of course, Riley and Sloane were still getting intimate every chance they got—so much that Riley knew she was too caught up in her passion and not concentrating on solving the mystery as much as she should. An entirely new occurrence for her—since her head was *always* in the case. Except for now. Sloane Bennett and the best sex of her life were dimming her focus.

When Aunt Mimsey invited Riley and Sloane to tea on her back porch, Riley knew it was trouble. And she was proven correct before even lifting her aunt's dainty flowered teacup to her lips.

"Winifred tells me you two are denying your feelings for each other," Aunt Mimsey said with a giddy, knowing grin that made Riley want to sink into the porch's wooden planks. It was bad enough that Aunt Mimsey and the Dorchesters had figured out something was going on between them, but a hundred times worse if they thought there were *feelings* involved. Because if Riley even *hinted* at having feelings for Sloane, she'd be humiliated. What she and Sloane shared was—at least in Sloane's mind, she knew—strictly about getting horizontal. Or, well, in some cases perpendicular, and once even vertical against one of the pear trees—but she harbored no illusions that Sloane Bennett cared for her in any lasting way.

So she swiftly changed the subject. "Winifred has a wild imagination. No one here has any *feelings* for anyone else—Sloane and I are simply trying to solve this case. Which reminds me, we've come up with lots of new clues. Mostly in the garden—a *secret* garden," she added, letting her eyes go wide. She suspected any sort of secret would catch Aunt Mimsey's fancy and detract attention from her and Sloane.

"Oh yes, the secret garden," Aunt Mimsey said, as if it were a boring piece of yesterday's news.

Riley blinked. "You know about the garden?"

Aunt Mimsey took a sip of her tea, looking a bit wistful. "Well, I never mentioned it to anyone, but your uncle Walter and I used to make out there when we were first married."

Sheesh, the secret garden was a regular lovers' lane! Although it was hard to imagine Aunt Mimsey and Uncle Walter making out. Riley suspected she looked horrified.

Aunt Mimsey went on. "I never knew why the garden existed—I assumed Winifred just wanted a pretty place to stroll—but when Walter and I went there . . . well, let's just say I spent a lot more time on my back than my feet." Then she winked.

And Riley grew even more aghast. Ugh. "You're not saying you and Uncle Walter . . . did the deed there?"

Aunt Mimsey narrowed her brow, her expression a bit befuddled. "Why, dear, I'm not sure what *deed* you're talking about, but we had sex there many, many times, right on the grass under the pear trees."

Riley and Sloane exchanged looks of rank disgust. "How . . . romantic," Riley said dryly.

"Oh yes, it was," Aunt Mimsey fluttered on, and before Riley could stop her, she regaled them with the tale of a particularly steamy August afternoon when she'd nearly swooned from the heat in the garden, but Walter had caught her—and made her "forget all about the weather," she concluded with a girlish titter.

Between Aunt Mimsey's continued stories of sex in the garden and further accusations of a relationship between Riley and Sloane, the next half hour was excruciating. When finally the teapot was drained and Riley managed to make their excuses, she and Sloane practically sprinted toward the arbor gate that would provide their escape from the yard.

"From now on," Sloane said once they were free, "when we go to the garden, we're taking a blanket."

"Maybe two," Riley concurred.

Although—even dismayed to find that apparently everyone they knew had indulged their sexual appetites in the garden before them—Riley never once thought about not returning there with Sloane. In fact, all this talk about it had her thinking she could use a little release right this very minute. "Want to go *now?*" she asked, tilting her head hopefully.

He didn't even blink. "Wait here. I'll find the blankets."

And it was only when Sloane left her standing in the lush green grass behind the Dorchesters' house that her mind cleared enough to realize a potentially frightening truth: if Aunt Mimsey knew about the garden, that meant, technically, she was a suspect, too!

Braden padded down the stairs, listening to the sound of Laura's fingers dancing across the keyboard. He couldn't believe anyone could type that fast and felt bad knowing he was about to interrupt her when her work was clearly flowing well.

Selfish son of a bitch, he thought. *You can't even wait a couple of hours, until the sun sets, to talk to her?*

But no, he couldn't. And as for being selfish . . .

All along, from the moment he'd seen Laura through the webcam, every move he'd made had been for *both* of them. Bringing *her* pleasure brought *him* pleasure. And this was no different. The only selfish part was the interruption, but he had a feeling she'd forget all about that very soon.

"Hey snowflake, take a break for a few minutes?"

The typing ceased as she looked over her shoulder. She wore another one of those skimpy tops he liked so much and had shoved her hair behind her ears. "You're really pushing your luck today," she told him, but teasing filled her voice. She rose to her feet as he plopped on the couch, patting the spot beside him.

As soon as she sat down, he eased his arms around her delectable curves and lowered a kiss high on her chest. From there, he lifted his mouth to hers—and damn, no matter how hot things got, he still got off on just kissing her.

"Well," she said, a bit breathless, "this is the kind of break I like."

He grinned but grew more serious as he lay her back on the sofa, still in a loose embrace, stretching his body out alongside hers. "You know what I've been thinking about all day?"

She shook her head.

"Last night," he informed her, his voice going deep at the memory— and the knowledge of where he was taking this.

"What *about* last night? Pizza with Tommy?"

He lowered his chin, gazing down on her as he ran one palm over her tummy, up under her top. "Yes and no."

She peered up expectantly, clearly waiting for him to go on.

"I was also thinking about how much you loved being filled with two cocks last night in bed."

A pretty—and predictable—pink blush stained her cheeks. She'd mostly gotten over her shyness about discussing their sex, but he'd known such a statement would bring it back out. "Don't go all nervous on me, honey. We both know it excited you—a lot."

She swallowed visibly. "You could tell?"

She thought she'd hidden it somehow? He couldn't hold in his smile. "Yeah, I could tell, and it got me really hot." He'd seen Laura in a high state of arousal many times now, but something about last night had been different. Perhaps a deeper surrender? Something he'd felt more than seen? He wasn't sure how, but he'd known it instantly.

"Well . . . okay. Yeah, it felt . . ." She swallowed again, a testament to her nervousness on the topic.

"Tell me."

"It felt like . . . I was being consumed, taken, from all directions. Just . . . an incredible fullness I can't put into words. Almost overwhelming. I . . . couldn't control my response."

He grinned, liking her answer, especially the last part. Then proceeded with what he'd come down here to say, lifting one hand to her cheek. "I want to give you the real thing now."

"Huh?" she asked, peering up at him, beautifully wide-eyed.

He let his voice drop an octave to tell her, "I want to give you two cocks, baby. Two men—at the same time. I want you to be with me and Tommy. Tonight."

Chapter Thirteen

Laura let out the breath she'd been holding. *"Braden."* She couldn't fathom what he'd just suggested. "Are you . . . are you serious?"

His hand skimmed up her side until the tip of his thumb brushed over her nipple, through her top. The pleasure bit through her as he replied, "I'm *very* serious."

She sucked in another deep breath, her mind whirling. She couldn't deny that she'd suffered hints of the same inconceivable desire when Tommy had been there last night. Yet . . . she couldn't possibly do something so very hedonistic. "God, Braden, I . . . don't know."

"Because the idea doesn't appeal to you? Or just because it sounds forbidden?"

An image flashed in her head—her, between the two men, their hands roaming her body, their straining cocks rubbing against her. Her pussy spasmed at the very thought, and she quietly admitted, "The second."

His eyes darkened at her answer, making her pool with wetness between her legs. Resting his forearm between her breasts, he tilted her chin upward. "It's all in your head, honey."

Her voice came breathy. "What?"

"The idea of it being forbidden. It's just something society taught you, but it's not real, it doesn't mean anything. And if you want it, you should have it. I *want* you to have it."

"Why?"

He slid his knee between her thighs, pressing warm against her cunt through the jogging pants. His large bulge pressed hot and hard at her side, giving her the urge to turn toward it, to take *that* between her legs. "I want to give you the ultimate pleasure, something most women just fantasize about but will never have."

"Oh." Her voice came too light, barely there. As always, she wondered how he managed to make such things sound almost normal. And was she truly considering this—two men, at once? She had to catch her breath as the thought—and the images in her head—struck her anew. Stung with harsh temptation, she swallowed nervously. "And you want to do this . . . tonight?"

"Yes." Spoken plain and simple and quietly commanding—classic Braden. He clearly knew it worked on her, made it easier for her to acquiesce and give in to her baser desires.

She bit her lip, peering up at him, still agonizingly aware of the stiff erection at her hip. "I know this shouldn't matter, because in a few days I'll probably never see you again, but . . . wouldn't you think of me differently afterward? Because when this is over, I want you to . . . remember me fondly."

His eyes softened, peering down on her. "There's no other way I *could* remember you, snowflake. Sweet. Sexy. Exciting. Brave. Nothing bad. I promise." He ended with a deep, tender kiss, his tongue twining with hers and making her pussy cream further.

She found herself lifting her hands lightly to his face, her fingers grazing the dark stubble there. Her breath came short. "What if . . . what if we were to . . . to start this . . . and I suddenly realize I just can't do it?"

Only a few inches separated their faces. "Then you take my hand, look into my eyes, and tell me you just can't do it. And we'll stop."

"Really?"

"Of course." He sounded a little surprised. "Laura, you may think I've made you do things you never would have otherwise. But I've never really *made* you do anything. And I never would—not if you truly didn't want to."

She nodded softly, instantly. It was true. She might like to think he almost forced her at times into the wild things they shared, but he never really had. He just knew exactly how to persuade her. And she feared he was frighteningly close to persuading her again right now.

"You trust me, don't you?" he whispered, his dark eyes connecting deeply with hers.

She nodded automatically.

"Then you'll do this for me."

She almost nodded again, but this time caught herself. "I'm . . . I'm still not completely sure. Part of me wants to, madly, *shockingly*, but . . . part of me just . . ."

"Just what?"

She drew in another long, deep breath. "Part of me worries how I'll feel afterward. Part of me isn't sure I can be that wild, even for you, Braden."

Now it was he who let out a labored sigh. "I can *tell* you how you'll feel afterward, honey. Well-pleasured. *Phenomenally* well-pleasured. That's all."

"You're so sure I won't have any regrets?"

He cast only the slightest of smiles. "This is your Vegas, Laura."

She tilted her head against the throw pillow, confused. "Huh?"

"What happens on the mountain stays on the mountain. It doesn't change your life or change who you are. It's just about pleasure."

She'd never believed that Vegas saying. Everything you did affected who you were. And Laura knew that if she gave into this temptation, this desire that burned deeper inside her with each passing moment, it *would* change her. She just wasn't certain if it would be a change for the better or the worse.

And yet, Braden had taught her so much about pleasure. He'd never asked her to do anything that didn't turn out to be an experience to savor. He'd shown her greater delights than she'd known she was capable of. Maybe he was right. Maybe she should simply turn off all her usual worries and let herself sink even deeper into the sensual world he'd built for her since coming here.

To her surprise, he sat up on the couch, the departure of his firm thigh leaving the spot between her legs woefully empty. He patted her knee and said, "Tell you what, snowflake. Tommy has a couple of new computer games he wants me to try out, so I'm going to head up to his place for awhile and let you work—and think. I'll set out some steaks to thaw before I go, and I'll bring Tommy back with me for dinner around seven. You can let me know your decision then."

She blinked, then sat up, a bit taken aback. He'd stopped pressuring her, persuading her, was truly putting it into *her* hands, letting *her* decide. "Um . . . how will I let you know?"

He cast the sexy grin she'd grown used to. "Oh, I'm sure you'll find a way."

Braden puttered around the house a bit before leaving, and Laura tried to write—but who could write *now*? She sat at the computer, staring out at the peaceful winter setting, trying to let it calm her—but her emotions ran wild.

The truth was, no answer seemed the right one.

Did she want this? Braden and Tommy, both of them, touching her, fucking her?

God help her—yes, she did. Her every nerve ending turned inside out just thinking about it. And God knew that the deeper she sank into this affair with Braden, the more she wanted to please him, the more she wanted to keep showing him she could be the exciting woman he wanted her to be.

And yet . . . this was a big line to cross, at least in her mind. Even Monica hadn't been with two guys at once. And what if five years down the road she met Mr. Right and felt compelled to tell him she'd done this and it made him think badly of her? No, Braden was wrong—once you did something, you couldn't take it back.

Of course, if it were a guy like Braden, she'd have no worries. She'd felt the need to ask, but had totally believed him when he'd promised he wouldn't think of her differently. She *knew* that about him now somehow—knew that he sincerely liked her, utterly respected her, no matter what. Maybe only a guy like that should qualify as a Mr. Right.

She let out a sigh. She had a feeling guys like Braden—truly free and forward thinking, truly into the deeper, more intense sorts of pleasures he wanted to bring her—were few and far between. Most men, deny it though they might, still lived by a double standard—they would probably think it was A-okay if *they* indulged in a threesome but wouldn't want to marry a woman who admitted the same.

Just then, her lover came trotting back down the stairs. "I'm taking off," he told her, approaching from behind, then squeezing her shoulder as he bent to lower a kiss to her neck.

She looked up at him. "Have you ever done anything like that before?"

"A three-way?"

She nodded.

She thought he almost looked a little sheepish as he said, "No," shaking his head lightly. And in all honesty, she was surprised, had been almost certain he'd had a long history of multiple partners.

"Then why do you seem so sure about it, so positive you want it?"

"I don't shy away from my desires, Laura, never have. I just never wanted this before. But now I do. With you."

Her stomach churned. He wanted to experience something with her that he'd never wanted with another woman. It seemed like . . . an opportunity to be special to him, to give him what he'd given her so many of: a memory of something new to take with him when this was over.

As he walked to the door, he paused to look over his shoulder. "Tommy has, though, just so you know."

"Oh?"

"He's been with two women before. A couple of times."

She gave a slight nod. She'd just started thinking they were all virgins at this only to find out Tommy was not. "Snow bunnies gone wild?" she asked.

He grinned, his eyes softening. "Something like that."

Another nod on her part, then she spoke quietly. "I'm more than a snow bunny, you know."

He didn't hesitate. "I know that, snowflake. I know that very well."

With that, Braden threw on a rugged-looking brown jacket, and Laura listened as the door closed behind him, leaving the house in silence.

Whew. She was still trying to wrap her mind around his suggestion and the fact that she'd almost actually agreed to it. Images still floated in her head. The two men taking off her clothes, touching her at the same time. Her body, between theirs, being buffeted by masculinity from both sides. And then, of course, the specific thing Braden had mentioned—two men equaled two cocks. At once. Her whole body tingled at trying to imagine what that would feel like, or if she could even handle it physically.

She still didn't know if she could do it. And she had no idea what would help make up her mind. Part of her knew she simply *couldn't* do anything so risqué. Yet another part of her knew she couldn't let Braden down, and that she couldn't pass up an invitation to what sounded like such overwhelming pleasure.

But it was early in the day, hours before anything would happen. And God knew she couldn't afford to waste half a day of writing on worries about what might or might not happen tonight. And if nothing else, work would provide a good distraction. Thinking about Riley's fictional affair with Sloane Bennett was considerably easier than dealing with her real affair with Braden. And possibly—*gulp!*—Tommy.

Which was when she realized that something *big* needed to happen in Riley's world—and she knew exactly what it was! Pulling her gaze back from the window, she focused on the screen and began to type.

As Riley and Sloane rounded the last bend before reaching the garden, he hefted the old quilts higher in his arm and took her hand. But as they reached the entrance—a white latticed arbor draped with hummingbird vines and bracketed by the tall, well-groomed walls of green shrubbery on both sides—Sloane pulled to a rough halt, jerking Riley back a step.

"What?" she asked, dumbfounded.

Sloane didn't look at her, but she could sense the darkening of his demeanor. "Wait here," he said and started inside.

"Why?" she asked, following.

He turned on her, his gaze serious and menacing. "Wait here, Riley—I mean it."

Riley drew in her breath, incensed. How dare he? She watched as he strode through the arbor into the garden, wondering what on earth was going on. Which was when she saw it: a foot! She gasped, covering her mouth with one hand. A man's lone foot stretched into her line of vision through the hummingbird vines—she spied the hem of simple dark blue pants, a black laced work boot sticking out from the bottom.

Just then, Sloane reappeared, scowling when he saw that she'd been peeking. "Who is it?" she asked, stunned. "And is he ...?"

"Hawthorne is dead," Sloane told her plainly.

"Oh my God!"

"You can say that again."

Riley had never cared much for the Dorchesters' gardener—in fact, he was generally quite surly. But that didn't mean she wanted to see him dead.

"Tell me it looks like a heart attack or something natural," she demanded. Because discovering stolen items in the garden was one thing—but a dead body was entirely another. She didn't want to find out they had a murderer on their hands.

"Well," Sloane said, "I'd love to. But given that the guy has a big knife in his chest, I don't think it's likely."

Riley gasped again. "A knife?" She found herself leaning closer to the arbor, trying to peer around it. The move revealed more of Hawthorne's leg, and the other, bent at an odd angle.

Sloane pulled her back. "Multiple stab wounds, Riley, and a lot of blood. Not something you need to see, honey—okay?"

She drew in her breath and knew she must have looked panicked as Sloane took her into his arms. She couldn't believe this! In all the cases she'd worked on, no one had ever been murdered!

"He was kind of mean," she whispered into Sloane's shoulder, echoing her thought from a moment earlier, "but I never would have wished him dead."

Sloane drew back slightly. "Mean how?"

Oh, she'd forgotten—Sloane wasn't here often, so he hadn't known Hawthorne well.

"He was just the grumbly sort. Just recently, in fact, he had several run-ins with Aunt Mimsey, yelling at her for parking her car over the edge of our driveway, getting one wheel in your aunt and uncle's yard and creating ruts. But she's getting older—her driving isn't what it used to be. And it's only one wheel, for heaven's sake—trust me, if you knew Aunt Mimsey well, you'd know it could be a lot worse."

Sloane's eyes narrowed. "How many times has this happened?"

Riley thought about it. "Three? Four? I'm not sure. I just know he was quite blustery about it, and she got very upset. Aunt Mimsey doesn't get angry often, but Hawthorne had her in quite a state."

She stopped blathering on when she caught the worried look in Sloane's gaze. And she understood what he was thinking even before he said it.

"Riley, honey, I'm sorry, but you know where this all points, don't you?"

She didn't answer—*couldn't* answer. The very notion was too horrifying.

"You know your aunt is starting to look guilty."

Riley sucked in her breath. Aunt Mimsey was such an important part of her life, and had been like a mother to her ever since her own had died. Yet her aunt *had* slowly become more addled over the years. And she *had* coveted Mrs. Dorchester's broach, as well as that Hemingway autograph. In fact, Riley feared that if she thought long and hard, she could find a connection between Aunt Mimsey and every item that had been stolen from the Dorchesters' home. What if she'd been hiding them, thinking to come back for them later, after their disappearance had been forgotten? What if she'd thought it too dangerous to have them all in her possession until the Dorchesters gave up on finding them and this all died down?

All silly speculation, she assured herself. And she found it impossible to believe Aunt Mimsey was capable of murder . . . except for one terrible thing that even Sloane didn't know about, because Riley had shut up before spouting it out. Aunt Mimsey had been so upset over her last row with Hawthorne that she'd said to Riley, "If that man yells at me one more time, I'm going to make him sorry."

What if that time had come? What if Hawthorne had pushed Aunt Mimsey too far?

"Sloane, make love to me," Riley pleaded, her voice rough with desperation.

He still held her but gently pulled back. "Riley, we need to call the police. We need to tell my aunt and uncle what's happened. And you and I need to put our heads together to figure out who's responsible." He glanced toward the arbor. "Besides, the garden's a little . . . occupied at the moment."

"I don't care—about any of that. Not right now. Just make love to me, Sloane—I don't want to wait! Make me forget everything bad for a little while. Take it all away. Make it so there's nothing but you—you inside me."

She watched as Sloane's eyes darkened—then began surveying the space around them. Taking Riley's wrist, he pulled her hurriedly away from the garden's entrance and into the shade of a large, sprawling maple tree, all green and billowy with summer. He threw the blankets to the ground, then pushed her to her knees, joining her there in a hard, urgent kiss.

This sex would be different than anything they'd shared in the garden, Riley knew. He'd taken her to heights unknown in that pristine setting, but this—outside the garden, in the tall grass, the heavy tree limbs dripping over them, swaying madly now in a sudden, warm breeze—would be something much wilder still.

Braden lounged comfortably on a sofa in Tommy's office, a laptop balanced before him, while Tommy sat behind his desk, manning a larger computer. They took turns in a two-player quest game involving medieval castles and damsels in dungeons. Braden was down to his last of five swords, and unless he slayed the dragon guarding the moat on this try, he lost the game. But he wasn't even sure they'd *finish* the game, given the topic he'd just broached with little warning. He'd just asked Tommy if he wanted to have a threesome with him and Laura.

Tommy stared at him around his screen. "Dude—you're sure you want this?"

Braden gave a short, definite nod. "Do I ever do *anything* I'm unsure about?"

Tommy shrugged in concession. "Nope—I'd say you're the most decisive guy I've ever met. But this is a little different than what ski run to hit or what you want on your pizza. Hell, it's even a little different than buying out a company, for God's sake."

Braden tilted his head. "This from the guy who's the official expert on three-ways. I thought this would be nothing to you."

Tommy's eyes narrowed. "It's not me I'm concerned about. I just have to make sure you really want to share her."

"What I *want* is to give her more pleasure than any man ever has—or ever will again. And this is how."

Tommy drew back. "Whoa—this sounds serious."

Now it was Braden who shrugged. "She's opened up to me in ways she never has for anyone else. I just want to take that further, keep that momentum going. I want to see her experience ultimate pleasure—I want to see her take both our cocks."

He watched Tommy draw in his breath. "Damn," he said, sounding more aroused now than concerned.

"Is that a yes?"

"Uh, yeah. I don't think I'm strong enough to pass this up even if I wanted to."

"Good. And besides, I figured it would end your sex drought."

Tommy nodded. "Hell of a way to end it, that's for sure."

"Just remember what I told you—we'll need to feel her out over dinner. I know she's into it—she just hasn't quite talked herself into thinking it's okay yet."

"Got it. We play it by ear, take it where she wants it to go."

"Exactly." Now that it was settled, Braden looked back to his screen and resumed wondering how he was going to slay that damn stubborn dragon and get to the damsel waiting for rescue inside the castle. But thinking of that damsel made him look back up. "One more thing."

Tommy peered around his screen again. "What's that?"

"You can do anything with her, anything she wants. But just don't kiss her. On the mouth, I mean."

Tommy blinked, clearly surprised. "Why? What's it matter?"

Braden's chest tightened slightly. He didn't have an answer, only knew he felt strongly about it. "Just don't."

An hour before Braden was set to return with Tommy, Laura finished her work and headed upstairs to shower. As she ran the soap over her body, she couldn't help thinking of the ultrasensual bathing she'd shared with Braden. She'd been in a state of semiarousal all afternoon—ever since he'd kissed her on the couch and gotten her so hot, then left without taking it further. Now, her nipples remained sensitive and erect, and her pussy tingled with want.

Biting her lip with a thought toward the evening, she reached for the shaving cream still on the shower bench and, sitting down there, shaved her legs and the sensitive mound between. Like before, each gentle stroke of the razor blazed a trail of fire over the aching flesh, getting her hotter still.

Was she preparing for a ménage à trois? She pulled in her breath, still unsure. She only knew she wanted to make of herself what Braden had made of her prior to this: a wholly sexual being. She *wanted* to be aroused. And she wanted her body to be smooth and soft and clean, and her pussy boldly on display, for *whatever* happened later, be it with one man . . . or two.

After, she stroked her fingertips between her parted legs to make sure she felt smooth to the touch. Smooth, wet, and slick. Knowing what she would feel like to Braden—or anyone else—amped up her excitement further.

Only when she exited the shower, letting her towel drop to the floor to walk through the room naked, did she notice the pretty little shopping bag on the bed, pink and shiny. As she approached, she also spied a card bearing her name.

Hurriedly, she opened it and read the small, precise script inside.

Snowflake—

I bought this for you before I came, and just hadn't found the right time to give it to you. I've been more concerned with getting you out of your clothes than getting you into sexy ones ☺. But I thought tonight appropriate—that is, if you decide you want that ultimate pleasure I promised. No pressure, though. I want to give it to you more than I want to breathe—but you have to want it, too, just as much as I do. I hope you're wearing this when I come home—but if not, I understand.

Braden

Her heart pumping fast, she reached in the bag. Nestled in pale pink tissue paper she found an ensemble of champagne-colored lace: a demi-bra, a pretty cami with triangular, curving cups, and a sexy thong. She remembered a time when he'd asked her for her bra size, and she supposed this was why. Only then, she'd imagined him having more items *delivered*—she couldn't have conceived of him coming here and turning her sexual world upside down.

Without hesitation, she stepped into the lacy undies, which sported a little bow in back where the tiny strips of fabric met, then put on the bra and walked to the mirrored doors of the closet. They fit perfectly and felt expensive. She had to let out a heavy breath just looking at herself—the rise of her breasts from the bra that barely concealed her nipples, the slope of the panties hugging her cunt.

Returning to the bed, she slid the cami on over the bra. Both were necessary if she really intended to don the cami as "outerwear"—its cups offered no support, and she wanted her chest to look pert and firm, wanted the curves to swell sexily above.

Which begged the question—was she really wearing this? Tonight? To dinner?

She bit her lip as she studied herself in the mirror again, then reached for the jeans she'd worn last night. She would have liked some strappy shoes to complete the outfit, but overall, the jeans and cami alone made for a sexy, confident look.

A look which, if it were summer, she would actually wear on a date or out with friends. But if Braden and Tommy showed up to find her in this, with snow outside, when only last night she'd worn a sweater and snowflake socks to dinner—it would make a statement. For Laura, it would say *Fuck me* as clearly as fishnet stockings and stiletto heels said it for Candy next door. They would come in, they would see her, and they would know what she wanted.

The question was: Did she? Could she? The answer didn't seem much clearer than it had earlier today.

Unless you considered that she stood here dressed for after-dinner sex when she knew her lover and his friend were due to arrive within the hour.

Unless you considered the way her pussy burned right now, and the sense that her breasts felt bigger than usual, aching to burst free from the champagne lace that held them.

Unless you considered that the very darkest part of her wondered what it would feel like, wanted to know, wanted to experience it, wanted to throw all caution to the wind for the first time in her life.

That's when she heard the door open below. Damn, they were early.

"Laura, honey, we're home. Are you upstairs?"

She rushed to the doorway and out onto the little bridge that overlooked the foyer. "Just on my way downstairs right now."

And the next thing she knew, she stood before both men, smelling the cold they'd brought in and watching them stomp the snow off their shoes, then seeing them peer up at her . . . and smile. Braden's look was particularly knowing, and particularly heated, as his gaze took in her top before rising to her eyes. "You look great tonight, baby," he said, lifting one hand to her cheek as he leaned in to deliver a short, slightly chilled kiss.

But Laura didn't feel the cold—only the heat, the slow fire that had just ignited in the room between the three of them. "Thanks," she said, trying to disguise a last somewhat nervous swallow. Then she turned to Tommy, ready to be bold, ready to show Braden she could be as adventurous as he wanted her to be. "I'm glad you could join us again tonight."

Chapter Fourteen

Tommy leaned in to kiss her cheek, his hand curling warm at her waist, and the simple contact sent a soft frisson of arousal echoing through her. "My pleasure," he said, and Laura forced herself to meet his blue eyes, just to see what she found there. Nothing smarmy or presumptuous but a tinge of sensual awareness that she couldn't deny. As she turned for the kitchen, her nipples rubbed against her bra.

So was it true? Had she decided she was really going to indulge in this wildest of fantasies? As usual, the very question sent a heavy breath *whooshing* from her, so she decided to cut herself a break and not force herself to answer. Instead, she pulled a bottle of wine from the fridge, since a glass of Chardonnay sounded welcome right now.

"Ready to put the steaks on the grill?" Braden asked—and from there, things turned amazingly easy. Since, after all, they were just three normal people having dinner. Sort of.

Braden and Tommy fired up the grill, putting on the steaks and potatoes, while Laura tossed the salad, then set the table. She turned on music, something low and soft in the background.

When they sat down to their salads, Laura chose the chair at the head of the table. Only when Tommy sat on one side of her and Braden on the other did she realize perhaps it had been a subconscious effort to put herself between the two men, to begin to get used to that, see how it felt—even if only in some small way.

And though conversation was easy—the guys telling her about the new computer games they'd tested today—everything inside Laura began to heat up, to swell with an inescapable and potent sexual consciousness. She wasn't sure if it was just her body, wound up from her thoughts through the day, or if it was more palpable than that, something they *all* could feel passing between them, hovering in the air—but a whole new element of sensuality pervaded her being. Everything she touched, she felt more. Everything she ate delivered more taste than ever before.

She found herself forking an entire cherry tomato into her mouth, letting her tongue run over its smooth skin as she luxuriated in its very roundness, until finally she bit into it and let the tangy flavor burst across her taste buds, wet and cool. She washed it down with a swill of wine, welcoming the fruity warmth as it passed into her throat, then lowered the glass back to the table, where her fingertips slid slowly up and down the stem.

When Braden went to check on the steaks, Laura emptied her glass and watched as Tommy reached to refill it.

"Braden tells me you had a rough breakup not long ago." She wasn't sure it was the right topic, but it had just popped out—with a little help from the wine. She liked knowing he was a guy with feelings, a guy who could take a relationship seriously—maybe more seriously than Braden, for all she knew.

He nodded, took a sip from his own glass. "Yeah. But it was my own fault," he admitted with an endearingly devilish glint in his eye. "Did he tell you *that*?"

She shook her head.

"I cheated on her," he said, then held up his hands as if in defense. "Don't let that make you think I'm a lousy guy, though—because believe me, I regret it. It was a stupid thing to do and I've learned my lesson."

She tilted her head, intrigued. "Why does a guy do that? Cheat on a girl he cares for?"

He grinned. "Easy sex?"

She laughed softly, despite herself.

"Seriously, the temptation was there and I took it—but I really don't know why. Now I think maybe I just wasn't comfortable knowing I was getting in so deep with Marianne. Maybe I wanted to sabotage it—or at least prove to myself that she didn't matter as much as I was afraid she did."

"And?"

A grin of admission. "She mattered as much as I was afraid she did. And now I wish I hadn't been afraid."

She tried to reconcile this guy with the one who had three-ways with ski bunnies—and realized it wasn't that easy to peg a person, to lump him into a category. She'd learned in her own way recently that she herself possessed a lot of different sides, varying and sometimes *conflicting* parts of her personality. She supposed everyone did, whether or not they chose to let it show.

She found herself reaching out to touch his hand on the table. "I'm sorry it worked out that way." Heat flew up her arm and her pussy flooded at the simple gesture. Yet it wasn't just her general attraction to Tommy causing it—it was knowing what they might do together later, with Braden, and it was knowing Tommy knew it, too.

Their eyes met, and her nipples tingled. "I think I'm starting to get over it," he said, his voice delivering a playful hint of flirtation.

She smiled but drew her hand back as one French door opened, admitting Braden with a platter of still-sizzling steaks and foil-covered potatoes.

"Although I gotta admit, I still miss her sometimes."

"Who's that?" Braden asked, lowering the platter to the table.

"Marianne."

"Ah. The famous lost love."

Laura couldn't help thinking Braden sounded less than sympathetic, even though he'd sounded more so when he'd first mentioned the breakup to her. A guy thing, she supposed.

As they all began reaching for steaks, she said to Tommy, "A breakup can be so hard." Although she was actually thinking ahead, to how she would feel when she left Braden, more than thinking back to any particular past pain. "You just miss so many little things about the person. And big things, too."

"I miss the sex," Tommy said, and his unexpected bluntness made her laugh.

Braden high-fived his buddy across the table, but afterward Tommy said to Laura, "Not just because I'm a sex hound, though. It was pretty special with her." He sliced into a baked potato, then took a large sip of wine. "She had this little place on her neck," he said, pointing to his own. "And when I kissed her there, she just went *wild*."

"Neck kisses *are* fabulous," Laura agreed. As she'd noticed last night, talking about sex with him seemed easier than it would with most guys she'd just met. Then she looked to Braden, who was swirling the wine in his glass as he cast a sexy grin. "When Braden kisses my neck, it goes all through me."

"You like it even better when I kiss you lower," Braden pointed out, his voice deeper than before.

The usual heat ascended her cheeks, but she still gave him a smile and let the wine wash away her inhibitions, as it had so many times. "You have a skilled mouth."

"You do, too, honey."

She found herself licking her upper lip in response, simply needing to *feel* something there, some sensation at her mouth. She cut into her steak and as she ate, like before, it tasted richer, juicier, her potato more buttery. She could barely make sense of it, but everything she put in her mouth felt like a tiny aphrodisiac. Even the fork and knife in her hands felt heavier, and it was sensual just to hold them, wrap her fingers about them.

At some point she realized her knees were touching both guys' knees under the table to either side of her—and that she wasn't pulling them back, and neither were they. Tommy asked Braden how his family was, and Braden turned the topic to Laura's career, yet beneath the table something entirely different took place. Her pussy rippled with excitement, nervous anticipation—but she found herself getting *less* nervous and *more* anxious with each passing minute.

For dessert, Braden unveiled a plate of sinful-looking frosted brownies.

"Where did *those* come from?" Laura asked. She'd have certainly honed in on such treats if they'd been here for long.

"Made them this morning while you were working."

She'd heard him in the kitchen for awhile but must have been completely absorbed in her story not to have smelled them. She blinked playfully. "Why, Mr. Stone, I didn't know you baked."

He winked. "Only for you, baby."

He set the brownies in the same spot as the platter, which he'd just removed—quite the little host, she couldn't help thinking. And when Laura bit into one of them, it was so chocolaty, gooey, and delicious that she actually moaned—and her pussy spasmed lightly.

"Sounds like I should bring these to bed with us," Braden said with a wicked, teasing grin.

"It would be messy," she said.

"You worry too much."

She kept her eyes locked on his. "You're right, I do." Her knees still touched both his and Tommy's. "And I'm going to stop. Right now." She meant it. She was going to quit thinking so much. At least for tonight. "All worries of any kind are officially . . . gone."

As if to prove it, she indulged in another big bite of the sticky brownie, letting out another soft moan as the scrumptious taste melded with her new sensual awareness to trickle, once more, all the way down into her panties.

"You have"—Tommy leaned closer to her, drawing her attention back to him—"icing on your mouth." Reaching up, he gently swiped it away with one finger—then held it out to her.

Wrapping her hand around his, she drew his finger near and licked the chocolate away. Fresh excitement blazed through her, making her stomach tighten as she broke a sexy gaze with Tommy to look at Braden.

Her lover's expression dripped with such dark desire that she felt it pooling within her, beginning to fill her. "Still a little more," Braden said, his deep voice barely audible as he leaned over to lick a bit of remaining icing from the corner of her mouth.

"Oh . . ." she heard herself sigh as pleasure fluttered downward. And she began to understand—fully now, and with no real fear—that this was going to happen. And that she was going to let it.

"More wine?" Tommy asked, noticing her glass was nearly empty again.

Sounded like a good idea. "Yes."

"I'll open another bottle," Braden announced and rose, partially clearing the table as he went. Tommy and Laura got up, too.

When Laura automatically began to help, stacking plates together, Braden touched her arm. "Leave it, honey. You and Tommy go in the living room, chat a little more."

She didn't answer, just put down the plates and picked up her wineglass to join Braden's friend where he now stood peering into the vast darkness out the floor-to-vaulted-ceiling window. Getting up had suddenly made her feel the alcohol a bit more, but she didn't mind.

"You live up *there*, correct?" She looked to the right, up the mountain, lifting a finger in that direction.

He pointed. "You can see my security light from here. Do you see it?"

She looked, but trees seemed to be blocking the light from her view. "No. Where?"

Tommy set his wineglass on the desk, then positioned himself behind her, placing his strong hands at her waist and turning her body just slightly. "It's hard to spot—you have to catch it at just the right angle through the pines." His breath came warm on her neck as he spoke, and the warmth spread downward.

Although the strangest sensation struck her just then: she liked Tommy a lot, but if she were here alone with him now, just the two of them, she wouldn't be nearly so anxious to fool around. Tommy was hot, but it was *Braden's* presence, *Braden's* desire for this, that made her want it, too, and that made Tommy's nearness so exciting, his touches so tantalizing.

"You haven't seen us fucking in the window, have you?" she asked. Another wave of warmth passed through her at her own shocking brazenness.

His hands remained firm at her waist, his body grazing hers from behind. "You fucked in the window?"

She nodded, still peering out into the black, aware that he was beginning to grow hard against her ass. She supposed if anything would make her pull away at this point, it was *that*—but she didn't move. "Right over there," she said softly, pointing. "Next to the telescope."

"No, I didn't see." His voice had deepened, and his musky scent enveloped her. "But I would have liked to."

She dared to peer over her shoulder at him, to meet his eyes, that close. "Braden asked me if it excited me to know someone somewhere might be watching."

"What did you say?"

Her own voice came out surprisingly raspy. "I said yes."

She didn't flinch when Tommy lowered a gentle kiss to her shoulder, his mustache teasing her skin. He whispered softly in her ear. "Is this okay? For me to touch you?"

I think so.

But no, no doubts—only certainty. "Yes."

It felt no less than surreal as he delivered another small kiss in the same spot, but this time she leaned her head to the side, arching her neck for him, thinking, *This is really happening, really happening.* And if any last vestiges of fear lingered inside her, they disappeared when she glanced toward the kitchen and found Braden watching. As always, his eyes fueled her.

He dropped the dish towel in his hand to the dining table and stepped into the living room. He moved his lips to say, *Don't be afraid. I want this.*

Which made her want it, too—even more than before, more than when it had been only a vague fantasy, a shapeless desire flitting around the edges of her mind. Now it was concrete, real, within her grasp, and she yearned for it—yearned to know how it felt, yearned to experience everything there was to experience with Braden.

He seemed rooted in place by the sight before him, and Laura knew stark passion transformed her face as Tommy continued to rain soft, tantalizing kisses across her neck and shoulders. Each was like a tiny pinprick of pleasure, accentuated by Braden's eyes, watching another man touch her the same way *he* normally touched her.

As Tommy's kisses went on, his arms slowly eased around, his hands sliding sensuously over her stomach like a warm vice. When one rose to gingerly cup her breast, she let out a hot sigh, astonished—still—at how Braden's gaze ratcheted up her every physical response to the other man.

Soon both of Tommy's hands closed fully over her breasts, beginning to massage and lift, letting the nipples pucker between the light pinch of thumb and forefinger. Laura's head dropped back with a thready moan as she arched deeper into his grasp, and behind her, his hard-on pressed more prominently against her ass. "Mmm . . ." she heard herself purr. And that quickly, she was losing herself to the moment, to the situation, to the two men.

When Braden came to stand before her, the very heat of his body made her feel delightfully sandwiched between them. She peered longingly up into his eyes as he lifted both hands to her face. Tommy's caresses spread over her breasts and belly now, and having them both touch her—despite Braden's touch holding some remnant of soft innocence—set off the fireworks of reality inside her. And the reality was . . . she liked being touched by both of them at the same time. And she was going to love what was to come. Her pussy wept with anticipation.

Braden's mouth melded hotly with hers, the kiss turning her even more inside out than usual. One kiss led to another, and another, each hot and needful, until Braden's thumbs slipped beneath the shoulder straps of her camisole, lowering them to her upper arms. The fabric dropped from her chest, revealing breasts that strained against the tight fabric of the bra.

"Ah, so fucking beautiful, baby," Braden murmured, his eyes locked on her cleavage. As Tommy caressed her waist and stomach beneath the crumpled cami, Braden's warm hands captured her aching breasts for a firm, full knead.

"Oh . . ." she moaned, but quick as that, Braden curled his fingertips around the demi-bra's lacy edge and pulled downward on the cups, just enough to reveal the taut pink peaks. He looked as weakened by the sight as she currently felt.

Tommy's touches grew bolder as he shifted his hands up to her bared breasts—replacing Braden's—to massage the soft flesh. She moaned and drank in the heated look on Braden's face, and her cunt pulsed with wild lust.

Braden's mouth dropped to one hardened nipple where it jutted between Tommy's fingers. He suckled deep and intent, making her cry out. She had, at some point, begun to lean back against Tommy, a necessity now for she feared her legs would crumple beneath her otherwise. She looked down, watching Braden's mouth closing over her as another man's hand held her.

As Braden moved to her other breast, which Tommy lifted like an offering, Laura knew the sound of her breathing was the loudest thing in the room, although Tommy let out heavy, labored sighs behind her, as well. Braden licked her beaded nipple now—long, languid licks that left it hard and glistening with each stroke.

Without planning it, Laura found herself thrusting her chest farther toward Braden's ministrations. She lifted her arms above her head and brought her hands down in Tommy's thick hair. His kisses fell to her neck again, and his hands eased to her hips as Braden took full charge of her needy breasts, caressing with both mouth and hands.

She felt her self-control beginning to wane—her ass grinding slowly against Tommy's hardness behind her as she watched Braden laving her delighted breasts with wet licks and kisses. And just when she thought she could exist happily like that forever, one of Tommy's hands skimmed inward, over her jeans, until he was stroking between her thighs.

A fresh cry escaped her as the hot pleasure rocketed through her. Her body fell into a natural undulation, against Tommy's hand and his erection behind her, against Braden's hungry mouth and kneading palms—*and for his eyes*. Because she still felt his gaze, felt him watching her every reaction, and she relished it.

Tommy's hand left her crotch only to unbutton her jeans, then lower the zipper. When he eased his fingers down inside, stroking into her wetness, they both moaned.

Braden drew back, looked down—then knelt before her. Wrapping his hands around the waistband of her jeans, he tugged them to her thighs, keeping his gaze riveted on the front of her miniscule panties, Tommy's fingers inside.

She couldn't part her legs far due to the denim, but Tommy's middle finger raked through her damp slit, making her all the more crazy given Braden's close-up view. She sighed her pleasure—then bit her lip when Braden's hands rose to her thong, drawing it, too, gently down to her thighs.

"Ah, God," he moaned at the sight of Tommy's fingers rubbing her, sinking deep now. "So fucking pretty, baby."

"So smooth," Tommy echoed.

"Tell Tommy," Braden said deeply, "how you shaved this pretty pussy for me."

She could barely speak amid the rampant lust pulsing through her body, particularly the part they were focused on right now. Tommy's large finger still raked through her moisture. "I shaved it . . . in the shower . . . when he asked me to . . . while he watched. And again . . . today. For both of you."

"That's so hot," Tommy purred, still touching, touching, and Braden didn't move, simply watching, up close, until she could have sworn her cunt gaped wider just for him.

When Braden leaned slowly inward, Tommy seemed to know he intended to lick her, so he withdrew his finger and used both hands to part her labia. She shuddered when Braden's tongue raked over her engorged clit, and she again suffered the yearning to spread for him, and tried even though she knew the jeans would stop her.

Dragging his wet tongue up her center, again, again, he pushed her jeans and thong down farther, all the way to her ankles until she was able to pull one foot free. Then—sweet heaven—she parted her legs so that she could feel each hot lick deeper. Tommy still used his fingers to part her pussy as Braden laved her whole slit from top to bottom. Behind her, Tommy's arousal pressed harder—so hard—into the center of her ass, so that as she moved instinctually against Braden's mouth, she felt deliciously stimulated from the back, too. Experiencing that "sandwich effect" again, she gave herself over to it, letting herself feel wholly taken by them both, wholly trapped between them, surrendering to their wants and whims.

Finally, her legs weakened to a point that she had to break through the heat to breathe, "I can't stand up any longer."

Braden ceased ministrations, ending with one soft kiss just above her clit, and murmured, "Come on, let's bring you over here."

He took her hands and led her swiftly but gently to the sofa. Her legs would barely move—she felt dazed, intoxicated more by the men than the wine now—so he guided her.

Yet being back face to face with him brought on a whole new bevy of desires that had to be acted upon. His clothes needed to come off. And she had to get to his cock. It wasn't a choice, but a raw need.

Drawing her knees up beneath her on the sofa, she pushed the open shirt from his shoulders, then scrunched the dark T-shirt underneath, trying to get to his broad chest and that six-pack stomach. He helped, ripping them off, and she reached for his belt.

Then she remembered Tommy, who'd sat down behind her on the couch, and he'd been so sweet and generous so far that she didn't want to leave him out. Turning, she reached boldly for the buttons on his shirt, and he leaned back, watching her undo them. She knew that surely Braden watched, too, and as always, his eyes injected in her a whole new wanton passion.

She followed her instincts, letting herself go more in this moment than ever before. Braden wanted to see her with another man—then see her he would.

As Tommy's shirt fell open to reveal the same muscular stomach he'd revealed at their first dinner, she began to kiss his broad chest, began to kiss her way *down* it. She didn't go slow—Braden's eyes pushed her, made her hungry, made her dirty, brought out the darkest sexual side of her being.

She undid Tommy's belt, worked the button on his jeans. She unzipped them over the large bulge there and kissed her way farther down. When his cock burst free, protruding from white briefs, she didn't hesitate to wrap her fist around it, release it completely from his underwear, and sink her mouth down over the head.

"Jesus," Tommy groaned.

And behind her, Braden rasped, "Ah, God, baby. Suck him for me. I want you to suck him." And as she took Tommy's erection deep in her mouth, moving up and down, making him wet, letting her lips stretch to accommodate him, she understood that Braden knew it was for him. He knew it was for his eyes, his pleasure, as much as hers. There was no jealousy that she'd gone down on Tommy before him, nothing but awe in Braden's voice, nothing but his wanting to push her deeper and deeper into passion. *Her* pleasure added to *his*, and *his* added to *hers*, so that it multiplied over and over, no matter what sexual act they indulged in, and even now, with another man, Braden knew, as she did, that it was all about him—no one else.

Tommy's cock was not quite as large as Braden's but still filled her mouth deep, and she relished working him over while Braden watched.

"Yeah, baby, that's so good," Tommy said.

Braden's hands rubbed her back and molded to her bare hips as he leaned over her, watching. "That's right, honey. You look so beautiful sucking him. So beautiful for me."

But soon enough, Braden's voice ceased, and kisses began. On her back, then on her sensitive ass—and she found herself arching it toward him. She sought as much sensation as she could get, her body hungry and longing for it.

Before she knew it, he was rubbing her pussy with circling fingers, and she pressed back against them, wanting more, more, moaning feverishly around Tommy's cock. When Braden's fingers slid inside her, she had to release Tommy to let out a gentle sob. "Oh . . ."

"You're so wet, baby," Braden said.

She answered by thrusting against his touch, welcoming it deeper. She could hear her own wetness as his fingers moved in and out.

She stroked Tommy's stiff shaft, studying the thick column of flesh, veined and smooth, before lowering her mouth back over him and listening to his hot sigh of pleasure above.

And as she took Tommy in at one end, and Braden's fingers at the other, she knew she wanted still more. She wanted exactly what Braden had known she wanted. Two cocks inside her at once. She pushed her bottom wildly against Braden's fingers, needing more thickness there, needing the glorious erection she knew stood between his legs. She thrust, thrust, finally whimpering her frustration and sensing he *knew* she needed it and was teasing her, drawing it out, just to make her lust for it more.

"What do you want, baby?" he finally purred. He was leaning over her now, the warmth of his chest pressing into her back, his voice near her ear. "You want my cock? Is that why you're wiggling that sexy ass so much?"

She looked up at him, her mouth still around Tommy's shaft, and their eyes met.

"Jesus, honey," he sighed.

She released Tommy, her lips swollen yet still hungry. "Please" was all she could say.

Braden kissed her—a quick, warm kiss on her well-stretched lips—and his eyes promised he'd give her what she craved.

A second later his majestic erection glided through the valley of her ass, parting her there, rubbing against the tiny fissure, making her wild with desire. She arched harder against him, which pressed her breasts around Tommy's damp shaft, and together, they all groaned.

The sweet stimulation was grand—but she still needed more. "Fuck me, Braden. Please fuck me—*now.*"

"Aw, honey," he ground out roughly through clenched teeth, then the tip of his long shaft pressed against her eager opening, pausing for just a second before plunging inside.

She cried out—amazed, as always, by the stunning, shocking pleasure of the entry, the very sense of fullness it provided. And she didn't hesitate to lift her head, reach for Tommy's erection, then lower her lips back over it.

Both guys moaned, and she sank into a deep and total bliss to have reached this unfathomable moment, to have two long, hard, beautiful cocks inside her body at once. Both of them moved in her, fucking both pussy and mouth in even, rhythmic strokes that took over her senses, made her stop thinking, made her do nothing but feel, absorb, drink them in, soak up their marvelous controlled power. She'd never felt so very taken before, so physically possessed. She delighted in the sense of utter wantonness that overcame her as she gave her body completely, thrusting her cunt at Braden as she vigorously suckled Tommy.

They moved that way together until she was drunk on it, until she felt mindless, an embodiment of pure sex, pure pleasure—nothing else mattered but physical fulfillment.

It was then that Braden's fingers snaked around her hip, dipping to stroke her clit. Wildfire seemed to ignite in her very core, spreading rapidly outward until it consumed her whole body. She drove harder against Braden's cock, taking it deeper, inviting more punishing strokes. *Fuck me, fuck me, fuck me.* She'd have screamed it if her mouth hadn't been filled with Tommy's thick shaft, but she wasn't willing to give that up, merely sighing hotly around it instead.

When Braden loosed his other hand from her hip to stroke his thumb across her anus, it was all the stimulation she needed to explode into orgasm—screaming around Tommy's cock as blinding pleasure burst through her nether regions in paralyzing pulses of heat and light. *Oh, oh, oh!* She shut her eyes, let the swallowing climax own her, stretch through her, as her two lovers continued to fill her.

When it was done, exhaustion gripping her, she released Tommy to sink to the couch, her head on his denim-clad thigh. The move forced Braden's cock to leave her, as well, and she turned on her side to look at him. His eyes, not surprisingly, already shone on hers, brimming with wonder. His warm hand squeezed her bare hip. "Are you okay, honey?"

She tried to smile, but her lips were too worn out at the moment. "Yes. Good," she breathed.

He leaned closer. "You are incredible. You know that, don't you?"

This time, she managed to wrench her mouth into a soft grin. "*You're* incredible. The things you make me feel, make me experience." It dawned on her then that her head still lay on Tommy's firm thigh, so she shifted her eyes upward. "You, too."

He let out a gentle laugh. "I haven't really done anything."

She bit her lip and glanced toward his still-erect shaft, not far from where her head rested. "But you have a nice cock." She even reached up to pet it, making him sigh as Braden chuckled softly.

"Damn," Tommy whispered. "I want to fuck you so bad right now I can taste it."

"Can you take it?" Braden asked her. "Can you take Tommy in your tight little pussy?"

Laura's cunt flared with desire as she purred, "Mmm, yes, I think I can."

Chapter Fifteen

"Then I want you to have him." Braden's voice dropped lower. "I want to watch him fuck you, honey, so, so deep."

With that, he took her hands and guided her, switching her position on the sofa so that she faced Braden, her ass turned toward Tommy. She didn't rise up on her knees—too tired—but instead pulled them up under her in a more relaxed pose.

Behind her, she heard the rip of paper and knew Tommy was putting on a condom. Then his hands closed warmly on her hips, massaging, whispering how hot she was, how sexy, how giving, and how well she'd sucked him. She peered at Braden the whole time, who lay stretched out across the end of the couch, naked now, and looking good enough to eat. Which was exactly what she intended to do. Her mouth was tired, but not *that* tired.

Perching between Braden's parted legs, she wrapped her hand around his erection as Tommy began to ease into her from the rear. She pumped Braden lightly as all three of them moaned in unison, then sank her mouth over him. He tasted salty, sweet, with her juices, and that somehow made the intimacy even deeper.

She pushed back against Tommy and knew she was taking him to the hilt when her ass pressed against his pelvis. Again, she was full with two gloriously hard shafts. She cupped Braden's balls in her hand as she moved her mouth up and down his length, and she sensed Tommy's colliding with her mound as he began to deliver short, firm strokes.

Releasing Braden from her lips, she licked him from bottom to top, then swirled her tongue around the head as Tommy drove at her from behind. All the while, she savored the ability to delight them both at once with different parts of her body.

She kept her eyes locked on Braden's as she used her tongue on him, still stroking with her hand underneath and sucking away the pre-come from the tip when it gathered there. Until finally she stopped her licks altogether, nestling his cock warm between her breasts. They still stood plump and pert with the help of the bra cupping their undersides, and he groaned as she began to fuck him that way, letting his still-damp cock slide deeply between. "God, yes," he murmured above her. "So nice, baby."

Behind her, the strength of Tommy's strokes increased until he was pounding into her, hard, harder. It made her boobs jiggle against Braden's cock. She barely understood the wild pleasure it brought to close her breasts so softly around his stiffness, but it had her sighing in hot joy, pleasing her almost as much as Tommy's erection.

Tommy pummeled her now, making her cry out at each powerful thrust, until she found herself wrapping her arms around Braden's torso, hugging him as she met each firm plunge in back.

"Is it good, baby?" Braden asked, smoothing his hands across her shoulders.

"Mmm," she managed, still taking in each hot drive Tommy delivered.

"Ah, fuck her sweet pussy for me," Braden murmured, and she knew he was watching Tommy ram into her, watching her take it, feeling the pleasure vibrate through her body as he held her.

"Oh God," Tommy said suddenly. "I'm gonna come. I can't stop. I'm gonna come hard." And with his hands still bracketing her hips, she listened to the long, heavy groan that left him as he delivered impossibly deep strokes that reverberated to her core.

Then he went still inside her, finally releasing a long, exhausted sigh. "Jesus," he whispered, and she smiled to herself with the feminine pride of having pleasured him.

When he withdrew, she rested against Braden for a moment, his cock still stretched long and rigid between her cradling breasts, but her cunt felt empty, and now she wanted to make Braden come, too. She lifted her head from his stomach to look at him. "I need you back in my pussy."

His eyes remained glazed, his mouth half open, and his deep groan told her how much her words had affected him. "Kiss me," he said.

An indulgence she never tired of. She rose, skimming her body upward over his until she could press her tongue warmly into his mouth. He moaned as they traded kisses, her arms circling his neck, his hands dropping to knead her ass. "Fuck me," she finally whispered. "Please fuck me."

He sat them both up on the couch, Laura on his lap. "Like this," he said, then positioned her so they both sat facing the window, his rock-solid length stretching up the crease of her ass. She understood what he wanted and, lowering her feet to the floor, she stood, then sat slowly back down, the move sheathing him.

They both moaned and he felt unbelievably huge, but adjustment to the position came easier now than when they'd first had sex.

She carefully began to move on him, pleasantly aware of her nudity as Tommy watched, aware this was the first time her body had felt so clearly on display since they'd moved to the sofa. She liked his eyes on her almost as much as she liked Braden's, liked knowing he watched her slide up and down Braden's shaft, liked the sense of her breasts jiggling slightly atop the tight bra with each movement she made.

Braden's hands curved over her thighs, squeezing, caressing—then parting. "Spread, honey," he whispered deep in her ear. Then he looked to their right, to Tommy. "Why don't you lick her sweet pussy for me while she rides my cock."

Tommy's voice sounded strained. "Happy to." Then he dropped to his knees, situating between her legs. Both hers and Braden's had opened wide to accommodate him, and she glanced down at her smooth bare flesh, open and pink and waiting for Tommy's mouth.

His first lick up her moist center was tentative, testing—but oh so welcome, and she sighed as fresh heat rippled outward. "Oh, more," she heard herself beg without quite meaning to.

"*Lots* more, sweetheart," Tommy promised. He drew his gaze from her cunt to her face, then let it drop back again just before sinking his tongue deeply, dragging it enthusiastically over her clit, again, and again.

"Oh God," she moaned.

Braden's hands rose to knead her breasts as Tommy's mouth worked at her below, his hands caressing her inner thighs. Once more, the multitude of sensations and the knowledge that more than one man delivered them nearly overwhelmed her. Tommy's skilled tongue raked upward, each time ending at her clit, and soon she no longer moved up and down on Braden, but simply gyrated in rhythmic circles on his cock that helped her meet Tommy's mouth with just the right pressure.

Tommy focused solely on the engorged nub then, licking, licking, each stroke sending a new burst of heat through Laura's pussy. "Yes," she whispered, "yes." Above, Braden tweaked her sensitive nipples between thumb and forefingers, adding to her growing excitement. She understood intuitively that *she'd* pleasured *them*, and now *they* were pleasuring *her*, their every action designed to push her closer to climax.

"Yes, lick me," she said on a hot sigh as she watched Tommy stroke his tongue through her feminine folds. "Oh, oh—now suck me. Suck my clit," she begged, barely aware that she'd suddenly started telling him what she needed.

He obliged, suckling the swollen knob of pink flesh deeply between his lips, until she was crying out, "Yes, like that, like that!"

"Mmm, I want you to come, baby," Braden purred near her ear. "I want you come so fucking hard."

"I . . . want you . . . to come, too," she managed between escalating breaths. "Deep inside me . . . fill me up with it, baby . . . fill me."

Releasing her breasts in order to brace his hands at her hips, Braden began pumping harder up into her as Tommy suckled her in rhythm with their fucking. As she met Braden's thrusts, her clitoris rose hard against Tommy's mouth, achieving perfect friction. She felt herself climbing, climbing, working her way rapidly toward the peak of pleasure, until Braden demanded, "Come for me⏤baby⏤*now*." And she did.

She toppled headlong into the deepest ecstasy of her life, the waves of release pounding through her body, stretching on longer than any orgasm she could recall. She rode it out⏤rode Braden's cock and met Tommy's hot mouth again and again⏤until finally the scintillating vibrations began to ebb.

But when Braden yelled, "Ah God, here I go, too!" and pressed her firmly down onto his cock as he drove deep into her in four harsh strokes, the now-faint sensations increased, stretching back through her body, lengthening the orgasm even more.

Seconds later, Laura found herself relaxing back against him, his arms enfolding her. Turning her head from where it rested on his shoulder, she leaned a small kiss to his neck.

Their eyes met. "Doing okay?" he whispered, sounding as spent as she felt.

"Better than okay," she assured him.

He flashed a sexy and very satisfied smile.

Braden relaxed on the sofa with Laura and Tommy, Laura's disheveled bra the only scrap of clothing among them. For the first time, it occurred to him that maybe he should feel a little weird about being this intimate with Tommy⏤they were guys, after all⏤but he didn't. They'd been friends a long while, they'd always clicked and been comfortable and frank when it came to sex, and even if it seemed a little odd to be lying naked on the same couch as his buddy, he didn't let it bother him.

He couldn't get over how amazing Laura had been. Just like every other sexual experiment she'd finally given into, she'd quickly abandoned her inhibitions and let herself go—beautifully. Even when he'd come home and found her wearing the lingerie he'd bought for her, he couldn't have imagined how hot she would be for him tonight, how sexy and willing with Tommy. His pleasure was quadrupled by knowing how far she had come in such a short time, that a couple of weeks ago, she wouldn't even masturbate in front of a guy but was now pleasuring two of them.

"Anybody hungry?" Tommy asked, apparently shaking free of the lethargy that had stolen over them all. Without waiting for them to answer, he headed to the kitchen, returning with the rest of the brownies and the bottle of wine Braden had managed to open but not pour right before the hot encounter had begun. They passed the wine, each drinking from the bottle, and everyone grabbed a brownie.

Of course, upon spying Laura's delectable nipples still jutting above her bra, Braden couldn't resist using his finger to dab a bit of the gooey icing onto one pointed peak, then bending to lick it off. "Mmm," she sighed, casting a shockingly wicked little smile in his direction.

Tommy followed suit, soon suckling more dark frosting from the other pebbled peak, and from the expression on his sweet Laura's face, she was content to let them suck as much chocolate from her breasts as they wanted. She looked like a sexy cat stretching, purring, as she luxuriated in the pleasure.

Braden continued applying the chocolate and licking it off, but before long he felt Laura's fist—around his dick. Groaning, he glanced to see that she'd reached out on the other side of her to grab on to Tommy's, as well. Damn, the girl was hot—everything she was doing tonight was driving him out of his mind.

Instinctually, he suckled her taut nipple harder, pulling deep, until she moaned. Next to him, Tommy continued laving the opposite peak just as enthusiastically. She tugged on their stiff cocks, stroking, stroking, until finally he realized she was tugging him *by* his cock, up onto his knees. He let himself be guided and realized she was resituating Tommy by means of his dick, too.

She didn't hesitate to draw their hard shafts right up onto her tits, raking the heads across the peaks, where they'd both just dabbed more chocolate. She dragged their dicks playfully back and forth across the pointed nipples, using them to wipe the chocolate away. "Jesus Christ," Tommy murmured, and Braden moaned at the delicate yet arousing sensation of her beaded nipple against his erection.

Next thing he knew, she bent, lifting his cock to her mouth, and began to suck off the chocolate she'd just collected there. His stomach clenched watching her impassioned ministrations, slow and deliberate, as she gazed up at him. He ran a hand through her hair and rasped, "Baby, so hot," the only words he could get out at the moment.

Then she gave Tommy a turn, lowering her beautiful mouth over him and suckling him clean of the thick frosting, too. He gritted his teeth, moaning.

Back and forth she moved between the two stiff shafts, and whichever one she wasn't sucking she rubbed across her nipple again. Braden wasn't sure he'd ever experienced anything so erotic as her slow, purposeful actions, executed with pure confidence—by a woman in charge of her men.

The brownies were long since forgotten as she generously took turns pleasuring them, until Braden finally said, "Christ, baby, stop—I can't take it anymore." He knew he could have just come, but he didn't want to, not yet. And he might have been well practiced in holding back, but sometimes Laura excited him beyond his limits.

"Then what would *you* like to do now?" she asked him softly, peering up, eyes wide, lips beautifully swollen.

This was supposed to be all about her, but if she was asking . . .

He drew a fortifying breath. "I'd like to watch Tommy fuck you again. But I want to see better this time, want to see his cock slide into your cunt." Before, he'd wanted to watch her reaction, wanted to see the heat and pleasure dance across her features, but now his desires had turned to something more feral and animalistic.

In response, she drew him down for a long, impassioned tongue kiss that, under the circumstances, nearly buried him.

He'd imagined him and Tommy giving it to *her* all night, making sure *she* was relaxed and pleasured—he'd never once envisioned her being so very giving to *them*. And as she eagerly stood from the couch and walked over by the fireplace, its glow lighting her pale skin, and as she dropped to her hands and knees to arch her lovely round ass toward them, he was overwhelmed by her hot generosity.

He and Tommy joined her, Tommy positioning himself behind her, also on his knees, as Braden dropped down beside him. Braden skimmed his hand along her porcelain back, the gentle curves of her body, and let his touch dip down to graze her breast underneath. And as Tommy put on another condom, Braden found himself pushing two fingertips into her warm wetness to make her ready for his friend.

She let out a soft sigh as he began fucking her with his fingers. She moved against them, and he fell that much more in lust with her beautiful enthusiasm. "So incredible, baby—you're so, so good," he bent near her ear to whisper. "And I'm so ready to watch this sweet, hot pussy take Tommy's cock."

"Mmm, I *want* you to watch," she answered breathily, and her words tightened his groin. He'd known from the start that his predilection for watching excited her as much as him, but she'd never actually said it until now.

Braden used his hands to part her for Tommy's entry. He watched intently as his friend eased deep inside her.

"Oh God!" she cried out, and he watched the primal movements as the two came together, watched Tommy's hard shaft disappear smoothly inside her opening, then slide back out, again, again.

The view nearly paralyzed Braden. Or maybe it was the stark realization. She was giving him so much. All of her. She was doing everything he asked, following his every whim. She wanted to pleasure him just as much as he wanted to pleasure her, even when it meant taking another man into her body so that Braden could experience the intimacy of watching it, of watching her pussy accept a cock other than his. He heard his own thready sigh—and needed more of her.

He'd wanted to watch, yes—but now he needed to be part of the liaison, too. It wasn't jealousy—it was simply hot, wild desire and rampant need that grew from his gut.

"Lay her down," he told Tommy softly. "Stay inside her, but lay her down on her side."

Tommy anchored one arm around her waist, then maneuvered them to the carpet on their sides as Braden had instructed.

Oh God, she looked beautiful, that pale lace outlining her gorgeous breasts, the rest of her curvy and naked, her pussy bare but for the light swatch of hair above it. She looked beautiful moving against Tommy, meeting his slow thrusts, her face etched with passion. She looked beautiful meeting Braden's gaze through it all—no more shyness now from his sweet snowflake, nothing but unadulterated heat and fearlessness, and she was putting it all out there, for him.

He lay down, too, stretching out along the front of her body, lifting his hands to her face. "I want to kiss you, baby, while Tommy fucks you."

She sighed and reached out, her hand stroking his chest as he moved in close. Threading his fingers through her hair, he slanted his mouth across hers, pressed his tongue gently inside.

"Look at me, Laura," he whispered when the kiss ended. "Look at me while he moves in you. Look into my eyes."

She obeyed the command, meeting his gaze as she met Tommy's strokes from behind. He saw her absorb each one, heard her sigh and moan. He kissed her again, ran his hands over her breasts, down the curve of her slender waist, up her arms and back to her face—for more sweet, hot kisses.

She reached for him, too, her hand closing firm over his bare hip. She pulled him close, as close as Tommy lay in back. His cock nestled in her slit, and she lifted her leg over his thigh, pulling him against her tighter. "Unh . . ." he moaned at the sweet, slick contact.

She moved against him and found her rhythm, letting his erection slide through the front of her pussy and over her clit. He knew every motion she made brought pleasure now—arch frontward and she met his cock, arch backward and she took Tommy deeper. He'd never seen her so lost to pleasure. Her cries sounded as if they echoed from someplace deep inside. She ground against him, harder, harder, each gyration seeming to draw her deeper into ecstasy.

"So hot, baby, so sweet and hot for me." He murmured and cooed to her but could tell she hadn't the strength to respond, too caught up in the joys he and Tommy delivered.

Until finally she broke, crying, "God, now!" as she thrust against him hard, moved faster, rubbing herself against him in hot, wild undulations that were pushing *him* closer and closer to the edge.

"So beautiful when you come, honey," he breathed over her, kissing her, touching her face, then stroking his thumbs across her nipples.

"Christ," Tommy groaned, and Braden knew his buddy was climaxing, too, emptying into her with hard plunges that echoed all the way through Laura and onto him.

The jerking sensations were the last thing Braden felt before he exploded, bursting in three powerful shots across her belly as he yelled out.

They all lay still for a moment—a bit of shock, a bit of recovery— until Braden and Tommy both rolled away and Laura lay on her back before the fire. Braden's white semen had left her wet and glistening from navel to cunt, and the erotic sight stymied him for a long moment, until he followed the urge to reach down and rub it into the smooth, bare flesh of her pussy. Tommy helped, too, both of them massaging, sensually working the fluid into her soft skin. She rose up on her elbows to watch, parting her legs to let them dip deeper.

The three of them drifted off for a few minutes, lulled further by the warmth of the fireplace, but Braden didn't think much time had passed when Tommy quietly got up to dress. He returned a few moments later, kneeling to lower a kiss to Laura's cheek. His hand rested on her smooth stomach.

She opened her eyes to find him hovering above her. "This has been amazing, sweetheart," he told her. "Thank you for letting me know you this way."

She bit her lip, still wearing the new coquettish expression Braden had noticed just this evening. "The two of you turned me into a very bad girl tonight."

Tommy grinned. "You do *bad* very *good*," he said, then glanced at Braden only to add, "Later, dude."

"Later," Braden said, then watched Tommy head to the door, put on his coat, and exit out into the cold night. He couldn't help thinking his friend had left seeming more like his old happy-go-lucky self, his smooth-with-the-ladies self, and though he hadn't concocted this idea even remotely for Tommy's sake, he hoped maybe this was that change of pace Tommy had needed to get back in the game.

Propping up on one elbow, he shifted his gaze down to the woman beside him. She'd seemed so cool tonight—startlingly so—but now that they were alone, he had to ask. "You still okay, baby?"

Her expression looked no less than dreamy as she nodded. "That was . . . unbelievable. I've never . . . felt so full."

He couldn't hide his knowing grin. "I knew you'd love playing with two cocks."

"And in the end," she said, "when I looked at you, I swear your eyes fucked me as deeply as Tommy's cock. When I was between you both, on the floor, it was . . . *perfect.* Like being fucked from the front *and* the back, those two beautiful cocks rubbing *in* me, *on* me, exactly where I needed them."

He couldn't help chuckling inside—he'd never seen Laura quite so animated or unguarded when it came to talking about such extreme sex. He had a feeling she was still a little drunk—on the wine or on him and Tommy, he didn't know—but he enjoyed her exuberance.

"You, my naughty little girl, were astounding." He leaned in for a short, sweet kiss.

"I just sort of . . . let myself go, I guess," she admitted happily.

Peering down at her in the firelight, he couldn't help but think back—not only on this night, but on all the days and nights leading up to this. Normally, he would keep this inside, but he knew he was a little drunk, too—on the wine *and* the woman—and hell, if Laura could be this open, so could he. "Want to hear a secret, snowflake?" he whispered.

She nodded, smiling up at him through sleepy eyes.

"You excite me more than any woman ever has. And probably more than any woman ever will." What he'd wanted to give to her, *she'd* given to *him*.

Chapter Sixteen

The sun shone through the window the next morning, forcing Laura's eyes open. She lay in bed naked next to Braden, who was already awake and peering over at her, his dark gaze gorgeous as ever, his hair rumpled and jaw covered in stubble. It was the kind of vision that made a woman wonder if she was dreaming.

Which made her think back to . . . something else that had seemed so surreal it *had* to have been a dream. Last night.

"That didn't really happen, did it?"

Braden's eyes widened with worry. "Oh God. Please don't tell me you're going to freak out and go all regretful on me."

She drew in her breath and stared up at the ceiling fan whirring above them. It *had* really happened. She'd fucked two men's brains out last night. Wow.

But before she proceeded to freaking out, she made herself stop and think through the situation. It had happened, and there was no taking it back now. And she'd *let* it happen, had *wanted* it to happen. And it had been the most delicious experience of her life, no denying it. She didn't think she'd ever felt more powerful, more feminine, more desired, more like a woman of her own than she had last night.

She pulled her gaze back down to the handsome man at her side.

"A week ago, I couldn't have handled that, no way. But somehow, now, because of you—I can. And I doubt it's anything I'll ever do again, but I'm glad I did it, I'm glad you pushed me to. You made me feel things I never would have without you."

A slow smile unfurled across his face. "I'm so glad, baby," he said, pulling her into his arms. "Because I want you to feel *everything*. I want you to be a woman who isn't afraid to seek her pleasure."

Despite herself, a slightly sheepish giggle leaked free. "Believe it or not, before we met, I *did* have sex, you know. I'm not *totally* as backward and old-fashioned as I probably seemed to you when we met."

"A lot?" he asked, looking curious.

"Well . . . with guys I was in relationships with, yeah, sure."

"But was it . . . like it is with me?"

She looked into his eyes, trying to read the real question there, trying to interpret his heart. But she didn't want to make the mistake of seeing more than actually existed. "If you mean were there vibrators and third parties and shaving involved—you already know the answer to that."

"That's *not* what I mean. What I'm asking is—was it as . . . *intense* as it is between us?"

Intense. That was putting it mildly. She shook her head. Then looked up at him, half teasing, half not. "You may have ruined me for all other men."

There was no mistaking his arrogant expression. "That wasn't my goal, but . . ."

"But?"

He grinned hotly. "But I like thinking I've given you experiences no other guy ever has."

A short, wild laugh escaped her. "Congratulations, you have—about a hundred times over. Which reminds me, you don't have any other surprises up your sleeve for me, do you? Other kinky activities, lingerie, toys?"

Still smiling, he shook his head. "Afraid not. Unless you want me to come up with some."

"No shoes?" She raised her eyebrows. "Not that I want them, but you once insisted on my shoe size, so I expected you to haul them out at some point."

He gave his head a matter-of-fact tilt. "You said you'd throw them out into the snow. I didn't want to waste a perfectly good pair of shoes."

She cast a smirking grin in reply just as his cell phone buzzed— across the room on the desk next to his laptop, where she guessed he'd left it yesterday when he'd been catching up on work. She watched as he flipped back the covers and padded across the room to answer, so beautifully naked that her mouth began to water.

"Braden Stone," he said upon flipping the phone open.

She could tell it was a business call, not only from the discussion but from the very tone he took—commanding and strong and authoritative—and she understood *exactly* how he succeeded in toppling corporations. "That's not acceptable," he was saying, "and you're going to make it right. Today. Within the hour, in fact."

She bit her lip, realizing that watching him give someone hell on the phone while he was peering out the window stark naked was perhaps, oddly, one of the sexiest things she'd ever beheld. She was also forced to realize that what she'd shared with him last night had been no less than profound.

She'd been trying to convince herself all along that this was just sex, just fun, just physical pleasure. But the worlds he'd opened to her now, the generosity he'd shown her, the way he'd encouraged her and excited her and made her feel safe no matter what . . . She sighed, knowing beyond a doubt that she was changed forever because of him. A sobering realization.

"Get back to me," he said, "and meanwhile, I'll call Phillips and First National." He flipped the phone shut and turned to face her, his voice returning to "normal Braden." "I can't believe this, but it looks like *I'm* the one who has to work today. Some complications with a pending merger, and I need to make some calls."

Laura drew in her breath. "It's just as well. I need to write, too."

She didn't mention that after what they'd shared last night, he probably could have finally talked her into spending the day with him, in bed or out.

She didn't mention it because this was a sign—a sign that she simply couldn't let herself get any more attached to him than she already was.

She knew leaving would be difficult now, no two ways about it, but she couldn't wallow in that—she had to be a big girl. And working—as usual—would be a good distraction from all the emotions swirling inside her.

"I have time for a quick breakfast, though, if you do," he offered.

She couldn't help smiling. Distraction could start in a little while. For now, she was going to relish the opportunity to cling to him for just a little longer after last night's intimacies. She sat up and tossed the covers aside. "I think I could squeeze it in. Want to make it *together*?"

He flashed a devilish grin. "Baby, I *always* like making it with *you*."

Over an easy breakfast of scrambled eggs and English muffins, Laura felt his gaze.

"You look deep in thought."

She switched her glance from the snowscape out the window to the man across from her, caught. "Guess I'm still just stunned by what I did last night."

He lowered his chin, his expression chiding her.

"Don't worry—still no regrets. I'm just thinking how very un-*me* it was. For you, I guess it's no big deal, but for me, it's . . . big."

She couldn't help being surprised when Braden set down his fork and stood up, walking around behind her chair to bend down and slide his arms around her. He spoke softly in her ear. "What you did—what *we* did—is okay, honey. It didn't hurt anybody, it felt good, and hell, it might have even *helped* somebody."

Laura looked up at him, surprised.

"Last night might have gotten Tommy out of his funk over Marianne. He hadn't had sex with anyone since then."

"Oh," she heard herself murmur.

Wow, was it possible their ménage à trois had really held some humanitarian value? She was letting sarcasm taint her musings, but it *was* nice to think maybe it had helped Tommy overcome his heartbreak a little.

A few minutes later, they cleared the dishes together, then parted ways with a kiss, and Laura padded to the computer as she watched her lover disappear up the stairs to his own work.

As she pulled up her book's file, she found herself realizing that Braden's mere hug had assuaged her lingering concerns over her actions, somehow made it all better. But where would she be when his hugs were nowhere to be found?

The truth was—if she and Braden had had a future, she wasn't so sure she'd have any concerns over last night at all. He'd made their threesome seem *more* than okay—he'd made it seem truly *right*. So if anything was really bothering her, it was likely the fact that she'd had the most intimate, outrageous sex of her life with two guys she would soon never see again.

Be a big girl, she reminded herself. *People have affairs all the time and don't self-destruct over it.* People probably had ménages à trois all the time as *parts* of their affairs without falling apart. She didn't personally know any of the latter, but she was sure they existed. She'd allowed herself into this world of sexual decadence—now she had to come out the other side unscathed.

But she feared last night had bonded her with Braden in an almost frightening way. She'd had to trust him so much to let herself go to such extremes. She'd had to open herself so deeply, uncovering parts of herself *she'd* never even seen, let alone shared with anyone else. And when she took the time to remember and realize all she'd shared with him, she couldn't deny the ugly truth: leaving him behind was going to hurt even more than she'd ever imagined.

*   *   *

"I have a confession," Riley confided to Sloane as they sat in the Dorchesters' back porch swing watching the stars overhead.

"You're the killer?"

She gasped, and he squeezed her hand.

"I'm kidding, honey. I'm kidding." Then he added a knee pat for good measure. "Relax and tell me what's on your mind."

She let out a sigh, then admitted what she'd done. "I went to Aunt Mimsey this afternoon, and I told her to run. I told her she was a suspect and that, although the evidence is thin, the cops know." When the authorities had come to investigate Hawthorne's murder, everyone in the Dorchesters' household, plus Riley, had been thoroughly interviewed. It had come up that both Mr. Dorchester and Edna the housekeeper had heard Hawthorne yelling at Aunt Mimsey and later found out how angry she was about it. Riley had been forced to admit the same. And although no one claimed to have *liked* Hawthorne, Aunt Mimsey was the only person in the vicinity who'd been found to have a grudge against him.

Sloane didn't appear in the least surprised. "How did she respond?"

"Very calmly. She refused to be frightened, simply stating that she hadn't done anything wrong."

"Do you believe her?"

Riley hesitated. She could still scarcely comprehend that anyone could think Aunt Mimsey a killer.

Sloane lifted her chin with one bent finger. "You can tell me, Riley. It'll stay between us—I promise."

Riley's heart warmed. She'd been so afraid Sloane would want to hold Aunt Mimsey accountable. To him, she probably seemed like nothing more than a dotty old woman—he had no way of knowing how loving and kind she could be.

"I really can't fathom Aunt Mimsey hurting anyone," Riley said, "even if certain evidence does point in her direction. She can barely stand to kill an insect. In fact, she got into a horrible argument with Hawthorne last summer when he was using those spiked mole traps to stop an infestation, insisting that they were cruel and——" Riley stopped, cringed. "I just incriminated her more, didn't I?"

He shrugged. "I'll keep the mole trap incident to myself."

"Thank you," she said, reaching up to give him a short kiss—which quickly turned passionate and left Riley breathless when it was through.

"But between you and me," Sloane said, "I'm afraid the cops may start taking a closer look at Mimsey soon, out of desperation, if no other clues turn up."

"Then we have to find more clues," she replied vehemently.

"I was just thinking the same thing."

"I have an idea." She lifted one finger in the air and offered a short, triumphant nod.

Sloane looked doubtful and spoke dryly. "I can't wait to hear."

"We stay out here all night."

He blinked in the moonlight. "And hope the clue fairy drops a few on us?"

"I was thinking," she began, "about all the things we've found—the stolen items and Hawthorne's body. When were they put in the places we found them—around the yard and in the secret garden? It couldn't have been during the day—because we've been out quite frequently in the daytime hours, and besides, who would lurk around hiding things or dragging dead bodies away in the middle of the afternoon? Our culprit clearly moves at night—so we need to do a *stakeout*!"

"You watch too much TV."

She harrumphed. "You think it's a dumb idea."

"No, I actually think it's a *good* idea. But I still say you watch too much TV if you think using words like 'stakeout' is enough to make you a detective."

Riley rolled her eyes, insisting she *was* a good detective, whether or not she'd had adequate chance to prove it to him yet, and Sloane ignored her, instead explaining that a good all-night stakeout generally required night goggles and snacks. He went to retrieve both as Riley stayed to man their post, eyes peeled.

A few minutes later, she heard the rustle of shrubbery. She looked to the right, toward the noise, but could see nothing in the darkness as the row of bushes in question was shadowed by the toolshed. Still, she realized someone had just walked past the porch into the backyard—thankfully, without seeing her.

Which was when her leg tickled and she glanced down past her shorts to spot, by the light of the moon, a large brown spider meandering up the side of her calf. *Sweet mother of God!* It was all she could do not to go shrieking through the yard, but she somehow managed to stay still. She needed, at the very least, to bat the grotesque intruder away—yet she bit her lower lip, knowing if she moved, even to knock the spider off, she'd be heard. Because she couldn't see who traveled the backyard, but she could indeed hear soft movements as whoever it was padded over the flagstone path toward the gazebo—which meant even the slightest sound resulting from *her* movements could reveal her presence.

Riley's eyes dropped back to the spider. *Go away, go away,* she willed it.

The spider apparently failed to receive her telepathic message, since it continued taking horribly tingly steps up her leg.

She tried to calm down and think. *If you carefully flick the spider away, it can be done silently. You just can't freak out and go running around as if you're on fire.* The act would require precision and composure. But a sensible and mature person could do it.

Still aware of movements beyond the porch in the dark, Riley leaned over, took bold, careful aim, and gave the spider a silent but strong flick. It disappeared into the night—and she still wanted to jump around and scream, but she restrained herself and forced slow, even breaths as she worked to remain very still in the swing.

She smiled to herself then, realizing she'd just dealt quite efficiently with one of her greatest fears. *Take that, Sloane Bennett.* She'd become a respected detective yet!

Just then, flames lit the gazebo! *She* might not be on fire, but the gazebo *was*! She gasped, stood up, and spotted in the light of the blaze none other than Edna Barnes, the Dorchesters' housekeeper!

Just then, the back door opened and Sloane exited with a picnic basket in one hand and what looked like a pair of high-tech binoculars in the other. "What the hell?" he said, seeing the fire.

"It's Edna!" she replied.

Edna looked up, clearly startled by their voices, then fled.

"I'll put out the blaze—you follow her!" Sloane said, dashing for the hose.

This was it—Riley's big chance to apprehend a criminal! And it would be a lot more fun than fighting a fire, so she was glad Sloane had taken that task and left her this perfect opportunity for glory.

She sprinted through the deep backyard, unable to see much as she descended under the cover of the trees that dotted the area, their thick boughs blocking out the moonlight. But she heard Edna's footsteps as the older woman rushed ahead in the distance, so she ran blind, hoping her knowledge of the grounds would keep her from bashing head-on into a tree trunk.

It was just past the vegetable patch, before reaching the path that would lead to the secret garden, that Edna was caught in a shaft of light and Riley yelled, "Stop or I'll shoot!"

Edna looked back only long enough to say, "I might believe that, Riley Wainscott, if you owned a gun!" Then she ran on.

Drat, Edna knew her too well.

Which meant it was woman against woman, sprinter against sprinter. Riley barreled ahead, breathless, remembering with regret that she kept meaning to join the local health club. But through pure will, she gained on Edna, closing the distance between them step by grueling, panting step—until finally she tackled the housekeeper in the tall grass in a field beyond the garden. They went down with an *oomph*!

A long moment later, as the two women lay panting, recovering from the impact with the earth, she heard Sloane's voice. "Riley? Are you out here?" She looked up to see the beam of a flashlight coming toward them.

"Out past the vegetable garden!" she yelled, keeping a firm grip on Edna as she pushed to an upright position, still straddling the other woman's body. "I've got her! She won't get away from me now!"

It was only as Sloane approached, shining his light down to capture Riley and her prey, that she realized she was using every ounce of force in her body to keep an elderly woman with arthritic knees pinned to the ground.

"You're hurting me, Riley! I have a bad back."

Riley let out a disgusted breath, trying to cover her overzealous actions. "Well, that's what you get for killing poor Hawthorne."

Edna peered up at Sloane. "I don't know what you see in her. She's mean to old people."

"Riley," Sloane said in his typical dry tone, "I think if you get off her, we'll manage to detain her until the police arrive."

Riley let out a sigh. Oh well, at least she'd handled the spider situation like a pro.

That night, they made love in Braden's bed, looking toward the mirrored closet doors. Neither of them *called* it making love, but to Laura, that's how it felt. In the tender moments, definitely—but even in the rougher ones, too.

He lay behind her, thrusting deeply into her, each stroke delivering a barrage of pleasure. As they peered into the reflecting glass, he said, "Keep watching us, baby." She obeyed.

She saw their bodies undulating together, witnessed his face wrenching in sweet, hot agony, and saw her own, as well. When he lifted one of her legs with his hand, parting her thighs, she saw his cock sliding smoothly into her. "Watch me fuck you. Watch how easily you take me inside."

She was shocked at how beautiful she thought herself that way, surprised at how differently Braden had made her view sex. It occurred to her that maybe—despite having had sex with other guys, even guys she'd sincerely cared for—she'd never really, *truly* been intimate with anyone before Braden.

She'd loved most of all watching Braden's face when he came—she'd never been so aware of taking a man to another plane, even if for just a few short moments.

Afterward, they lay talking, letting the ceiling fan cool their bodies after sex that had grown sweaty.

"So," he said, "day after tomorrow?"

She sighed. She'd told him over breakfast that was when her retreat would end, when she was flying home. When she'd arrived here, she'd had no idea her *writer's* retreat would turn into a *sexual* retreat, as well. Nodding against her pillow, she answered. "Yeah."

He stayed silent for a moment, then softly met her gaze. "I'm gonna miss you, snowflake."

Temptation filtered through her, the temptation to say what she was thinking. *Maybe I could just stay here with you forever.*

But then she remembered that he didn't even live there—his real life, real world, was in L.A. And *her* real world was in Seattle. Just like Riley and Sloane's secret garden, this was merely an escape, and this affair would be only a brief albeit powerful interlude in her real life. So instead, she said, "I'm going to miss you, too. This has been a . . . pretty amazing time for me."

"Not just for you, snowflake," he said quietly, and her heart soared.

She smiled over at him, reached out and found his hand. God, she was going to miss just being close to him, just being able to look into his dark eyes or touch him whenever she felt the urge.

He rose on one elbow next to her. "Let me steal you away for awhile tomorrow—just half a day. For some skiing and lunch. Then you can write all afternoon. Besides, I hear all work and no play makes Laura a dull girl." He grinned. "What do you say?"

"I say if I was ever a dull girl, it was before I got *here*. But that aside, sounds like an offer I can't refuse."

"Good. Otherwise, I'd have to strap you into some concrete snowshoes and make you sleep with the fishes." His brows narrowed slightly, as if thinking it through. "After the spring thaw, that is," he added with a soft, sexy laugh.

Ah, how she wished they would both still be here after the spring thaw. But she had two more nights in his arms, and a day of fun with him tomorrow, so she reminded herself again to be a big girl, act like a grown-up, and enjoy these last couple of days with him for all they were worth.

"You're doing great, snowflake."

The ski lift gradually took them skyward up the mountain, and Laura smiled over at Braden, replying with a kiss. She thought she'd never shared a more romantic moment with a guy—with pristine snow falling all around them, the solitude of a lift ride made her feel much more as if they were alone than at a busy ski resort.

They'd started out early, Braden helping her put together a suitable winter ensemble from his large foyer closet, promising—when she asked—that the ladies' skiwear belonged to his mom and other family members who'd left it behind for return visits. His mother's skis had been stored there, as well, and he'd assured Laura it was okay to borrow them. "Especially since I bought 'em for her," he'd added with a wink. Upon taking to the Vail slopes, they'd stayed on only the easier blue and green runs, and so far, she hadn't yet fallen.

"I'm glad I came skiing at least once before heading home," she said. "Despite wanting to get my book done, this is nice."

He cast a soft grin. "Are you looking forward to that? Heading home?"

She answered honestly. "In some ways yes, in others no. It'll be good to see Monica, and my mom. But I'm going to miss *you* . . . *us.*"

He leaned in for another soft kiss, his tongue pressing lightly between her parted lips, and even now, a mere kiss from the man made her pussy tingle.

"But all good things must come to an end, right?" he said. He seemed lighter about her departure than he had last night in bed—and she supposed that sealed her fate, if there was ever any doubt.

She'd found herself thinking about Braden's mom—given that she wore the woman's parka and was using her skis. When Tommy had casually brought up Braden's family over dinner the other night, Braden had quickly changed the subject, so she and Braden had never discussed them. "Do *you* see *your* family a lot? Do they live in L.A.?"

He shrugged, looking ahead of them at the snow-covered pines dotting the rocky outcrop the lift currently traversed. "I see my mom every couple of weeks, but my dad . . . eh, not often."

"Why not?" she asked, but his expression had grown a bit distant, that quickly, so she added, "I mean, if you don't mind telling me."

"They divorced when I was eleven and I never really forgave my dad. He was a drinker, and a cheater. They think I don't know that, but I do."

Laura's heart contracted to suddenly envision her strong, commanding Braden as a little boy, having his heart broken by his father's hurtfulness. She let out a sigh, not sure what to say. "Wow. I'm sorry. My dad died when I was a teenager—a heart attack—but I'm blessed that my parents had a happy marriage."

Braden's gaze shifted briefly back to hers, but he still spoke matter-of-factly. "I didn't know many people with happy marriages growing up. Still don't, I guess. There have been a lot of divorces in my family."

"Monica's mom and dad are together and seem happy."

He leaned his head back, offering a wry grin. "The white sheep of the family." But at least his humor seemed restored now.

"So I guess that's why you're a thirty-five-year-old bachelor," she said, gently teasing but also serious.

"Probably so. And why I'll be a *forty*-five year old bachelor, and eventually a *fifty*-five year old bachelor . . ." His voice trailed off into soft laughter, which she joined in, but part of her felt sad. She knew some people never married or found a lifemate and still lived satisfying lives, and if anyone was capable of that, she suspected it was Braden. Yet it still sounded lonely to her, especially when she thought of growing old.

"You must like being single a lot if you plan to stay that way forever," she offered cautiously.

But he only shrugged in his easy-going, man-of-the-world way. "It's what I'm used to, and it has a lot of perks. I don't have to be responsible to anyone else. I don't have to worry about the complexities of marriage and family. And I can sleep with whoever I want, *when*ever I want." Seeming completely back to his normal self, he gave his head a rakish tilt as he peered into her eyes. "Think about it, snowflake—if I were the marrying kind, I'd *already* be married, and you and I never would have happened."

A sobering thought that tightened Laura's stomach.

"You wouldn't know what it's like to be fucked in the window where anyone can see you," he went on, the timbre of his voice dropping to a sultry, seductive level. "You wouldn't know what it's like to be with two men at once. Hell, you still wouldn't even have played with a vibrator."

She let out her breath, a bit stunned. "God, you're right." It seemed unthinkable now, like the experiences of the past week had already woven themselves so deeply into her existence that it felt as if they'd been part of the fabric of her life for much longer. And she realized again that it had begun to seem normal, all the wild things they'd done—but only with Braden. She couldn't imagine it feeling normal, or right, with anyone else.

As the unloading ramp came into sight and she lifted the tips of her skis, ready to *whoosh* down, it struck her that she must have had all these darker desires floating around somewhere inside her all along—and had simply never known it until Braden had helped her find them.

Standing to ski away from the lift, she couldn't help regretting that the ride was over.

By the time Laura sat down to write late that afternoon, she found herself feeling a bit melancholy, yet also insightful—and for the first time, she allowed herself the freedom to be utterly pleased, maybe even *thrilled*, that Braden had opened up her deeper, darker, more adventurous sexual self.

If she'd suffered any lingering hopes that he would suddenly announce his unending love for her, however, their conversation earlier had squelched it. She had a gnawing suspicion that *she* had fallen in love with *him*, but she somehow knew now that she could handle parting ways with him like the adult she kept reminding herself she was. What they'd shared had been amazing, mind-boggling, and life-altering—but she understood fully after today that he wasn't the type of man who got attached to women. And she harbored no delusions that a week of hot, naughty sex was going to change that.

And it was okay. Life would go on. She would be fine.

And so would Aunt Mimsey. And so would Riley. Riley's current story was beginning to come to a close, and Laura felt as if Riley had learned as much about *her*self in this book as Laura had gleaned about her own personality while writing it.

As Laura typed, a colossal secret made its way onto the computer screen—something even *she* hadn't known until she'd realized Edna was the criminal. Mimsey explained to Riley that many years earlier, when she was young, she and Edna had been friends—but then, in high school, Mimsey had aggressively stolen Edna's boyfriend! Not only that, he'd turned out to be Mimsey's lifelong love and now-departed husband, Walter—Riley's beloved uncle!

Edna, it seemed, had held a grudge their whole lives, and all the crimes she'd committed were poorly-thought-out attempts to frame Mimsey. As for Hawthorne, it turned out Edna and he had indulged in a wild affair that had ended badly, so knocking off the gardener had seemed a convenient way for Edna to turn much greater suspicion toward Mimsey when her other feeble tries had failed.

Despite the shock of finding out that Edna was apparently crazy, Riley's emotions instead focused on what she'd learned about her aunt.

Riley sat across from Aunt Mimsey at the table on the back porch, utterly stunned. Sweet, docile Aunt Mimsey had been a boyfriend-stealer in high school? It seemed impossible.

Yet, on the other hand, she supposed it had been meant to be. She'd never known two people more dear to each other than Mimsey and Walter had been before his death. So maybe, she thought, even if a relationship seemed a bit illicit in the beginning, it could be worthwhile and have a meaningful ending. Maybe life was not as cut and dried, as black and white, as Riley had always thought.

"Are you okay?" Aunt Mimsey asked, setting down her teacup to take Riley's hand.

Riley nodded, still a bit numb. "Just hard to picture you as a girl who would go after a friend's guy. Not that I love you any less for it," she was quick to say. "I'm just ... trying to wrap my mind around it."

"Think of it like this," her aunt said. "The way you feel about your Sloane, no matter how you deny it—that's how I felt about my Walter, even then. I didn't want to be that kind of girl, but it was bigger than the both of us."

Riley nodded somberly, even if she still wasn't comfortable admitting her affection for Sloane. "I understand. I guess I'm just ... starting to realize there are sides of you I don't know."

Aunt Mimsey cast a knowing, assured smile. "Well, of course there are, dear. *Everyone* has secrets. *Everyone* has desires they can't push down. We may not talk about them, but they exist quietly, in the background, and life goes on."

That evening, Laura and Braden prepared an easy meal of burgers and fries, tired after skiing. The mood was relaxed as they sat down at the table, but Laura couldn't help remembering she was leaving in the morning. Somehow her departure had snuck up fast.

"What time is your flight?"

She swirled a fry in ketchup. "Eleven fifteen."

"Eagle's a small airport. If you get there an hour early, you'll be fine. I'll drive you down."

She drew in her breath at the offer, at the chance to spend one more little chunk of time with him. But then she imagined the anguish of kisses in the airport, the stretching-out of it, the painful finality of it all. She'd do better if she left on her own—and besides, it was more practical. "No," she said, explaining, "I have to return the rental or you'll be stuck with two."

"I don't mind. I could return your car for you and get Tommy to pick me up."

But she held firm. "It's not necessary," she said, peering down at her plate, then taking a big bite of her hamburger to distract her from the slight awkwardness of the refusal.

He sounded reluctant but said, "Okay, if you're sure."

She tried to speak lightly. "When will *you* head out?"

He sighed, leaned back in his chair. "I think I'll hang out a few days more, unwind, watch the snow, veg a little." Then he grinned, teasing her. "You've worn me out."

She flashed a sexy smile, thinking she hoped to wear him out again, at least one more time, before the sun rose.

"So how's the book? Did I ruin your writer's retreat too badly?" He looked as if he might have mixed emotions on it—she suspected he hoped it was going well but would also take some arrogant pride in learning she'd not managed to accomplish much amid all their naughty play.

"I'll have you know it's almost finished, and I'm very pleased with it. I have to write the last chapter after I get home, but it won't take long now, and I'm actually going to make my deadline." A giddy sort of giggle escaped her. "I've never written a book so fast. And who'd have thought I could do it in the middle of a wild, crazy sextravaganza."

Braden let out a rich laugh and said, "I must be good for your creativity."

And she thought, *You have no idea, baby.*

After dinner, she announced she was going to pack. She grabbed the CD on which she'd saved her book file, then scurried up the stairs before she started looking too depressed.

She really *was* going to be okay without him, but saying good-bye would be torturous. Each piece of clothing she wadded into her suitcase, each little item, even hair clips and dirty socks, drove it home more. Worst were the items Braden had given her—the sheer black kimono, the champagne-colored ensemble, the velvet corset. In a way, it seemed weird to take them—she couldn't imagine ever wearing them for another guy. Yet it would feel just as odd to leave them behind—they were gifts from the man she'd come to care for, and even if they sat in her lingerie drawer forever, when she saw them they would bring her back here in her mind, back to the most glorious days of her life.

She didn't pack the red bra-and-panties set from Monica, though—the set she'd worn for him on the webcam back when he was just words on a screen. She wanted to look pretty and sexy for him on this, their last night together. After a quick shower, she donned the red lace, then put her standard cotton cami and joggers on over them, thinking she'd surprise him a little later.

Yet when she headed back downstairs, *she* was the one who got a hot surprise.

Braden lay on a thin quilt stretched out next to the star-filled window, beautifully naked, his majestic cock erect and ready for her. Two full wineglasses rested nearby, and an array of candles dotted the floor around him, like more twinkling stars in the low-lit room.

But her eyes stayed on her gorgeous man, his darkened eyes, and his commanding expression. He didn't smile. "Take your clothes off, snowflake."

Chapter Seventeen

Heat rose to Laura's cheeks, as well as other key parts of her body. Stopping in place across the room from him, she slowly pulled the drawstring on her pants, then wiggled her hips a little to help them fall. They dropped gently over her hips to her ankles, allowing her to step free of them. She could have sworn she saw Braden's eyes twinkle with lust at the sight of her tiny red thong panties. "Nice, baby," he murmured deeply, and the very sound of his voice made her pussy swell within the tight lace.

Next she lifted her hand to lower one shoulder strap of her cami, then the other. Where the white cotton remained stretched across her chest, she reached up both hands to slowly peel it down. It required a push and more hip-wiggling to help it the rest of the way before she finally stood before him in her red lace bra and undies. As always with Braden, she enjoyed being the object of his possessive gaze.

"Come to me, honey," he said, and she padded across the carpet to where he stretched out, well-muscled and bare. She knelt next to him on the blanket, and he handed her a glass of white wine, taking up the other himself.

"To keeping the lights on," he said, lifting his glass in a toast, "so I can see every beautiful inch of you."

She released a small, thoughtful smile and raised her *own* glass. "To my sexy voyeur, who made *me* see so many new things."

They sipped their wine, but quickly set the glasses aside. Laura found it difficult to sit that close to his full-on erection without touching it. So as soon as her hands were free, she reached out to stroke him, wrapping her fist around his length, loving the silk-over-steel feel of him, loving the way she made him moan. She bit her lip, studying his perfect cock, memorizing every long, lovely inch, watching the pre-come welled at the tip—and only eventually remembering to be surprised that scrutinizing him so boldly no longer made her feel sheepish.

Braden pulled in his breath as she squeezed and caressed him, and he couldn't resist sliding his palm from her hip up to the curve of her breast. They looked beautiful tonight, captured in snug red lace, her cleavage deep and round. Damn, he was going to miss this heat, this connection he shared with her. He'd had more than his fair share of hot women and exciting affairs, but he'd never felt such trust from a woman—and he couldn't help thinking Laura was the first girl he'd ever truly and wholly seduced in the purest sense of the word.

Her small hand pumped his dick with slow, aching precision, the sensation sweet enough that a selfish man would have been content to lay back and let her work him over that way all night long. But this was his last night with Laura, a fact he was all too painfully aware of, so he felt the urge to take control, to make sure he got all of her he could before they were done here.

Sitting up, he slipped his thumbs into the red straps of her bra and eased them off her shoulders. His groin tightened further at the sight of the lace falling just past her lush pink nipples, hard and pointed. The bra still cupped the bottoms of her breasts, underlining them with lace. He simply beheld them for a moment, then stroked his thumbs across the pert peaks. She drew in her breath a soft, scintillating sound— and he found himself tweaking the pink tips, twirling the taut buds between his fingertips until her breath came harder, harder.

He leaned in to kiss her and the sensation ran all through him, heightening his reaction to her continued strokes between his legs.

"I love when you touch me," she said on a ragged whisper.

The words ignited a fresh blaze deep inside him. "I love to hear you say that. When we first met, you never would've said something like that."

Her eyes appeared glazed, and her chest heaved with labored breathing. "You changed me."

He met her gaze—and had to have more of her.

Capturing her wrists in his hands, he pushed her to her back on the quilt, shifting to hover over her, let his body graze the slopes of hers. His erection skimmed her soft belly. "I want you so damn much," he ground out through clenched teeth before he pressed his mouth hungrily back to hers. Her fingers wound through his hair and her thighs parted beneath him so that he could nestle his hard length where she was the softest.

Breaking the kiss, he dropped his mouth to her breasts, suckling first one then the other, his cock going harder every time she moaned. He held the outer curves of her breasts with both hands as he switched back and forth between them, sucking soft and sweet, using his tongue to lick, then pulling harder, wanting to take them deep, wanting to feel her nipples elongate even farther between his lips. She whimpered beneath him now, lifting her crotch against him, and he loved making her so wild, taking away her control. That's what he'd yearned for from the beginning—to make Laura drop that shy little shield of protection, to take away all her inhibitions. And now he had it, sweet Laura writhing and trembling beneath him, responding to his every touch.

"I need to taste your pussy," he rasped over her, then kissed his way down her smooth stomach, listening to her breath catch with each inch he descended.

"Yes," she breathed before he was even there. "Yes, baby, please."

A bolt of masculine satisfaction shot through him, spreading outward when he lowered a kiss to the front of her pretty panties. Her breath still came heavy as he hooked his thumbs through the elastic at both hips and proceeded to roll them slowly down. His blood ran hotter the second his eyes fell on that lovely pussy she'd bared just for him.

Tossing the thong quickly aside, he parted her legs again, wide, and knelt to kiss her moist pink folds. She sighed, and he used both thumbs to play with the delicate creases of warm flesh as he lowered another kiss to her clit, swollen and damp. This time she moaned.

He kissed the hot nub again with both tongue and lips as she lifted against his mouth in a slow, sensual rhythm that drove him wild. Dropping lower, he licked deeply into her, drinking of her, wanting to take her juices inside him, wanting to feel her welcoming wetness in his mouth, *on* his mouth, on his face. If ever there was a place a man wanted to drown . . .

God, he needed still more of her, needed to have her in other ways. He always tried to be a generous lover, with Laura especially—giving her pleasure brought *him* more pleasure than he could easily understand—but at the moment, he needed to take, just a little. His cock ached for her.

Rising up over her again, peering down into her sweet, impassioned eyes, he said, "I need to fuck you, baby."

She sighed hotly in reply and the sweet desire on her face drew him in, made him focus on her perfect mouth, made him think of how incredible she looked sucking him. He ran the tip of his index finger in a circle around the edge of her parted lips. "I need to fuck you . . . *here*," he whispered, then let his finger dip inside. She sucked it wetly as he pulled it back out, then shifted upward so that his knees rested on either side of her head, and used one hand to slowly ease the tip of his shaft between her lips.

She opened eagerly, moaning her pleasure. God, she was beautiful taking his cock into that pretty mouth, letting him move in and out, in and out—so good, so very good. When she reached up to cup his balls, he groaned and slid in a little deeper.

But he forced himself to slowly extract his wet length from those sweet, moist lips, backing down her body just enough that it came to rest between her supple breasts. "And I need to fuck you *here*," he breathed, using his hands to press the two soft mounds around his erection as he slipped wetly back and forth in the valley between.

"Oh . . ." she cooed, hot and aroused, and he loved that she enjoyed this as much as he did. Her eyes fell shut in sheer delight, and he fucked her slow and deep that way, the lace of the bra underneath abrading his skin lightly, teasing his balls.

Finally, he released her breasts and headed south once more until he knelt between her legs, nudging his shaft at her beautifully parted cunt. "And I need to fuck you *here*," he told her, then drove into her warm, tight passageway, amazed at how easily her body accepted him now.

She sobbed heatedly, lifting to take him deeper, and as he drove farther into the welcoming tunnel, she let out a severely pleasured moan. "Love when you're inside me, Braden. Love how big you are in me."

He still knelt, upright, with her thighs hugging his hips. He braced his hands on her ass and pulled her toward him, again, again, listening to her hot little cries at each deep thrust. "Do you want to ride me, my naughty little girl?"

"Mmm," she purred, looking lost in the heady passion. "Yes, baby—yes."

Bending over her, he slid his arms up the length of her back and said, "Wrap around me." She did so, with both arms and legs, allowing him to haul her up into his lap without disconnecting their bodies.

"Oh!" she screeched at the deeper impact of sitting up on his cock. He watched as she bit her lip and absorbed the hot pleasure the position provided.

"I love that you feel it deeper this way," he told her. And he also loved fucking her with their faces so close, her nipples grazing his chest, their limbs entwined. He loved everything about the woman, and he wanted this hot little ride to take her to heaven.

Laura began to move on him, her body responding instinctively. His erection felt like it stretched forever inside her, like it must be expanding the depths of her pussy with every thrust. She gripped his strong shoulders and started to grind against him, her clit rubbing against the flesh above his shaft.

He leaned back against the window, seeming to relax a bit as she recaptured control. They kissed, their tongues touching, lips lingering, and Braden's sure hands caressed her breasts above the bra.

"Suck them," she said, looking boldly into his eyes.

"Ah, damn," he groaned, his voice brimming with the usual heat, and when he bent to take one of her needy nipples into his mouth, it pushed her closer toward the orgasm building inside her.

"Oh God, baby, yeah," she murmured amid the swallowing pleasure.

She rode him hard, concentrating on his firm cock inside her and the way her clit brushed against him with every undulation of her hips; concentrating on the hot pull of his mouth at her breast, on the sound of her breathing. He lifted his head and she looked into his dark eyes, took in his handsome face, and she saw in the periphery the multitude of stars surrounding him, seeming close enough to touch even though they were millions of miles away.

"I'm gonna make you come now," he promised, and she wondered how he could possibly say such a thing with so much confidence, yet at the same time, she totally believed him.

With his hands on her bottom, he pressed the tip of one finger to the fissure of her ass—and sent her exploding into space. The pleasure swept through her from head to toe, the mind-blowing orgasm nearly swallowing her, somehow seeming all the more engulfing for the view of the cosmos out the window at his back.

When the intense, jolting sensations finally passed, she found herself spent, leaning to rest her forehead on his shoulder.

She could almost feel his grin when he said, "Think you'll recover?"

"I don't know," she said, breathless. "Sometimes, with you, the way I come . . . it's just so powerful. You make me crazed." She lifted her head to see his smile unfurl farther.

"So I noticed. Anything I can do to make you feel better?"

She tilted her head. "Um . . . a backrub, maybe?"

He laughed. "Are you kidding?"

She shook her head. "If you want me to be able to go on, you're gonna have to relax me a little, restore my energy."

He gave his head a chiding tilt. "Be it known, little miss snowflake, that I don't usually stop mid-fuck to give a backrub." Yet even as he said it, he was lifting her off him, turning her over on the quilt, then straddling her hips to begin slowly massaging her shoulders.

"Then I must be special."

He dropped a quick kiss between her shoulder blades and said near her ear, "Yes, you must be. How's that feel?"

"Mmm," she sighed. "Nice."

"I aim to please."

"You aim quite well—especially with that big tool of yours."

The remark earned a laugh from him as he continued with the soothing massage. "Who'd have thought you'd turn out to be such a bad girl?"

"You, apparently," she reminded him. "You worked awfully hard to make me into one."

He gently unhooked her bra to continue the rub but before long reached around beneath her, seeking her breasts. She found herself lifting, to give him access, moaning as his hands closed back over the soft flesh, catching the nipples gently between his fingers. "You're right, I did. And now that you're such a naughty girl, I'm going to have to spank you."

She looked over her shoulder, bit her lip. His cock rested in the valley of her ass. "You said we'd get to that, but I'd forgotten about it."

His voice dropped to a low whisper. "You need to be punished."

The truth was, Laura had no idea what the fuss was about spankings, but she figured if anyone could show her, it was Braden. "Discipline me," she said.

As Braden eased off her, she found herself spreading her legs so he could kneel between, bending over her. The tip of his hard shaft still jutted slightly into her ass, making her feel the vague desire to shift, so it would fall in the middle. She did, and they both sighed—just before the flat of his hand struck her rear.

"Oh!" she cried, flinching.

She'd barely recovered when he slapped his palm down again.

This time, she held in her shriek, but emitted more of a grunt, gritting her teeth.

By the time the third strike came, she realized that the little shock it sent through her already aroused body heightened the sensation—all over.

And as his spanking continued, as he told her again what a naughty, naughty girl she'd been, the blows began to reverberate through her ass down into her pussy, making it tingle hotly and burn for more stimulation. She realized her cries now sounded a lot more like moans, and that she yearned to be fucked again. She found herself lifting her ass in the air, higher, higher, seeking more of his hot spanking, as he said, "Have you been sufficiently punished yet? Or do you need more?"

"I—I'm not sure." She peeked over her shoulder again. "But I definitely need more of *something*."

His wicked grin said he could read her state of excitement loud and clear. Slowly, he hooked one arm around her waist, warm and firm, and leaned over her back, pressing his chest there, to whisper slowly, deeply in her ear, all seriousness. "Is there anything else I can do for you, baby? Anything we haven't done, haven't tried—any games we haven't played that you want to play? Any pleasure I can bring you that I haven't brought you already?"

His hard length had slid fully into the crease of her ass again, and she found herself desiring more sensation there, and peeking numbly over her shoulder at his face, then lower, but not saying anything.

He rubbed gently against her, and she moaned.

The next time she looked back at him, his eyes twinkled darkly. "You want me to fuck your tight little ass." A statement, not a question.

She shivered and replied honestly. "Actually, I'm afraid of it. Afraid it will hurt and ruin the night."

His face was only an inch from hers when he said, "I would never let that happen." And without waiting for her to answer, he pulled her up with that anchoring arm onto her hands and knees and dipped two fingers from his free hand into the damp flesh between her thighs. "Oh God," she said at the unexpected touch, surprised when he pushed them deep, all the way inside her pussy. She responded, unable not to, thrusting back against them, taking them to the hilt. She let out hot breaths with each stroke, aware she could hear them moving in her wetness.

Which is when he pulled them out.

She tossed a look over her shoulder, ready to protest—when he slid one wet finger smoothly into her asshole.

"Oh!" she cried out, both startled and weakened. She'd never felt anything like it. New, fresh, hot sensation in an entirely different opening.

Just like with her pussy, he began sliding his finger in and out—and she followed her instincts, starting to move gingerly against it, meeting the soft drives. Her face flushed with heat as she tried to get used to this new sort of fucking, and her arms began to feel weak. But her body continued moving, taking, accepting, wanting more.

"How's that, baby?" he asked. "Feel good?"

She couldn't deny it—although an "mmm" was the only answer she could manage.

"That's right," he said softly. "Fuck my fingers. Fuck my fingers with your sweet little ass."

She was about to think, *Fingers? As in more than one?* when she felt a second enter. "Oh God, Braden."

"Good?"

"Yeah," she breathed.

Soon, he thrust harder, rougher, and she heard her hot whimpers but was barely aware of making the sounds. She was losing herself in the odd sensation, feeling her body filling with heat, and aware she wanted more.

"You want my cock there, baby?" he leaned near her ear to ask.

She knew it was a rhetorical question, knew he was planning to give it to her whether or not she was brave enough to ask for it. But a sense of self-preservation made her utter one word amid her intense arousal. "Scared."

He slowed the drives of his fingers and spoke soothingly. "Nothing to fear, honey, I promise. Just relax. And enjoy. Think about how good your ass feels right now. Think about how you want more, how you want my cock deep inside you there." Then his voice dropped to a sultry whisper. "I have to do it, Laura. I have to be the man who takes that last little shred of virginity from you. You know that, don't you?"

She understood what he was saying—it only made sense. If she wanted it, he was the right man to give it to her. And it had to be now, tonight. And if she got this close to it without experiencing it, she would always regret it, always wonder how it would have felt. "Yes," she finally said, her voice small but sure.

He moaned at her acquiescence, then changed how he used his fingers. Her anal opening was wet with her own juices now, and he began turning his fingers in circular motions, as if trying to widen her, make her even more ready. "God . . . oh God," she heard herself moan.

When his fingers left her, she took a deep breath.

"Relax for me, baby," he said. "Relax and want me."

Yes, I do. So much. She was too drained and excited to say it, but she wanted to give him that last piece of her virginity now more than she wanted to breathe.

The tip of his cock felt hard yet moist against her, and she knew a deep, primal yearning to accept it there, in that impossibly tiny opening. He pushed, and she thought the head began to enter. She heard an "unh" escape her.

Behind her, his breath grew heavy, his hands tightening on her waist.

She bit her lower lip as he delivered another gentle thrust, then began to rock rhythmically against her. She rocked back, trying to meet him, take him, the sensitive fissure of her anus hungry for him.

The opening stretched, and a soft burst of pain came with it. She cried out but then realized just as quickly that he'd found entry and his cock was sliding, sliding, slowly into her ass.

"Oh my God," she heard herself whisper as the most bizarre sense of fullness she'd ever experienced assaulted her. It was as if he'd found a new part of her body that she'd never known existed.

"So tight," he said, but his voice sounded weak now, too, as weak as she felt. "And you're so amazing, baby. So fucking amazing."

"I can't believe . . . you're in me there."

His hands massaged her hips and the cheeks of her ass. "I am, honey. Oh God, I am."

And then he began to move—slow, small, light thrusts clearly designed not to hurt her. She met them, arching higher, eyes shut, lost in an entirely new world of strange, heady pleasure that stretched through every inch of her body from head to toe, all-consuming.

And she thought she'd absorbed just about as much sensation as she could when something cool pressed between her thighs in front, and as it began to buzz she realized it was the vibrator. She hadn't even seen it on the quilt with them in the dim lighting, but apparently Braden had thought they might want it and was now reaching around to glide the toy cock back and forth in her slit while he fucked her ass.

The arc of pleasure was immediate—the orgasm coming mere seconds later, bursting through her with all the power of an exploding star. "Oh God! Oh God! Oh God!" She heard herself practically howling with the intensity of it, felt almost disconnected from her body. At some point, she realized she was no longer supporting herself on her hands but had collapsed, slumping down in front, resting her head on the quilt.

Behind her, Braden still fucked her ass, but every tight stroke came with a hot, masculine moan—until he said, "I'm gonna come in your ass, honey," and then let out an enormous groan as he plunged deeper, harder, again, again, then crumpled atop her, spent.

After falling asleep on the quilt for a while, Laura felt Braden nudge her awake, take her hand, and lead her to the shower. They cleaned up, then fell naked into bed together, where they wordlessly made love again, Laura on top for a while, then Braden, lifting her ankles to his shoulders as he drove relentlessly into her welcoming cunt.

Three more times through the night they fucked, until morning came and they realized they'd barely slept. "You'll sleep on the plane," he said gently, kissing her forehead.

After a quick breakfast of bagels and coffee, they returned upstairs so Laura could dress and finish packing. Braden came up behind her to tuck the penis-shaped vibrator into her suitcase. She looked up at him, surprised. "I'm supposed to send this through the X-ray machine at the airport?" It was a carry-on.

He grinned, winked. "I'm sure it's not the first one they've ever seen. Be bold, snowflake." And that easily, she decided she would be. It was a vibrator, not a machete—she could travel with it through the airport if she damn well pleased. "And I want you to use it," he said, leaning close, "and think of me."

"I will," she said on a whisper, without hesitation.

"Good. That'll give me some nice fantasies."

They stood in the bedroom, staring into each other's eyes, and Laura felt like there was so much more to say—but she had no idea what.

Finally, she spoke softly. "Last night was . . . well, there are no words. I'm glad you took that last little piece of me."

"I'm glad you gave it to me."

She sighed, said, "Well . . . I should go," and reached to zip her bag.

But he grabbed on to her wrist so that she looked up at him. "Not just last night—this whole time, Laura, has been . . . unforgettable."

She nodded, and knew she needed to leave quickly before she burst into tears and asked him to love her forever and then had her heart smashed to bits when he looked horrified. "I should go," she said again.

Braden wheeled her suitcase to the stairs, then carried it down to the foyer. He wore flannel pants, thick socks, and a gray thermal pullover but said, "I'll take this out for you."

She was putting on her coat and looked up to reply. "No, I can get it. You don't even have shoes on." When he started to protest, she lightened the mood. "I have to get used to toting around my vibrator without you, don't I?"

The corners of his mouth quirked up slightly, his eyes smiling. "Yeah," he said softly, "I guess you do."

They stepped out onto the porch and he lifted his hands to her face. She looked up at him as the cold air chilled her—and fell in love all over again with his deep, expressive eyes and the dark stubble on his cheeks. He kissed her, slow, soft, letting his mouth linger on hers. It sent skitters of pleasure all through her—as much as the first kiss from him had nearly a week ago.

"Bye, snowflake."

"Bye," she said and hoped to hell he couldn't tell she was close to tears. She quickly wheeled her bag down the walk over a covering of fresh-fallen snow and to the back of her rented SUV.

"Drive safe," he called as she opened the door to climb inside.

She only waved. Shut the door. Started the engine. And backed up the long driveway, aware that he still stood on the porch watching her go.

And as she backed out onto the road and put the car in drive, a tear descended her cheek as the stark truth hit her.

It was over. Just like that. No more kisses. No more sex. No more cuddling or moaning, or breakfast with him, or dinner. No more snowflake.

Chapter Eighteen

Laura sat at her desk in her apartment in Seattle, putting the finishing touches on the book. Edna had been charged with murder, attempted arson, and numerous counts of theft. And Sloane was preparing to depart back to his P.I. business in L.A.—but not before he was lauded for single-handedly solving a murder while simultaneously putting out a fire. Of course, Riley got *no* credit for *her* work on the case—the local police chief giving her nothing more than a bit of halfhearted recognition for "detaining the culprit on the instructions of Sloane Bennett."

But for once, Riley wasn't all that upset over the lack of respect for her detective skills. Not only was she used to it, but her heart was already occupied with another sorrow—having to say good-bye to her lover, Sloane.

Riley looked up when the doorbell rang. Maybe it was a reporter, coming to interview her about her part in Edna's apprehension! But no, the *Gazette* had spent all its coverage on Sloane, touting him as "the mysterious private investigator from California who solved a local murder completely on his own!" Or maybe, she thought, still holding out hope for something good, it was her boss, Mr. Kelsey, coming to tell her he was finally ready to promote her from secretary to private eye.

Yet, again, no—nothing had happened to change Kelsey's poor opinion of her investigative abilities.

Ah well, she'd been thwarted once more, but there would be other mysteries to solve, and one of these days, Riley was going to get the recognition—and the job—she deserved.

Sighing, she pushed to her feet and opened the door—shocked to find Sloane standing on the other side, looking as dark and handsome as ever. He held out a pink rose.

She bit her lip, touched that he'd remembered the day in the garden when she'd mentioned it was her favorite flower. Reaching out to accept the rose, she raised it to her nose to breathe in the sweet fragrance, then smiled up into his eyes.

"It's cut from the secret garden," he said.

"It's beautiful. Thank you."

Sloane took her free hand in his, lifting it to his mouth for a gentle, lingering kiss. "I know the garden turned out not to be ours alone, Riley, but when we were there, it felt like it belonged only to us."

She nodded, a bit numb and trying not to cry. She knew this was it, that he was leaving, even before he leaned in to kiss her forehead, then her lips, and said, "Good-bye, Riley Wainscott. I won't forget you."

Riley stood at the door, peering blankly out at the stone path and lush green lawn long after Sloane had walked away. She girded herself with what Aunt Mimsey had taught her: *We all have desires we can't push down—but life goes on.*

Sloane had opened Riley to parts of herself she'd never known. And he'd made her a better detective, too. Her heart was a little broken right now, but life *would* go on. And she'd be a happier, more complete person for having known him.

Laura sighed, having written the last words of the book she'd decided to call *Dirty Little Secrets*. The title had struck her on the plane, and it seemed perfect. The book was *filled* with secrets—Aunt Mimsey's, Edna's, her own with Sloane, and even the Dorchesters had their secret garden.

It also seemed the perfect title to sum up her memories of what had happened on the mountain. She'd told Monica she'd slept with her cousin, but she'd given her friend none of the naughty details—not about the webcam or about Tommy, not about every other new experience Braden had opened to her, and she never would. Those secrets would belong to Laura alone. Well, and Braden, too, of course.

She'd handled their good-bye like a pro—a few tender kisses at the door, and out she'd gone, a brave new woman, ready to face the world now changed and emboldened because of him. And she'd remained strong since then—but also a little torn inside, if she was honest with herself.

A sensual exhilaration still echoed through her when she remembered the things she'd shared with him—Braden had given her ultimate thrills, and he hadn't judged her for her decisions; he'd truly wanted only to give her pleasure. She knew she would cherish the memories they'd created in the mountainside house together for the rest of her life, even if they *were* so outside her normal world that they almost seemed dreamy and unreal now.

But at the same time, she couldn't deny the sadness still lurking inside her from missing him. Missing the intimacy they'd shared, and even just his company. She feared she'd never experience that much intimacy with a man again. No other guy could ever open her up like that, get to those parts of her, make her so comfortable with things that had started out seeming so forbidden. How on earth did a girl just say good-bye to that kind of trust, that kind of sharing?

Hard to believe, she thought, still staring at her computer screen, that it had all started with a secret camera, and the man behind it. One more dirty little secret, she thought with a melancholy sigh.

Two weeks after turning in the book, Laura sat down at her computer in her snowflake-print flannel pajamas and lowered her coffee mug to the coaster on her desk. After a brief glance out the window at the morning quiet of her Capitol Hill neighborhood, she hit the button to retrieve her mail. She clicked to open one from her editor, Karen, sporting the subject line: *DIRTY LITTLE SECRETS INDEED!*

```
Love it! Love Sloane! About time Riley
had a real love life! I feel as if you've
tapped into a whole new part of Riley's
personality. Will we see Sloane again in
the next book? Karen
```

Laura sat before her computer, stunned. She couldn't have been more thrilled with her editor's response to a book she'd truly fallen in love with as she'd written it—but her editor wanted Sloane back in Riley's life? She hadn't even considered such a move. And though she immediately understood the appeal of such an idea, she was more than a little reluctant to give Sloane a recurring role in Riley's stories. She'd envisioned the dark stranger as someone Riley would simply remember fondly and think of wistfully. And the truth was, given that Braden had been the character's inspiration, Laura feared it would just be plain painful to keep writing about him.

Taking a deep breath, she hit reply.

```
Karen—so glad you like the book! I'm re-
ally proud of it and, like you, feel I know
Riley even better than I did before writ-
ing it. About Sloane, I'm not sure. I had
envisioned Riley being changed by their
affair—perhaps more outgoing, more sexually
confident, and more determined than ever
to prove herself—but I hadn't considered
bringing him back in the future. Let me mull
it over. Laura
```

She sighed at having been forced to think about Braden this early in the morning. Not even 8 A.M., and there he was, on the brain, where he would likely stay all day now. She sometimes thought he filled her thoughts as much as he had when she'd been at the house in Vail. The only difference was, instead of being able to fuck him at night, she only lay down in her bed and *remembered*. Every touch. Every penetration. Every spine-tingling, soul-stirring kiss.

The next e-mail she opened was from Monica.

Well? Are you going out with the Starbucks dude?

Laura actually shivered. A cute guy who hung at the Starbucks a few blocks away had asked her out last week, and she hadn't exactly given him an answer, even as Monica had stood elbowing her and telling the guy how much Laura loved Mexican food.

A couple of months ago, she would have definitely accepted the invitation. He was good-looking, had a great smile, and whatever he did for a living, it required wearing a well-cut suit and tie. But for some reason she hadn't been able to put her finger on, she'd hesitated, telling him she'd have to get back to him. Now, having thought about it, she *could* put her finger on what the problem was—she didn't feel especially comfortable with the idea of anyone touching her but Braden. And since dating customarily led to touching, it just seemed like a bad idea.

She e-mailed Monica back.

I don't think so.

The next thing she knew, an IM box popped up from her friend.

SEXYPSYCHIATRIST: Are you out of your freaking mind? He's a total hottie.

RILEY: I'm just . . . not into dating anyone right now.

SEXYPSYCHIATRIST: Oh God. Please don't tell me you're hung up on my cousin.

Laura sighed. Then lied. *RILEY: It's not that. It's just that I need a break from guys. First there was David. Then Braden. I'm not ready for another big thing just yet.*

SEXY PSYCHIATRIST: Hmm, let's see. You'd

broken up with David at least a month before
Braden came along. And it's been a few weeks
since you came home from Vail. And I'm not
sure a date qualifies as a "big thing."

Whereas Laura would normally just continue to argue, she instead stopped to consider Monica's words. She'd hoped her affair with Braden would make her bolder, more outgoing—not less so. And yet, she was turning Mr. Starbucks down for no good reason. And Monica was right—he *was* a hottie. Not as hot as Braden, certainly, but still a very handsome guy. And unlike Braden, she *did* want to marry someday, and for all she knew, Mr. Starbucks would turn out to be her soul mate.

RILEY: Okay, you talked me into it.

The screen stayed blank for longer than usual before Monica's answer popped up. *SEXY PSYCHIATRIST: Okay, now I'm scared. Since when do you see reason?*

RILEY: Since now. The next time I see the coffee hottie, I'll tell him yes.

SEXY PSYCHIATRIST: Wow! That's my girl.

She still didn't really *want* to tell him yes, deep down inside. But she doubted Braden was sitting around pining over *her*—so maybe it was time to really *be* Riley. Riley wasn't going to let Sloane's departure hold her back—she was going to let their affair change her for the better. Laura felt a fresh determination to do the same thing, her heart be damned.

Braden opened his eyes—fresh from a nice, naughty dream—and turned in bed expecting to find Laura beside him.

But the space next to him was empty. Shit—he wasn't in Colorado anymore. Hadn't been for weeks, in fact. Beyond his large bedroom window, he caught a glimpse of the deck that overlooked the Pacific, then heard the call of a seagull.

He couldn't believe he was still missing her. He'd been sure that would fade after he came home to L.A. And *then* he'd been sure it would go away once he got back involved in his work. But concentration had become difficult ever since his hot vacation with Laura in the mountains.

Don't freak out about it, man. When he looked at it logically, there were reasons. Laura was the only woman he'd ever done such extreme things with. And the only woman he'd ever spent longer than a weekend with in one stretch. So it made sense that he'd grown accustomed to seeing her face beside his in bed. It made sense that he missed her body. It made sense that he missed her smile.

So it was a month later and he found himself in the same rut Tommy had been in back in Vail. He'd talked to Tommy just yesterday, and his buddy sounded fine now—he was dating again. "A cute girl from over in Avon who works at the Christie Lodge, and damn, dude, she looks *hot* in her little pink ski pants," he'd said. He'd gone on to explain that it was nothing serious, but that he thought he was done with one-night stands. "Just getting too old for it, I guess."

Braden hadn't asked what that meant, but now he wondered if this was the first sign of a guy getting ready to settle down, a notion that made his stomach pinch. Not that he begrudged his friend happiness, but if Tommy got married at some point, it would change things—frankly, it would make Braden a little less likely to try to get away to Vail several times a year. He'd never thought of the Vail house as lonely, but after Laura's departure it had seemed that way. If he didn't even have Tommy to hang with whenever he wanted, it would *definitely* feel lonely.

Either way, though, he'd been glad to hear his buddy sounding happy.

Now . . . he just wished he was, too.

The fact was, he hadn't slept with anyone since Laura.

He'd *tried.* He'd even once got so far as bringing a girl home with him. But for some reason, in the end, he hadn't gotten into it.

Maybe Laura had made him realize that what Tommy had said when they'd been discussing Marianne was true—maybe Braden, too, wanted a girl with some substance. Even if it was just for fooling around, he suddenly didn't feel satisfied by the same old shallow chicks.

Only, he had the weird feeling that even if he found a *less*-than-shallow chick strolling up the beach right now, he probably wouldn't really want to fool around with her, either. He just kept thinking about Laura.

Six months later, autumn had arrived, *Dirty Little Secrets* had just made the *USA Today* list, and Laura's life had become a drudgery.

She'd tried to date Mr. Starbucks back in the spring, and they'd had a nice enough meal at El Camino, her favorite Mexican restaurant over in funky, artsy Fremont. But when he'd asked her back to his place, she'd claimed she was tired, and when he'd tried to kiss her at her door, she'd actually turned away. She'd felt both mean and as if she were behaving like a bit of a freak, and the parting had been utterly awkward.

Since then, she hadn't even *thought* about trying to date anyone. Monica had spent most of their time together lecturing her, so even her "girlfriend time" had been less than appealing lately. Which had led to much wearing of joggers and renting of sad movies. She couldn't even remember the last time she'd actually put on a pair of real pants.

And if that wasn't bad enough, as she'd sat down to start on her next Riley Wainscott Mystery this morning, she'd encountered her old nemesis—writer's block. Actually, she'd been encountering it every morning for the last few months—but at the moment, it felt even worse than usual, overshadowing her current book's success.

"God, Riley," she murmured in frustration toward the computer screen, "you're supposed to be a whole new woman this time around, ready for new adventures, new relationships, new beginnings of every kind. So what *are* they?"

All she could do was picture Riley and Aunt Mimsey having tea, or visiting the Dorchesters. Or maybe Riley wandering wistfully and lonely through the secret garden. *Wow, what a catchy hook for a story: wannabe detective takes walk.*

Once upon a time, Monica had been sure Laura's writer block had been caused by a lack of sex. And the results of her visit to Colorado had seemed to support the claim. God, she hoped that wasn't true, given that she didn't seem to want to have sex with anyone other than Braden Stone.

She was just about to wonder, for the first time ever, if maybe all of Riley's stories had been told, if all of her adventures had already been lived—when an Instant Message popped up on her screen. She flinched when she saw who it was from.

FLYBOY1: Are you there, snowflake?

Her heart threatened to burst through her chest. He suddenly felt so nearby—even if also still far away. RILEY: Yes, I'm here. Hi.

FLYBOY1: How are you?

What a loaded question. She lied, of course. RILEY: Great, thanks. And you? Busy buying up unsuspecting corporations?

FLYBOY1: I told you, I'm not ruthless and conniving in business. Just ruthless. <g>

RILEY: You're pretty ruthless in bed, too, as I recall.

FLYBOY1: Let's just say I know how to get what I want. :) Did you have any complaints?

RILEY: None.

FLYBOY1: I just finished reading Dirty Little Secrets last night.

Damn—she'd never even *thought* about him seeking out her book. Her poor, put-upon heart pounded even faster at the news.

RILEY: And?

FLYBOY: I want to know where Riley and Sloane Bennett stand.

Because of the same reason her editor had—because it was an appealing story line? Or was there more to his question? How obvious was it that she'd loosely fashioned Sloane after *him*? She almost couldn't breathe. `RILEY: Well, as you read, Sloane had to return to his business. So . . . they're finished, I suppose.`

`FLYBOY1: I think that's a bad idea.`

`RILEY: Oh?`

`FLYBOY1: I think you're missing an opportunity. They were good together. In fact, I think Riley should hook up with the dark stranger again.`

Laura considered her answer, still unsure of what they were really talking about. For at least half a second, she seriously considered typing *I love you* into the box. But then she came to her senses and remembered how hurt she would be when he didn't know what to say to that, and when it became clear that she'd just humiliated herself. She took a deep breath and tried to compose a reply. `RILEY: I'm not sure how that would happen. They live three thousand miles apart. It seems unlikely they'll bump into each other again on accident.`

It took a little while for him to answer. `FLYBOY1: Would you be surprised to know I still miss you, snowflake?`

Laura's throat clogged with emotion. She considered things she could say.

I miss you every day.

Every night.

Then she thought of the Braden she'd come to know and love in the mountain home, and she instead told him something she knew he'd be thrilled to hear. `RILEY: Sometimes I use the vibrator you gave me, and I think about you.`

FLYBOY1: *God, honey, that's nice. You just made me hard.*

Hot desire fluttered through her. RILEY: *Feels like old times. <g>*

FLYBOY1: *I love to think about you fucking yourself with it, moving it in and out of your perfect little pussy. Do you keep it shaven?*

Laura pulled in her breath. The truth was *no*—she had no reason to. But she didn't want to spoil the fantasy, didn't want him to think she hadn't remained the bolder, more sensual woman he'd made of her. RILEY: *Sometimes.*

FLYBOY1: *Ever think about installing a webcam on your end? <wink>*

The mere act of communicating with Braden, even just over the computer, was making Laura feel alive in a way she hadn't in months. *Keep the playful, naughty banter going,* she commanded herself. Besides being exciting and fun, and a way to keep him in her life, maybe some cybersex would be enough to revive her creativity again.

Yet to her surprise, something inside her slowly began to sink. She wanted to excite him, wanted to rekindle all that forbidden pleasure that had first brought them together—but she couldn't.

Knowing the things they'd done together, face to face, body to body, and knowing how very close to him she'd felt, how very trusting, how very attached—she knew already that dirty cyberchat wasn't going to make up for what she lacked. Already it felt empty. Like moving backward. She couldn't do it. She typed her answer in sadly. RILEY: *No.*

FLYBOY1: *Would you?*

RILEY: *No again.*

FLYBOY1: *Did I just accidentally do something to make you mad at me?*

RILEY: No.
FLYBOY1: Then is something wrong?
RILEY. Yes.
FLYBOY1: What?
RILEY: I love you.

She sent it without giving herself a chance to even consider it. It was gone, and it couldn't be brought back. She felt sick, her stomach churning, every nerve ending in her body tingling so intensely it was painful.

When he didn't answer, she feared she would throw up.

And then a message appeared.

FLYBOY1: I didn't know that, honey.

A far cry from *I love you, too.* Oh God, she'd made a horrible mistake.

RILEY: I shouldn't have said that. I can't believe I did. Forget about it, okay?
FLYBOY1: I don't know how to forget about
something like that.

Laura made a stressful decision—to barrel ahead to the heart of the matter. She had to—nothing else made any sense.

RILEY: Well, since I'm pretty sure you
don't feel the same way, I want you to at
least TRY to forget it, okay? I want you
to remember me fondly, not like the dork
who just spouted out something without
thinking about it.
FLYBOY1: I never said I didn't feel the
same way.

Her chest ached from the intense beating of her heart. RILEY:
But you didn't say you did, either.

A long, painful hesitation on his end that made tears well in her eyes.

FLYBOY1: I don't even really know what love
is, Laura. That kind of love. I've never been
in it. You know me—bachelor forever and all
that. I'm sorry.

Well, that was all she needed to know. She still possessed the ability to excite him, but he didn't love her. And he was a nice enough guy that he was trying to let her down easy. The person on the other side of the situation, though, never seemed to understand that there could be nothing *easy* about it.

Taking a deep breath, trying to hold back the tears enough to type, she constructed an answer. *RILEY: I understand. Thank you for reading my book and letting me know. I have to go now.*

And she shut down her Instant Message program and Internet connection as quickly as she could, before he could reply. Then she even shut down the computer altogether.

Methodically, she shed her jogging pants for a pair of jeans, left the apartment, and started walking toward Starbucks, even at the risk of seeing the guy she'd refused to kiss, because she simply had to get out of the house for a little while.

She couldn't believe she'd told Braden she loved him.

You could have had lots of fun IMing him. You could have had a secret little Internet affair for weeks, months, years. But thinking of "years" brought back the original problem she'd figured out during the exchange: it just wasn't enough, and she couldn't survive on that. Back when she'd first arrived at the Vail house, she'd questioned whether or not she even knew what it was to be in love—but now she definitely knew. She was in love with Braden, and nothing less than him loving her back was going to make her happy.

Which probably meant she was destined for a long life of dirty clothes, sad movies, and writer's block.

Chapter Nineteen

Part of Braden couldn't believe he was in a Seattle cab speeding toward the address he'd gotten from his cousin, Monica. But another part of him couldn't believe he'd managed to wait this long.

It had been a week since Laura had told him she loved him. A week since she'd rushed abruptly off the computer and ignored his every IM since.

Maybe it was just as well—because he hadn't even been sure what he wanted to say, only that he'd hated feeling he'd hurt her, and hated the idea that they might never come into contact with each other again. The more he'd imagined it, the more unthinkable it had become.

He still didn't know for sure about love. He'd never let himself be an emotional guy. His job demanded that he block emotion out, and it had always come easy for him—in fact, now that he thought about it, it was probably why he was so good at what he did. Maybe it was due to his parents' divorce—he'd just never believed in monogamy very much after that, that it could work, or maybe that it was even natural. Happy couples seemed few and far between in his life.

But Laura's tenderness and the genuine way she'd opened herself to him and put herself at risk affected him in a way he couldn't keep ignoring. From touching herself on the webcam for him . . . to experimenting with a three-way . . . to telling him she loved him. He'd never had anyone trust him so very much, and each time it had stirred something deep inside him, made his heart feel like it was bending, stretching, in his chest.

"Thirty-four Woodview," the cab driver said, pulling to the curb in front of a small, quaint-if-slightly-funky-looking apartment building from another era. Braden glanced toward the front door and, palms sweating, heart racing, realized he was actually nervous—an emotion he wasn't very well acquainted with.

He paid the driver, picked up the rose he'd laid gently on the seat next to him, and got out, striding boldly to the door and inside. Then he found the apartment number Monica had also supplied and, without hesitating, knocked firmly, ignoring the doorbell.

When Laura opened the door, he feared she might faint. Her mouth dropped open and he'd never seen her eyes so wide. "What are you doing here?"

Good question. He still wasn't sure. "I just couldn't leave things the way they were, snowflake." Then he held out the flower, a pink rose just beginning to open.

Her eyes dropped to the rosebud and she let out a heavy breath. "How did you know this is my favorite flower?"

He shrugged. "It's Riley's favorite, so I took a shot."

Trembling now, she accepted it from him. She stood with her hair falling tousled around her face, wearing a pale yellow strappy top, blue jeans below. Her nipples jutted softly through the fabric. Damn, she was just as beautiful as he remembered, maybe more, and only then, in that moment, did he realize just how stupid he'd been.

He should have come here the day after she'd left Vail, the day he'd realized he missed her so much. He just hadn't known then, or the week after, or the week after . . . he hadn't known for sure until right this moment. *He loved her.* He loved her so fucking much. Being without her had physically hurt. For the first time since February, he felt happy.

"I have a plan for Riley," he said. "I think she should move."

Laura blinked. "Huh?"

"I think Riley should pack up and move to L.A. with Sloane. I think they should keep solving new mysteries together. And I think they should find their own secret garden. If they can't find one, they should make one."

She blinked again. "Braden . . ." she began uncertainly, her eyes reaching out to him needfully.

And he understood. That he had to just say it. Because she needed to hear it. And he needed to tell her. He didn't even know how to say things like this, but he had to learn—right now. "Come to L.A. with me, Laura. Let me make love to you every night for the rest of our lives. I know it seems sudden, probably risky—but I love you."

Laura's knees nearly buckled beneath her, and she reached out to press her hand against the wall to steady herself. He wanted to make love to her. He *loved* her. Actually *loved* her. "I . . . I thought you didn't know what love was."

"I just figured it out, snowflake. I'm in it. With you. And I have been since we met. I just didn't know it, because . . ."

She tilted her head, trying to understand. "Because you're . . . a virgin?" she suggested. "When it comes to love?"

He nodded, the corners of his mouth curving softly upward. "I guess that's an accurate way to put it." Then he stepped up closer and slid his arms smoothly around her waist, and her whole body ached for more of him. "And I want to give it to you, that last little piece of my virginity, the same way you gave me the last little piece of yours."

Oh God. It was too unbelievable, too perfect. "Braden," she said, nearly breathless. "Please kiss me."

His mouth came down on hers in a hot crush, and she could feel how long he'd yearned for the connection, too. The kiss reverberated through her whole body as their tongues thrust together. His hands dropped to her ass, making her pussy throb.

"I can't believe you love me," she murmured when the kiss ended.

He pulled back to peer down at her with those dark, possessive eyes. "I do, baby. I love you so damn much. I can't live without you."

She could barely breathe, too overcome with emotion. "I can't live without you, either."

"Then you'll come? To L.A.?"

She didn't even hesitate. She'd miss Monica and her mom—but that's why they made airplanes. She nodded emphatically. "God, yes!"

"Thank God," he whispered, pulling her back to him in a deep hug.

Mmm, he felt so good—but she still needed more of him, all of him. "Fuck me, Braden," she whispered.

A low groan left him, and after that, there were no more words.

They rushed frantically, pulling at each other's clothes. She dragged him to the sofa, opening his jeans so that his cock burst free. She moaned at the sight of it—so big and hard. She'd never needed anything so desperately.

Discarding her jeans and panties, she straddled his thighs and lowered herself onto his stiff, beautiful erection with a low cry that came from her very core. Braden moaned, too, and they peered deeply into each other's eyes as she began to move on him.

"So long," she murmured, grinding against him, "I've needed this for so, so long."

"There's been no one since you, honey," he told her. "This sweet body is the only one I wanted. This sweet pussy wrapping around my cock is the only thing that could make me happy."

She slid wetly against him, loving when he thrust up into her deep, deeper.

"God, yes," she purred. "Fuck me, Braden. Fuck me hard."

His fingers dug into her ass as he plunged into her with rough strokes that reached her very center. Ah yes, so good—she just needed to feel him, filling her.

She found her rhythm against the hard drives and knew it wouldn't take long to come, since he was so much better than her vibrator. "Soon, lover," she told him—which was when he pressed the tip of one finger firmly against her anus, and she exploded into pure ecstasy. "God, baby!" she cried. "God, yes! I'm coming! Coming!" But she didn't stop there, adding, "I love you! I love you, Braden, so much!" Because she could say that now! Because she didn't have to hide it anymore!

"Ah—baby," he growled on a low groan, and she knew he was coming, too, pushing deep, his eyes falling shut, and she watched his handsome face, watched the way his lips softly parted, the way his features softened as the orgasm tapered into relaxation. She smiled afterward, so glad he'd taught her how beautiful it could be to witness your lover's pleasure.

"What you said made me come," he whispered when his eyes opened again.

" 'I love you'?" she asked, eyebrows raised.

He nodded, then grinned. "I think I like that."

"Then I'll say it again." Her voice deepened. "I love you."

He smiled into her eyes. "I love you, too, snowflake."

A few kisses later, though, the new, slightly softer side of Braden she was seeing faded back to the masculine demeanor she was more accustomed to. "One rule, though, about me loving you."

Still in his lap, still enjoying the fullness of having him inside her, she asked, "What's that?" At the moment, she thought she'd agree to anything.

"There will no longer be any other guys involved. That's an experience I wanted you to have, and I'm glad we did it—but I'm done sharing."

Laura's heart swelled, secretly thrilled that he now even possessed the capability to be jealous! "I can live with that."

"Of course, I might allow a vibrator or two. And we'll still be doing it with the lights on. In front of mirrors. And maybe even the occasional window."

If any other man had told her such things, she'd have flipped out. But as always with Braden, she could deny him nothing—and imagining the sexual joys he'd show her at her new home in Malibu practically had her creaming around him again already. "Your wish is my command."

He grinned. "I think I'm going to like this being in love stuff." Then he added, "God, I've missed your kisses, snowflake."

And as his mouth pressed once more against hers, she basked in the knowledge that both she and Riley were heading to Los Angeles—to be with their mysterious strangers, to solve new mysteries, to discover new gardens, and to give their lovers every new pleasure they could find.

About the Author

Lacey Alexander's books have been called deliciously decadent, unbelievably erotic, exceptionally arousing, blazingly sexual, and downright sinful. In each book, Lacey strives to take her readers on the ultimate erotic adventure and hopes her stories will encourage women to embrace their sexual fantasies.

Lacey resides in the Midwest with her husband, and when not penning romantic erotica, she enjoys history and traveling, often incorporating favorite travel destinations into her work.